WATCHERS OF THE NIGHT

Charlene Parris

HARLEQUIN
ROMANTIC
SUSPENSE

Recycling programs
for this product may
not exist in your area.

ISBN-13: 978-1-335-59389-4

Watchers of the Night

For questions and comments about the quality of this book, please contact us at CustomerService@Harlequin.com.

Harlequin Enterprises ULC
22 Adelaide St. West, 41st Floor
Toronto, Ontario M5H 4E3, Canada
www.Harlequin.com

Printed in U.S.A.

Charlene Parris has been reading books for as long as she can remember and romance stories since high school, after discovering her mother's cache of romance books. She loves smart, sharp-witted, independent heroines, strong heroes who respect them and, of course, happy endings. Charlene writes for the Harlequin Romantic Suspense line because she loves adding twists and turns to her stories. When she's not writing, Charlene is working her full-time job. And for fun, she reads, walks and is learning yoga.

Books by Charlene Parris

Harlequin Romantic Suspense

The Night Guardians
Watchers of the Night

Visit the Author Profile page at Harlequin.com.

This one's for Kimberley Troutte. Your mentorship, unwavering support and experience have been beyond whatever I could have achieved. You rock!

Chapter 1

York Regional Police 4 District—
Greater Toronto Area, Ontario, Canada

Detective Adam "Knight" Solberg tossed his badge, wallet and keys onto his desk before sitting down, his swivel chair squawking in protest as he dropped into its familiar embrace. He turned to face a corkboard wall decorated with paper. Each sheet described an assignment currently under investigation and there were too many for his liking.

The phone on his desk rang. Adam tapped the speaker button. "Solberg."

"When the hell are you going to get down here?" a gruff voice demanded.

Adam smiled. "Old man, have you forgotten I have a job to protect your sorry butt from criminals?"

The caller laughed. "Don't I know it. You remind me

every time I see you." His voice quieted. "Seriously though, son. Is everything okay?"

He caught the change in his dad's voice. "Remember the serial killer case I talked about? Our forensics team found more clues that make me want to puke. When I catch the bastard—"

"Don't stress. You will." A short pause on the phone. "Are you coming by the club later?"

The Chariots of Chrome Motorcycle Club was Adam's one spot of solace. Consisting of active and retired law enforcement officers, it felt like a second home to him. His dad, Magnus, had been the club leader for several years now, but every time Adam went in, he wasn't treated like a son; he was a valued member of the pack, and he appreciated Dad's insistence on that.

"Let me see how things are going first. I'm waiting to hear back from Forensics on the DNA results."

"That could take a while," Dad said.

"I don't think so. Ever since Cornwall joined the forensics team with the Investigative Services Unit, we've been getting results back in half the time. I'll call you later."

Adam dropped the phone in the cradle. As much as he wanted to call the ISU to check on their progress, he knew it would sound like nagging. If they had their best team on it, he could get results back within a few hours.

Maybe he should go to the club after all. He needed to surround himself with friends and clear his head for a bit before diving back into the criminal cesspool.

Hanging out with Dad and the guys had been the right decision. Adam had gone back to work feeling refreshed and determined to nail down his killer. Forensics had come through with a name and address, and the perp was now cooling his heels in jail.

It was three in the morning, and home—and his king-size bed—never looked more inviting. He managed to wolf down a snack and strip off his clothing before falling naked onto the cool, smooth sheets.

However, dreamland was rudely interrupted by his cell phone. Yawning, he grabbed it and looked at the screen— it was eleven o'clock in the morning, and someone was buzzing from the lobby. It must be a mistake. He put the phone down, but it buzzed again almost immediately, and a tendril of adrenaline sparked through him when he answered. "Who is it?"

"Adam, it's Bruiser, open the damn door!"

He hit "0" on his phone, the adrenaline now turning to icy fingers of fear. What on earth would bring Dad's best friend here?

Now alert, he quickly pulled on a pair of sweatpants, hurried to the front door and swung it open. A couple of minutes later, the elevator pinged, and Bruiser jogged toward him. Adam immediately noticed the white bandage on his friend's arm, and sensed something wasn't right. "What the hell's wrong?"

Bruiser's dark brown skin had paled to an ashen gray. "I—I don't…" He placed his large hand over his face.

"Come in." He closed the door behind them. "What's going on?" A prickling of dread raised the hairs on the back of his neck.

"My God, my God," Bruiser repeated. He wrapped his arms around his chest and rocked on his feet.

"Talk to me." When the big man didn't answer, Adam grabbed his friend's muscular arms, shaking him. "What is it?"

Haunted brown eyes looked at him. "There was a fire at the club."

Adam processed the information as he stared at Bruiser. "And?" He shook the Black man harder. "What?"

"Your dad got me and Dawg out, but…" he sank to his knees, his body shaking as he cried. "He's dead, Adam. I am so freaking sorry."

"Who's dead?" His gut twisted with agony, but he needed to hear the words. He knelt in front of his friend, holding on to a tiny light of hope, feeling it start to sputter within him as Bruiser kept shaking his head. "Dammit, Bruiser, who died?"

When Bruiser finally looked at him, Adam's heart sank. "I'm sorry, we tried, but…" He fought to catch his breath. "We couldn't save him. I couldn't get your dad out."

Bruiser's quiet sobbing cut through Adam, confirming the impossible.

It wasn't true. Adam wouldn't—he couldn't—believe it.

He had lost his best friend, his mentor.

He'd lost his father.

It was midafternoon when Forensic Investigator Cynthia Cornwall stepped out of the van and into organized chaos. Police cars, fire trucks and ambulances created a barricade around the Chariots of Chrome Motorcycle Club. Firefighters aimed their hoses at the smoking husk, water arcing with precision into smoldering hot spots.

A large crowd had gathered beyond the barrier. Some had their cell phones out, filming the action, while others talked and pointed at the building. A few stood off to one side, inconsolably wailing in grief. Two men were arguing with some police officers, one in particular trying to shove his way through. A muscular dark-skinned man finally wrapped his arms around his companion, lifted him up and walked toward a nearby police van. She watched as the man slumped against the side of the vehicle, his expression twisted in anguish.

She caught all of this with one glance, her mind processing the human reaction to the catastrophe. Now she took her time, letting her gaze linger over the scene. She'd been told during the ride here that active and retired law enforcement members who had formed the club had been in the building at the time of the fire.

Cynthia looked over what was left of the structure. Previously, it had been a variety store with apartments above. The MC members had gutted and renovated the building, adding their Chariots of Chrome insignia above the door. That was all gone now.

It must have been one hell of a fire. The thick metal supports that held up the clubhouse were actually warped. Heaps of black ash and charred wood lay in messy piles around the destroyed building. However, she also noticed that a chain link fence bordering the property had been blown apart.

This had been an explosion.

She would have to locate the fire marshal and discuss his findings.

"Ready to go?" Her forensics partner, Daniel Oostermann, stood nearby, waiting.

"Yeah." She wasn't, not really. People dying in fires hit a particular sensitive spot for her.

Despite the shouting, Cynthia could still hear crying. It hurt to hear the suffering. All she could do was mentally prepare herself and put her best effort toward finding some answers.

The marshal stood by his van. "Cornwall," she introduced herself, displaying her badge. "Can you give me a rundown of what happened?"

He took off his helmet and wiped his face with a towel. "Damn, it was terrifying. That fire burned so hot we didn't dare get too close."

"Did the building contain material to make it burn like that?"

"It was a stone and wooden building with a metal structure, and it hasn't rained for a while, but it shouldn't have burned like that." His expression was grim. "I found traces of an accelerant."

That would explain the force of the blast and the condition of the building. "Any evidence of bomb material?"

"What? I—I don't know. I didn't see anything to suggest that."

"Any concerns of a gas leak, or other volatile substance?"

"No, everything's clear."

She nodded, her mind already processing several possibilities. "Thank you, Marshal."

She and Daniel got dressed in protective gear, then followed the marshal to the back of the building. "The men are still hosing down the charred wood as a precaution," he explained. "The back area is clear, but we need to be careful."

"Understood."

The area was covered in soaked debris and the mangled remains of motorcycles. Cynthia stood near the rear of the building and looked out across the small parking lot to the six foot high chain link fence. Most of the barrier had been completely destroyed, the rest hanging on by single links. "Do you know how far the explosion reached?"

"It hit a couple of houses beyond the fence. Broken windows, scorched grass."

"Did you find the point of origin?"

The marshal led them inside. "According to the scorch marks, the fire started here." He pointed to the left. "This area is just inside the back door."

She studied the cement floor. The burns were wide and deep. As she looked around, she noticed several skeletal remains surrounded by small heaps of ash. The flashback of a screaming child hit her hard, and Cynthia swallowed the lump of helpless anguish that threatened to overcome her. She kept her trembling hands busy by pretending to go through her pockets.

She believed the fire had only one purpose—completely obliterate any evidence that might be found. However, nothing could be entirely destroyed, as long as one looked in the right place.

"Any idea how many victims were in the building when it exploded?" Daniel asked.

"Witnesses think about seven or eight. One man escaped with cuts and bruises, three went to the hospital with extensive burns over most of their bodies."

"Is the man with the minor injuries still here?"

The marshal nodded. "Yeah, a tall Black man named Bruiser, retired cop."

Which meant there were at least three victims left in the clubhouse.

She took a couple of deep breaths to reassure herself and let her brain and its logical thought process take over. "Right. Better get to work." She pulled on a pair of plastic gloves.

There was little left of the building's original shape— almost everything had been reduced to cinders.

Cynthia worked closest to the origin of the blast, using

a powerful flashlight to better see what was around her, while Daniel moved farther into the building. They had agreed to inspect the clubhouse together in order to speed up the examination. As the only two forensic investigators at the precinct, priorities shifted on a constant basis—on the odd occasion that two current investigations were in progress, they would each take one, but she and Daniel would consult with each other, acting as sounding boards to solve discrepancies. Thankfully, the physical work involving the serial killer case had been finished last night, with only the final reports to write up.

She pulled out a brush and started sifting through the debris, her gaze sharp as she looked everything over. She wouldn't ignore anything, no matter how tiny or insignificant.

There were several streaks of what looked like white powder emanating from the centre of the blast, and she collected a sample. Something small glinted beneath her flashlight. Using a pair of tweezers, Cynthia picked up the object to inspect it more closely. A ball bearing. She placed it in the plastic bag attached to her hip and looked for others. Soon, she had found about a half dozen of them. During an explosion, these metal bearings would turn bodies into Swiss cheese—not a pleasant thought.

She carefully took off one glove and pulled out her cell phone. A couple of taps, and the map of the building appeared. Lining up the front and rear doors to the image, the picture gave her a good idea how the building looked before it was destroyed.

In the area she stood in, the picture showed a long counter to her left, with a fridge at the other end. To her right were images of tables and chairs. Near the front doors, a staircase led to second- and third-floor units. Six large windows in total on the ground floor. A good-sized space, roomy enough for several friends to hang out and socialize.

And hopefully small enough to find the crucial evidence they needed.

"I found ball bearings," she announced.

Daniel swore. "This was deliberate."

"But why attack a motorcycle club?"

"I've heard the Chariots of Chrome make their presence known within the nearby neighborhoods." Daniel picked something up—it looked like a ring—and dropped it into his plastic bag.

"You mean they still patrolled?"

"Yep, something like Neighborhood Watch. Everyone felt safe with them around. And if there was any trouble, they'd handle it."

Cynthia frowned. "They're allowed to do that?"

"Within reason. I'm sure they would call the police for official backup, but these weren't the type of retired officers to ignore something bad happening on their turf."

Which possibly meant some form of retaliation.

She kept looking and found several pieces of very thin copper wire. And there, under a pile of blackened wood, was the cracked face of a watch.

She studied it carefully. She didn't recognize the interior mechanism, nor the faint detail of a symbol above it.

She put it in a plastic bag, and continued her investigation, working in sections. She discovered a cuff link near the front door, in the shape of skulled figure riding a motorcycle. Nearby were charred human bones, and she took a moment to steady herself before examining them.

Judging by their position, she surmised that the victim had crawled toward the exit, but the dense smoke or fire had become too overwhelming. She placed neon markers around the body and continued her search, fighting the emotions that threatened to flood her mind with painful memories. She couldn't locate the other cuff link.

"I found three bodies," Daniel announced. He worked fast, but his attention to detail sometimes suffered as a result. She would have to keep her eyes open for more clues.

His markers indicated that these victims had been closest to the back door and the blast radius. They didn't stand a chance. Fighting back the sadness, she asked in a strained voice, "Any identification?"

"Well, this guy's wallet survived, so we have positive ID. Someone wore expensive shades." He shook an evidence bag with a pair of twisted frames tucked inside. "The third victim owned this." He held up another bag.

It contained a fob watch, not something a person saw every day. "There's one body near the front door," she told him. "And I found a unique cuff link. We should be able to get an ID on it."

"So, what do you think happened?"

Cynthia put her thoughts carefully together. "Someone brought a bomb in here, with a watch as its timer." She held up the object in question. "The marshal said he found traces of an accelerant. That makes me think it was beside the bomb when it detonated, but I can't be sure. However, if the victims arrived at the clubhouse before the perp could finish, then they didn't have a chance of spreading the accelerant around the building. Looking at the building's layout, the only place to hide the bomb was in the counter that extended the length of the wall."

"That explanation holds up."

"These three got hit first and I believe died instantly."

Daniel cocked a brow.

"A timed bomb with ball bearings, plus accelerant? At that close range?"

He nodded, watching her.

She faced the front door, using her imagination to give her a better grasp of the circumstances. "As for the other men, the victim near the front door rescued the survivors, then tried to get out, but couldn't. The smoke or the flames got to him first."

"Sounds like a good summary. Now all we have to do is figure out why."

"I saw something on the watch, but I want to analyze it further at the lab first."

"Theory?"

Cynthia opened her mouth, then closed it. "Not yet. I want to be sure on this one. Let's finish up."

They carefully collected the human remains, making sure that everything was bagged and marked in proper sequence. A few more critical pieces of evidence were located, because she had kept her gaze focused to spot anything that Daniel might have missed. Two gold teeth, more ball bearings, some smudged with a dark substance that could be the victims' blood and a warped belt buckle. And in a far corner, underneath rubble and the remains of an office chair, a small metal safe in surprisingly good condition.

She also located the second cuff link, which she carefully placed in a bag beside the first.

"I'm not sure how we can properly seal off the area," Daniel stated as they headed out the back door.

"We can place tarp over everything then set up the tents," she said. As they approached the front of the building, she noticed that the crowd had grown substantially. "I'll ask the officer in charge to help us."

With all evidence secured, she stripped off her forensic gear and walked over to the largest group of officers while Daniel waited at their van. The men were talking amongst themselves, and she felt the anger and frustration from this distance.

"Excuse me." When they all turned as one to look at her, she asked, "Could some of you help us to secure the scene? We need to place tarp and forensic tents over the area."

"Have you found any answers?"

Cynthia looked at the officer who asked the question, keeping her expression and emotions neutral. "We found evidence that should help move the case forward."

"Listen, our friends were murdered in there," the officer growled. "If someone wants revenge, they've picked the wrong men to mess with."

Others voiced their agreement, raising the tension.

"Until that's proven, I need to preserve the crime scene. Are you going to help or not?"

He looked her over. "You're a bit mouthy for a forensic specialist."

"I'm the one who finds the answers, so yes, I can get as mouthy as I want." She knew raw emotions could grab anyone at any moment. She had learned to keep hers behind a thick wall a long time ago—it was the only way she could continue working this job.

The officer who challenged her stepped forward, but a second officer who stood behind him grabbed his shoulder. "Quit it, Spade," he said. "She's doing her job. Come on."

"My colleague will help you." She pointed at Daniel, who had watched from the van.

The men left, leaving her to tune in to another confrontation. The man she had seen earlier stood face-to-face with Captain Gregory Boucher. "I have to be on this case!" The man yelled. "My dad was in there!"

"All the more reason for you to stay away, Solberg," the captain retorted. "You're too close to this."

Cynthia recognized the name—Adam Solberg was the detective who had been hunting the serial killer. He had found excellent clues relating to the criminal's MO, which had helped her find the fingerprints the officers had initially missed. He had been thorough, leaving virtually no stone unturned. He had the work ethic of an experienced, older detective.

So it was a shock to see that Solberg was younger than she expected, actually closer to her age. And Solberg was *hot*. His face had traces of classic Nordic features combined with smooth, tanned skin. His rich brown hair was cut a little too short for her liking, but the early evening sun picked up its golden highlights. The blue chambray shirt with rolled-up sleeves couldn't hide the muscles that stretched taut as the detective gestured angrily at the captain.

Cynthia turned around and fiddled with her cell phone, praying that no one had seen her face. Dammit, she was in the middle of a very important investigation. Why the hell was her brain taking time to discover the fineness that was Detective Solberg?

"So what am I supposed to do? Wait until you decide what information you can feed me?" Detective Solberg asked.

"Keep it civil," the captain warned.

She looked over her shoulder. Detective Solberg's expressions of grief and anger were very visible, but he fought to regain some semblance of control over his emotions.

So, his father was a victim. She had no idea if he was one of the survivors.

However, she understood his reactions better than anyone.

Cynthia took a few slow steps back until she hid behind a police vehicle. She wanted to watch and listen without being seen.

"I have every right to know what happened in there," Detective Solberg growled.

"We all do. In case you've forgotten, your dad was a friend of mine too."

"And you just told me you'd be involved." Solberg stabbed a finger into Captain Boucher's chest.

The Black man who had remained with him grabbed his friend's arm and pulled him away. "Stop it, Adam," he said. "You're embarrassing yourself in front of everyone."

"Bruiser, I don't care!" He shook himself free and glared at the captain. "I expect to be informed on everything that's going on. If you and your team find out anything—*anything*—I want to know."

"That's my call, Solberg," the captain said.

The detective's hands bunched into fists, and Cynthia held her breath. Solberg wouldn't dare hit a high-ranking officer.

Captain Boucher glanced down at the detective's hands, as if wondering the same thing. "Solberg, I'm putting you on an extended leave of absence. Starting now."

She didn't have to see Solberg's expression to imagine his reaction. "Are you serious?"

"Yes. Get the hell out of here before I decide to arrest you for obstruction."

Silence. Detective Solberg had moved closer to the captain, his body vibrating with rage until, with a snort of disdain, he turned on his heel and stomped off, his friend following behind.

Detectives and officers usually bore the brunt from victims' families. While she rarely had to deal with the aftermath—the accusations, the judgment, the demand for answers—she witnessed it. And Cynthia had just seen an almost mirrored version of the scene from her own life that played out too often for her liking. Cynthia knew what it felt like to be ignored, to be pushed down the priority ladder, to be slotted into a cold case file.

It had been over ten years, but the pain and anguish were still fresh. She grabbed her chest as grief threatened to break through the wall she had built around her heart.

It had taken her that much time to find a sense of closure. Cynthia decided that Detective Adam Solberg would not wait that long.

Chapter 2

"So, did you hear? They caught a suspect."

Cynthia's attention was so intent on the object beneath the microscope that it took her a few seconds before realizing Daniel was addressing her. "What suspect?"

"A couple of witnesses had seen a Black teenager running from the club before the explosion. They provided a pretty good description too, including the scarf he was wearing."

"Scarf?" Her intuition blared a warning. "What kind of scarf? What color?"

Daniel shrugged. "I didn't ask for details. Although I did hear that Captain Boucher plans on being in the interrogation room."

"Dammit." She carefully placed the watch found at the MC clubhouse back into its plastic bag and snapped off her gloves.

"What's up?"

"I want to find out some answers. Finish analyzing the items and try to get a hit on some fingerprints. I'll be back later." She hurried out of the forensics lab.

She ran to the elevators and smacked the up button, holding on to her frustration. She had specifically asked if she could question the suspect about the bomb found at the scene when he was found. Judging by the pieces she had painstakingly collected and studied under the microscope, this wasn't just handmade, it was meticulously put together, which pointed to someone with serious experience.

The elevator pinged. Cynthia got on and pressed the button for the floor above her, which contained the interrogation rooms.

She saw two officers standing guard outside a room at the end of the hall. "Hey there," she called out. When one of the men looked at her, she flashed her badge. "I understand Captain Boucher is interrogating a suspect in the MC clubhouse bomb case. Is he already finished?"

"No, he's coming down in a couple of minutes."

Thank goodness, she had made it in time. "Okay, thanks, I'll wait."

She barely got the words out before the elevator doors opened and the man in question strode toward them. "Ms. Cornwall."

Captain Gregory Boucher was an intimidating giant, standing at six foot, four inches and about two hundred and twenty pounds. His aura and his position commanded respect, and the two officers didn't disappoint. While she admired his no-nonsense personality and honesty, Cynthia had made sure to cultivate some of that respect for herself during her employment. "Captain," she called out as he was about to enter the room. "I'd like to listen in and·ask some questions, please."

Boucher glanced over his shoulder. "You've never needed to do an interrogation. Why now?"

"I have some specific questions I want to ask the suspect about the bomb that was used in the club." *He was going to question her justification? Fine, bring it on.*

"Anything I can help with?"

"No, sir, my questions are tied to the forensic evidence I found and my findings. It'll take too long to explain to you what I need to know." Although she kept her words polite, Cynthia made sure Captain Boucher got the subtle, but assertive hint.

He nodded. "Come in."

Fluorescent lighting illuminated a bolted table and two office chairs within the dull green room. The suspect sat in the chair farthest away from the door, his hands clasping and unclasping, his head bowed to hide his face.

The captain eased his large frame into the remaining chair. Cynthia wasn't annoyed—in fact, this gave her the perfect opportunity to stand where she could watch both men and their expressions.

"Larry," Boucher called out.

The teenager looked up, then glanced at her before sitting straight and letting his long, slim legs extend in front of him. "Yeah."

"What's your last name?"

"If you know my first name, you gotta know my last name too, right?"

Kid had a point, but Cynthia kept quiet.

Boucher frowned. "You getting smart with me?"

"No, sir." Larry crossed his arms. "Mind telling me why I'm here? I've stayed clean the past two months."

"You heard about the explosion at the Chariots of Chrome motorcycle club near Keele Street and Barrhill Road?"

"Near the 7-Eleven? Yeah, I heard about it." Larry's expression was sad.

"Where were you yesterday afternoon?"

"Met some friends at Vaughan Mills Shopping Centre, checked out some clothing and shoe stores, played video games, hung out, the usual."

"And where were you between eight this morning and twelve o'clock today?"

He shrugged. "Had an appointment."

"With whom?"

"A friend who helped me get clean."

Cynthia stared at the young man, wondering who this "friend" was.

"And what did you and your friend talk about?"

"Business you don't need to know about."

"Larry, I have witnesses placing you at the club before the explosion."

Larry didn't say anything, but his restless hands spoke volumes.

"And I know the club has security cameras both inside and outside the premises. The members had problems with break-ins in the past." Captain Boucher leaned forward. "Don't make it harder on yourself by lying."

The captain's demeanor was calm and encouraging, not the frightening image Cynthia had expected. He hadn't shouted or threatened, and that impressed her. When Larry looked her way again, she gave a slight nod.

"I went to see Mr. Solberg. He's been helping me a lot, and I wanted to return the favor."

So Larry's friend must be Detective Solberg's father.

"Before we go any further," she interrupted. "I want it to be clear that we're interviewing Larry, not interrogating him—is that correct, Captain?"

"Larry is a suspect in the murder of active and retired police officers at the Chariots of Chrome Motorcycle Club," Captain Boucher growled. "If he can prove his innocence, I'll let him go."

"Hey, man, I was told that you all only wanted to ask some questions!" Larry rose from his seat and paced the length of the room, rubbing his face with his hands.

"Calm down." Cynthia moved closer, holding out her hand. "You're a suspect, that's all. Can you tell us why you were at the club?"

Larry stopped and braced his back against the wall, glaring at the captain. "I was helping Mr. Solberg."

"Helping him with what?" she asked.

The young man took a deep breath. "Like I said, I got clean, but I still hear about stuff."

"Stuff like what?"

"He's talking about drug deals." The captain shifted in his chair.

Larry nodded. "I won't rat on my gang—you all have tried getting me to talk before. But anyone else coming on our territory? They're fair game."

"So you're an informant," Cynthia surmised.

"Something like that. Doing my good deed for society."

"What a load of crap." The captain stood up, and she noticed something different in his body language, something more menacing. She stayed still, keeping herself in between the two men. "So, Mr. Good Deed," Boucher continued. "What was this tip you coughed up?"

Larry sidled closer to her. As much as Cynthia didn't

want to see the captain go ballistic on the teenager, she also didn't want to be used as a shield. She gave Larry her *don't mess with me* expression, which stopped him in his tracks.

"Like you're going to believe me," Larry accused.

"We have evidence," Cynthia said. "We can confirm or deny your statements."

Larry shoved his hands in his pockets. "I told Mr. Solberg yesterday there's a new drug gang trying to mark their turf in my crew's zone. They were supposed to make some kind of deal last night, but I heard it didn't go down. I went to the clubhouse this morning to tell Mr. Solberg I didn't know what happened, but he got pissed and told me to leave. That's all I know."

She glanced at the captain, who nodded in confirmation. "Are you sure your gang isn't involved too?" Boucher demanded.

"No way, man, I swear to God."

"Okay, Larry, take it easy. Could you sit down? I have a few questions I'd like to ask you," Cynthia told him.

"Cornwall, I'm not finished," Boucher growled.

"If you're talking about the explosion, that's my area of expertise." She watched the captain, her heart pounding so hard it tried to climb up her throat. She had overstepped her authority in the past, but it always resulted in the right answers and capturing the criminals involved. She wouldn't do this unless she was sure of her evidence.

The captain cocked an eyebrow, then finally nodded and sat down.

"That's a unique-looking scarf," she said, pointing at the item sticking out of Larry's front pocket. "Your gang's colors?"

Larry stared at her in surprise. "How did you know?"

"Come on, Larry, you think the police don't know who your gang is? Give us some credit," she scoffed. "But I'm not talking about that. I need to know if you're responsible for that explosion."

"I didn't kill anybody," he muttered.

"But your gang has been responsible for shootings in the past," she countered.

Larry looked away. "I've got nothing to say about that."

"Okay, so let me ask you this. Has your gang changed their MO recently? Are they using a different method to kill their targets?"

The teenager turned back to her. "Why are you asking?"

"Because the explosion was man-made." Cynthia watched carefully as Larry's expression morphed into fear.

"You mean a damn bomb?" The poor guy clawed at the wall behind him, as if trying to escape. "Are you serious?"

"Very." Cynthia had brought some pictures of the crime scene with her, and she wanted to observe Larry's reaction to them. But she hadn't expected this. "Why are you so freaked out? Are you trying to tell me that your gang isn't responsible?"

"We don't do bombs, man!"

"Are you sure? Don't forget, you're not part of the posse anymore. How would you know?"

"I don't hang out with them, but I talk to them, you know? They told me about that drug deal. They knew I had a guy I can talk to about scaring off the competition. Makes their life easier."

"Riiight." Captain Boucher snorted with disgust. "And it would make your life easier if you bombed your competition."

Larry glared at him. "You kidding? Bombs destroy

everything. How can gangs steal from each other if they blow up the drugs and money?"

The teenager had another good point. "So you're saying you knew nothing about the bomb in the MC clubhouse," Cynthia said.

"No, ma'am. Why would my gang kill the guys that helped them out? In a manner of speaking."

"Don't you love it when suspects try to justify their actions?" Boucher laughed.

"Hey, if you got info on my posse, you know we don't do explosions," Larry argued.

"First time for everything," Boucher countered.

The captain's comment wasn't exactly true. Gangs usually threatened people based on their particular specialty. Mostly, it was guns, knives and threats to injure or kill. Other gangs conducted drive-by shootings. Arson was another way to scare victims into silence.

Larry's gang, the Desperados, were the guns-and-threats type of group. They'd been busted a number of times on small charges. Cynthia didn't believe they'd suddenly changed tactics.

"Captain, I don't have any other questions to ask."

"What?" Boucher narrowed his eyes at her, as if trying to read her mind. "Aren't you going to ask him about the bomb itself?"

"No, sir."

"Why?"

"Because there's no need to." *Please, Captain, trust me on this.*

Cynthia knew he wasn't pleased. He had friends who were hurt and killed in that explosion too. Like the officer who had challenged her back at the crime scene, Boucher was upset, but refused to show it.

He stared at her for several tense moments. "Fine," he grunted. "I'm deferring to your judgment."

"Thank you, sir."

"Doesn't mean I think you're right." He turned to Larry. "You're free to go. I'll have an officer escort you out. If you hear of anything, you know where to find us."

"Hey, Captain," Larry called out as Boucher opened the door. "I hope you catch the son of a bitch. Mr. Solberg was a good guy."

At Boucher's terse command, Cynthia followed him to his office on the second floor. She'd been in here once before, after she was transferred from Forensic Identification Services. When he had questioned her decision to come here, she only told him that she wanted a change of scenery. He hadn't quizzed her further, and Cynthia was grateful for his discretion.

Now she sat in an office chair facing his desk. On the wall beyond were plaques commemorating his achievements. A few pieces of neutral artwork graced the other walls, while three picture frames sat on the desk. She assumed them to be family photos.

"Ms. Cornwall, I trust you can explain why you didn't question Larry about the bomb."

She swiveled in her chair. Captain Boucher was standing at the large picture window, his back to her. Saying *Ms. Cornwall* was similar to a parent yelling out their child's formal first name—it meant she was in trouble.

"Sir, he doesn't know anything about it. You saw his reaction. He was terrified."

Silence.

"It simply isn't his or the Desperados' MO. I don't

think they had anything to do with the clubhouse explosion," she surmised.

"Based on what?" Captain Boucher demanded. He still hadn't turned around.

"Evidence and past history on their crimes." She jabbed at the folder on her lap. "That bomb wasn't just a complicated mechanism—it was also designed to do the most damage possible. Add an accelerant to it, which I discovered was gasoline, and the clubhouse burned hotter than Hell itself."

"What are you trying to tell me?"

"I think…" Cynthia hated guessing. Solid evidence was supposed to point her in the right direction. "Based on the current evidence we've collected, and knowing the patterns of criminal activity in our district…" She blew out a breath. "Sir, I think there's a new player in town."

Chapter 3

Adam recognized anxious family members in the waiting room of Sunnybrook Health Sciences Centre. Dawg's wife, Elizabeth, was a slim, pretty blond-haired woman with a backbone made of steel. Bruiser approached her and engulfed her in a tight hug as Adam spotted his aunt and uncle.

Aunt Michelle and Uncle Henrik were talking to a doctor as he approached. "Adam!" Aunt Michelle cried out before collapsing into his outstretched arms. "What's going on?" Her confused expression pulled at his heart. "What happened?"

It was natural for her to turn to him for answers. "All I know is that there was an explosion at the club." He choked, fighting to hold his emotions together. "Dad didn't make it."

Uncle Henrik, Dad's younger brother, hung his head.

"Adam, I don't understand." Aunt Michelle's face was streaked with tears. "Why would anyone do this?"

"Because Magnus got too close to something." Uncle Henrik looked at him knowingly.

"I—I don't know. Dad never told me anything." Adam's mind flashed back to a particular scene at the club yesterday afternoon. His father had stood near the back door, speaking to a young Black teenager who looked vaguely familiar. "Dad was talking to some punk about another drug gang possibly dealing in the area."

"Drugs?" Aunt Michelle whispered. "What the hell was Magnus doing?"

"Keeping our neighborhood safe. Do you think those punks have something to do with this, Adam?" his uncle asked.

Adam shook his head, more out of frustration than denial. "I have no idea. I'm not on the case."

Uncle Henrik's steely gray eyes locked on him. "Why?"

"Because I'm too close to it." He hesitated. "I may have also gotten mad at Boucher."

"Adam, don't tell me you hit your captain." Aunt Michelle made it sound so matter-of-fact that he almost laughed.

"I was tempted, believe me."

"So who's going to keep you updated on this?" his uncle demanded.

"You are. Insist on answers and keep Captain Boucher on his toes." Adam placed his hand on his uncle's shoulder. "I'm counting on you."

"Right."

Adam knew Uncle Henrik would be all over the police anyway, but the added incentive should help.

Aunt Michelle linked her fingers with her husband's. "Have you told Leila yet?"

Oh God—Mom. Adam's mind had been so focused on everyone else, he had forgotten about her. "No...no." Dammit, he was going to get upset again.

"We'll give her a call." Aunt Michelle kissed his cheek. "But you have to talk to her as well, okay?"

Inside the hospital's chapel, Adam stared at his personal phone, with Mom's number displayed on it. He hadn't hit the dial button—he'd been trying to think of how to tell her that Dad had been murdered.

But there was no way to make the traumatizing news easy. No matter how much he thought it through, it didn't change the fact that Dad wasn't here anymore.

He forced the misery back down his throat, took a breath to steady himself, then dialed her number. She picked up on the first ring.

"Adam."

The tone of her voice told him she'd seen the news. "Mom." His voice cracked, and the anguish tried to take over his body.

"Oh God." He heard her gasp. "Magnus?"

Despite the divorce, Adam knew Mom still loved him. Telling her about Dad would tear her apart—he was close to falling to pieces himself. "He didn't make it."

He squeezed his eyes shut as Mom cried, punctuated with wails of grief that tore his soul to pieces. It continued for what felt like an eternity, before her sobs grew quieter. "I'm sorry, *abni*." My son.

"There's nothing to be sorry for," he whispered gently. Poor Mom.

"What is being done about this sick atrocity?"

"The detectives I work with are investigating."

"And you?"

Adam shook his head, still furious at Captain Boucher's command to stay away. "I'm not on the case."

"I see." He heard the simmering anger in her voice.

"They're good colleagues, Mom. I'm sure they'll solve it." He had to have faith in his team, and if he knew Cornwall, she'd do everything in her power to bring the bastard to justice—her work on the serial killer case proved that. "Uncle Henrik and Aunt Michelle are at the hospital with me. Some of Dad's friends survived."

"Thank God at least for that." She sniffed.

"Aunt Michelle is going to call you." He didn't know what else to say, other than… "I love you."

"I love you too. Come and see me when you can."

After he hung up, Adam allowed his grip on his emotions to break. His sobs echoed and surrounded him, tightening their hold until he slid from the pew to sit on the cold floor. He wrapped his arms around his chest, afraid he would fly apart from the intensity of his grief. He leaned his head back, tears blurring his vision as he allowed his body to do what it needed. Dad had been his anchor, the lighthouse in the storm who always guided Adam in the right direction. Now he was left adrift, buffeted by waves of loss and emptiness.

He wiped his face with both hands, his body contracting as he fought to breathe normally. He slouched against the wooden bench, long legs extended, and took another couple of deep breaths. It helped a little.

Bruiser stood several feet away, hands in his pockets, the white of the bandages a stark contrast to his dark skin. His face was turned away, giving Adam a semblance of privacy while he pulled himself together. He slowly got to his feet, used the hem of his shirt to wipe his face again and approached his friend.

"Sorry I took so long," Bruiser apologized. "I was talking to Elizabeth." He spoke as if he hadn't seen Adam go through his meltdown, and Adam silently thanked him. Bruiser was the kind of guy Dad called a softie, but it was the wrong label. The big man had a knack for understanding when it was okay to talk, and when to remain quiet. Adam's old man busted through doors—Bruiser would knock first before entering.

Adam appreciated his approach at this moment. Bruiser didn't ask if he was okay—he knew Adam was hurting.

"How is she doing?" Adam managed to say.

"She's a strong woman. Dawg's a lucky guy—she'll get him through this."

Adam hated this feeling of helplessness. Always the one to get involved, he now felt directionless. His job was his life—now, it felt hollow. "Bruiser, did you notice anything weird at the club?"

"Just the kid."

"Kid?"

"Name's Larry, the young dude who was talking to your dad yesterday. You saw him. Used to be a weed dealer with a gang called the Desperados."

"I remember," Adam mused. "Slick little eels that slipped out of my hands before I could charge them." He tilted his head. "Why was he at the clubhouse? I heard Larry talk about another drug gang. What the hell's going on?"

"Larry feeds your dad intel. Seems that he owed Magnus big time. The kid was there this morning too."

"He's an informant?" Adam asked.

"Something like that. I understand Larry struck a deal between himself and his former gang. He wanted out but would let them know if anyone tried to muscle their turf. Larry told your dad any news that crossed the pipeline. We'd take care of the problem, and Larry's gang continued their small-time dealing."

"Will wonders never cease." Adam swore and suddenly slapped his hand hard against the nearest wall. He would have to trust Hawthorne and Timmins to find the killers responsible.

"You have a good team," Bruiser said quietly, as if reading his mind.

"Yeah, it's just…" This helpless feeling was going to get old, real fast.

"Why don't you go home? I'm going to stay here. I'll let you know when they're out of surgery."

Adam nodded, too mentally drained to say anything.

The doors opened with a quiet whoosh as Adam stepped into the cool evening air. Glancing at his watch, he noticed that only a few hours had passed. God, it felt like a lifetime.

The streets rang with car horns and late rush hour traffic. He stopped and looked around, debating on hitting the nearest bar and getting drunk. His emotions were raging, urging him to do something rebellious. It felt like his teenage years were boiling to the surface, pushing him to do something rebellious.

Adam wasn't going to fall for it. He had proven to Dad that he was a responsible adult—he wouldn't screw that up, not now. Not ever.

His cell phone buzzed, but he wasn't in the mood to answer.

A short ping caught his attention—someone had left a

text message. As it was his work phone, he figured he'd
better check in and explain that he wouldn't be at the station for the foreseeable future. Captain Boucher could be
a jerk sometimes, but now…

Blowing out a frustrated breath, Adam turned back
and discovered a small take-out shop tucked next to a
corner of the hospital. After grabbing a hot drink, he sat
down and pulled out his cell, checking his messages. Two
from Hawthorne, one expressing his condolences, and
the other updating him on the status of evidence against
the serial killer.

The third message… Adam flinched in pain as the
coffee burned his tongue.

Detective Solberg, my sincerest condolences on the
loss of your father. I've also heard that you will not be
on the case to solve his murder, which I find unjust, to
say the least. I, however, will be involved and will pull
out every trick of the trade I know to solve it. Officially,
I shouldn't even be texting you—it could cost me my
job. Please call me at this number so that I can meet
with you tonight. C. Cornwall.

"What the hell?" Adam knew this wasn't protocol.
To have any knowledge of his dad's murder case while
on leave was dangerously crossing the line. He needed
to tell her that, but her text mentioned that she already
knew what was at stake. So why?

He stepped back outside and found a secluded area
with a couple of benches. He called the number she gave
him and waited. It clicked on the second ring. "Cornwall."

"Why are you doing this?" Hell, he hadn't meant to say

that first. He wanted to be polite, introduce himself then lead into the reason for her text. "Dammit, I'm sorry—"

"It's all right, no need to apologize."

Despite his rudeness, Cornwall's voice remained calm. It held a slight lilt, and its unexpectedly sexy low tone caught him unaware.

"You've read my text."

"Yes, and I'm not sure whether to be angry or relieved. Boucher would have your head if he found out."

"Then let's make sure he doesn't."

This was the super-smart forensic scientist, so she knew what she was getting into. Adam rubbed his jaw, wondering if the risk to their reputations was worth it. "Look, I appreciate you doing this—"

"But you believe the risk might outweigh the reward. I'm willing to take that risk. Don't you want to know who murdered your father and friends?"

"Of course I do!"

"Do you know where The Artful Coffee Shop is?"

"No, but I'll find it."

"Excellent. I'll see you there in half an hour." The phone clicked off.

Adam stepped into The Artful Coffee Shop, located in a vibrant renovated community close to the Metropolitan Centre. His took in the surroundings. There were only eight tables in the cozy whitewashed building, each with a pair of large cushioned chairs that invited relaxation and intimate talk. Classical music played softly in the background, and in front of him, the coffee counter covered the length of the room. With eclectic, colorful pieces of art decorating the neutral walls, it was the kind of place his mom would love on first sight.

There were five people in the café—two couples and a single woman. She sat beneath the largest painting farthest away from the large windows, an open laptop in front of her. She looked at him as he walked farther in, and Adam sucked in a breath. Her dark gaze was intent as she stared, and rather than feeling admired, he internally squirmed with discomfort.

She rose from her seat and walked toward him, and Adam couldn't help but notice the alluring sway of her hips, the way her buttoned shirt molded her breasts and thick, black curly hair tied into a ponytail. Her dark-brown skin glowed beneath the warm ceiling lights.

Her eyes never left his as she finally stopped and held out her hand. "Detective Solberg, I'm Cynthia Cornwall. A pleasure to finally meet you in person."

Her grip was firm and warm. "Likewise." He was nervous, and for the life of him couldn't figure out why. It wasn't as if he was on a date, but he felt like a piece of evidence beneath her scrutiny.

"Please." She indicated the chair opposite her own. "Would you like something? I'm buying."

"Café mocha. And it's my treat."

She gave him a look. "No, I insist."

Her stance gave Adam the distinct impression that Ms. Cornwall felt she needed to prove something. He wasn't in the mood to argue—it had been a long day, as his stomach forcefully reminded him. "Thanks. I'll get myself a sandwich."

"I said I would buy. What would you like?"

He asked for the Cuban sandwich, then sat down while she approached the counter to place the order. Beside her laptop was a closed notebook and a unique-looking pen. It looked like she was working on an investigation. Dad's, maybe?

The coffee shop, in his mind, didn't fit with Ms. Cornwall's personality, but who was he to say? He never figured Bruiser to be a choir singer, either.

He took a closer look at the paintings. A few were abstract. One was either an original Salvador Dalí or an excellent copy. And he recognized a Group of Seven landscape hanging near the door.

The one over their table was distinctly Middle Eastern—what caught his eye was the lone pomegranate painted in the lower corner. The home in the painting was a simple two-story building with a balcony on the upper level. The colors were so vibrant that if Adam closed his eyes, he could almost see his own grandmother standing out front. He sighed, knowing he would have to call her as well to break the news of her son-in-law's death.

"The artist is a friend of the café owner," Ms. Cornwall said quietly. "I love the colors, and the impression of a simple, but happy life living in that home."

Adam spied the name of the artist, a woman whose work also hung in his mother's home. He turned, watching as her expression softened while she looked at the painting. His detective senses picked up a trace of nostalgia, or maybe wishful thinking. Adam felt a tug of emotion he hadn't felt since Else. *Nah, that wouldn't happen again.* "My mom has several pieces of this artist's work. Stills of simple Lebanese living. This house almost looks like…" He caught himself. "One of my relatives has a house similar to this."

"Really?" She sat down, her smile replacing the wistful look, but he wouldn't forget that open, honest expression. "This one is so beautiful. It's peaceful and calming, which attracted my attention."

It felt almost like a betrayal of his dead father and his friends, but Adam was glad to get his mind off what happened, if only for a few minutes. And seeing this unexpected side of Ms. Cornwall was pleasant. "They're my mother's favorite works."

"Art has been my one indulgence, a way to escape what I deal with every day." She glanced down at her laptop. "But you didn't come here to listen to my daydreaming, Detective."

Maybe one day I will. The thought came out of nowhere, heightening his awareness of the woman across from him. "Call me Adam."

She looked up, her dark brown eyes catching the light from the small lamp on the table. "Thank you. I'm Cynthia."

Their drinks and his sandwich arrived, and he took a big bite out of the Cuban, now suddenly aware of the sharp grumbling of his stomach. He hadn't eaten since he chowed down that snack the night before. He ate about half of it before coming up for air. "Cynthia," he started, then took a sip of the mocha—it was hot and damn good. "I have to ask again, why are you doing this?"

"My answer hasn't changed. Captain Boucher's actions at the crime scene weren't fair. You were angry, and he should have taken that into consideration."

"Wait, you heard me talking to him?" That wasn't Adam's finest moment.

"You were loud—I'm sure everyone did."

He chewed another bite of sandwich as Cynthia swept her notebook and pen into a leather satchel hanging on the chair behind her. Closing her laptop, she pushed it

aside and brought her drink in front of her. "I'm still analyzing evidence," she said, turning the cup around in her
hands. "But that explosion was intentional."

He almost choked, surprise and fury swirling within
him like a vortex. He put the sandwich down with trembling hands, and then took a long, slow sip of his drink,
mentally counting to ten so that he could calm down. A
bit. "It was a setup?" he asked.

"Yes. Captain Boucher and I interviewed a teenager
named Larry, except the captain was trying to lay the
blame at the kid's feet." Cynthia suddenly reached out
for her laptop, opened it, hit a button. "Bring your chair
around and put the headphones on," she instructed, hand-
ing him a pair of earbuds.

Adam scooted his seat over so that he sat next to her.
The table wasn't large, and in order to see the laptop
screen, he had to get really close and personal. His leg
brushed hers as he tried to maintain a respectful distance,
which wasn't working. As he put in the earphones, his
elbow hit something soft, and he suddenly realized it
was her breast. *Crap.*

She didn't comment or look at him, and instead hit
Play.

The screen displayed the interrogation room, with
Captain Boucher, Larry and Cynthia. As he listened to
the clip, Adam couldn't help but notice Boucher's aggres-
sive behavior. The man was usually a cool cucumber, so
seeing and hearing his gestures and Cynthia trying to
calm him down was unnerving. However, the captain
was good friends with Dad and the others, so it wasn't
unexpected.

Cynthia's demeanor was the complete opposite. During the interview, her voice was calm and reasonable.

However, she was completely aware of her surroundings, emphasized by the warning look she gave Larry as he got too close to her.

When it finished, Adam pulled the earbuds out. "I didn't think you'd be allowed into the interrogation room."

"I had some specific questions I wanted to ask the suspect." She clicked the video off. "The kind that Captain Boucher wouldn't have enough knowledge of. The bomb."

"Gotcha." Cynthia knew what specifics to ask that no one else would. "So, what do you think?"

"He and The Desperados aren't the suspects."

"How can you be sure?" For a moment, Adam thought she wouldn't answer. Her expression remained neutral, but he thought he sensed a quiet tension building around her.

"Are you questioning my methods?"

He was right—she interpreted his inquiry the wrong way. "No," he said in a steady voice. "I'm asking what made you sure it wasn't Larry and his Desperados gang."

"You know the gang and how they operate?"

"Yeah." Every bust Adam made on them didn't have enough evidence to keep them in jail for long, or they'd call their slick lawyer and get bail within a week. They were cunning, but not smart enough to build a bomb…

And just like that, he had answered his own question. "Okay, it wasn't Larry, unless he or the gang hired someone to do it."

"I don't think Larry would kill the man who helped him get clean."

"And yet Larry admitted in the interview that he still helps his gang with insider information." He was exhausted, mentally and physically. It had been a long, stressful and utterly depressing day. He wasn't thinking straight, and memories of Dad would pop up unexpectedly, forcing him to hold on to his already unsteady emotions.

Cynthia glanced at him, her expression thoughtful. "You didn't finish your sandwich. Maybe this was too much for you," she said, closing her laptop and slipping it into her satchel.

"No, it wasn't. I think it was the distraction I needed. I was at the hospital when you called."

Her beautiful face frowned with concern. "Oh my God, I'm sorry. I should have realized... I didn't mean to—"

"It's okay." He placed his hand over hers. They were still sitting side by side, and it felt so easy, so natural.

"How is everyone?"

"I don't know. They were in surgery when I left." He'd have to call Bruiser and find out their status, or he could just go back. But his friend would physically put him into a taxi and send him home. "Bruiser promised to call when he heard something."

"The Black gentleman who would put a certain green, angry monster to shame?"

He smiled. "The one and only."

Cynthia slipped her hand out from under his. A moment of warmth lingered before he snapped out of it and moved his chair back so that he sat opposite her. "Was there any other evidence you found that seemed suspicious?" he asked.

"The fire marshal found an accelerant near the bomb's location." Her notebook reappeared, and she flipped through several pages. "It was gasoline."

"I see." Not just a bomb, but a whole new level of overkill.

"I believe it was the kind of setup that was supposed to guarantee no survivors."

"Except we have several." Another problem to think about, how to keep his friends safe from further harm. He rubbed his forehead, trying to calm his distress.

"I've already talked to Captain Boucher. There should be several officers arriving at the hospital soon. We'll make sure your friends have 24-hour security while they recuperate."

It felt like this nightmare would engulf him. The only lifeline he had at the moment was Cynthia's—steady, sure and constant.

He provided her the information for Bruiser, Dawg and the others, which she wrote down. She grabbed her satchel, a hint that it was time to leave the pleasant ambiance of the café.

Outside, the sun had gone, leaving in its wake the brightness of harsh streetlamps. Traffic was still heavy, and its noise grated on Adam's nerves. "Want to share a cab?"

She smiled. "Thanks, but I'm going back to the precinct."

He glanced at his watch out of habit and was surprised that two hours had already passed. "It's pretty late."

"I'm used to it."

Adam used that exact phrase more times than he cared to admit. He saw a taxi coming toward them and waved it down. "I know you don't need me to tell you this, but I'm going to say it anyway. Be careful. If the captain gets wind of this…"

"I promise he won't."

The taxi stopped and Adam opened the door. Just as she was about to get in, he grabbed her arm. "Hey," he said, then stopped. Saying thank-you didn't seem to be enough, considering what Cynthia was about to do. "If you need anything at all, let me know, okay?"

She nodded, her dark gaze watching him curiously.

He lowered his head and kissed her cheek, hoping it didn't come across as a flirtation, that she would know he was grateful for her help. Cynthia's surprised expression lifted his spirits a little as he shut the door and watched as the cab sped off into the night.

Chapter 4

The Forensics floor was silent as Cynthia's footsteps echoed in the hallway toward the lab. The creepy vibes she got from the area when she first started working here had died away within the month. Now it was like another home, and when it was quiet like this, it was easier to concentrate on her work.

However, as she powered up her laptop and settled in, work wasn't the only thing on her mind. Despite being all business during their coffee meeting, she'd been completely aware of Adam Solberg. When she'd asked him to sit next to her to view the interview footage, she'd been surprised by how big he was. It had been a tight squeeze, and when his elbow bumped her breast, she had flinched but didn't admonish him. Normally, she'd browbeat a guy if he got too close.

And when his hand covered hers, it felt so natural, and

that had unnerved her. Adam impressed her as a gentle-man, despite the grief surrounding him. Maybe that explained why she was more tolerant of his actions.

Don't kid yourself, Cyn. You didn't say anything when he kissed your cheek, either.

"Argh, forget it." Cynthia double-clicked a file folder. One piece of evidence in particular had bothered her, and she needed to figure out why.

As she scrolled through the pictures, it finally came into view: clear, yet so vague.

The watch looked just as innocent as before. Its leather strap was mostly gone, but there were small fragments still attached. The watch face was more interesting, featuring a second dial and what looked like moon shapes within it, telling her this was a chronometer. These particular watches were tested and certified by independent laboratories for their incredible accuracy. But searching the internet for watches with this feature came up with too many hits, so she had to narrow it down. What made recognizing the watch so difficult was the glass casing—it had cracked, but didn't shatter, attesting to the mechanism's quality.

Cynthia zoomed the picture even larger, her laptop adjusting quickly to the change, then rotated the image, hoping to catch a glimpse of something that would help her identify…

Wait. She squinted at the watch face again, spying the odd shape located at its twelve o'clock position. She zoomed in even more until she reached the highest percentage, then rotated the picture slowly, hoping to catch it at the right angle.

There it was—a symbol she instantly recognized. Pleased that she had discovered this bit of information so quickly, she decided to go home instead of hanging around at work any longer. Daniel might also give her some fresh perspective tomorrow morning.

"A Rolex, huh?" Daniel raised his head from looking at the item nestled in his gloved hand. "Pretty hard to tell by just looking at it."

"I assumed a reliable, but cheap watch. Who would destroy a Rolex?" Another mystery piece to add to the puzzle.

"Are you sure it's not fake?" Daniel asked. "There's some really impressive knock-offs out there."

"I'll have to get it analyzed by a Rolex dealer, but I don't think it is. That should have melted with the rest of the clubhouse, but other than the shattered face and burnt straps, it's pretty intact."

"Makes you wonder who would sacrifice a piece of jewelry worth, oh, twenty thousand dollars." Daniel turned it over. "No fingerprints at all?"

"Nope."

"Hmm." Daniel dropped the watch back into the evidence bag and leaned against the counter. "So, I wanted to ask you something."

"What's up?" Her senses were on alert.

"I understand Detective Solberg isn't working on the bombing case."

She felt herself relax. "No. It's too personal for him."

"Yeah, I get that. But I thought he'd be here to wrap up his serial killer case. Why hasn't he come back to the precinct? He worked his ass off to nail that son of a bitch. If I was in his shoes, there's no way I'd let another detective take lead to finish it."

"So what would you suggest?" she asked.

"Since you're the forensic genius that helped crack the

case, I suggest that you talk to the captain about bringing Solberg back."

"Me, huh?"

"Yeah. Boucher listens to you. And we are short-staffed. So long as Solberg doesn't interfere with the bombing investigation, I don't see why he can't return and complete it."

"Enough said. I'm going to try your idea."

"Come in."

Cynthia stepped inside Boucher's office and shut the door behind her.

"Cornwall." The captain faced her from his favorite spot, the large picture window that looked out onto the street below and the forest park beyond. "What is it?"

"A couple of things I wanted to update you on, sir." Despite discovering the make of the watch, she really didn't have much more information, which annoyed her.

"What have you found out?" The captain sat down, and indicated for her to do the same.

Cynthia sat on the edge of the chair, anxious about her lack of results. "Daniel and I haven't found any distinctive fingerprints other than those belonging to the MC members so far. That explosion was meant to erase anything that could link back to the criminal. But the watch used to set off the bomb was a Rolex."

"What?" Captain Boucher's eyebrows lifted.

"It was difficult to identify as the watch face was extensively cracked, but I managed to figure out the symbol at the top. I'm going to take it to a certified Rolex dealer to confirm."

"You might discover the identity of the owner. Excellent. Anything else?"

"Whoever set this up was good. I'll need more time to go over the evidence we found."

"Understood."

She hesitated, and the captain caught it. "Something else on your mind, Cornwall?"

"Yes, sir." Now was the time, and she steadied her nerves. "Daniel's finishing the serial killer case for me, but he's feeling a bit—frustrated with Hawthorne and Timmins."

"In what way?"

"Well, they don't know the case. They've been asking questions Solberg already knows the answers to. Plus they're also working on the bomb investigation." She hoped the captain got the hint. "Everyone's stretched pretty thin."

"So you're requesting that Solberg return to finish his case?"

"Suggesting."

"Hmph." He rose and went again to his spot by the window. "You know that I ordered Solberg to take time off?"

"I heard about that, sir." Cynthia wasn't going to let the captain know she had eavesdropped on the conversation.

"Solberg's dad was one of the men killed at the club-house."

"Yes, sir."

"Then I'm sure you can put two and two together."

"With all due respect, Captain, we're short-staffed. Solberg knows the serial killer case like the back of his hand. He can wrap this up fast and it's one less thing on our plates."

Boucher turned to look at her but remained quiet for

several tense seconds. She kept her gaze on Boucher, refusing to turn away or show any signs of retreat.

"All right, Cornwall, you got your wish. I'll call Solberg later and ask him to return to finish his investigation."

She stood, keeping her stance businesslike even though she felt like collapsing with relief. "Thank you, sir."

"Let me know what answers you get from the watch dealer."

"Of course." She left, keeping her expression and stride tight and focused until she got back to the lab, where she wearily sank into a chair.

Daniel, his face hidden behind protective goggles, looked up. "You're back fast. What's the verdict?"

She gave him a thumbs-up. "Boucher's going to call Solberg back."

"What? Are you serious?"

"Yep, thank God. Now we can get that serial killer case out of our hair and Mr. Anderson into jail where he belongs."

"I didn't think that idea was going to work."

"It did, thanks to you. Let's hope Solberg is here sooner rather than later." Cynthia glanced at her watch. "I'm going to see if I can talk to a Rolex dealer today about our find. Wish me luck."

Cynthia held her police identification in front of the door, letting the man on the other side read it. He nodded and punched in a code, and the entrance buzzed, signaling her to come in.

"My apologies for the extra security, Ms. Cornwall,

but as I hope you understand, our merchandise is exceptionally valuable."

"That's quite all right, Mr. Vogel, I understand." The Rolex store was located on a main street in downtown Toronto, surrounded by high-end condos and a mixture of posh and take-out restaurants. She looked around the small space, decorated in rich wood, stainless steel and soft, luxurious leather. *Wow.* "Thank you for seeing me."

"Of course, anything to assist the authorities." Mr. Vogel was a handsome man, with dark brown hair cut stylishly short. He wore a well-tailored, navy three-piece suit that looked like it would cost two months of her very decent salary, and black leather shoes. A pair of steel-rimmed glasses completed the look, and as he reached overhead to lock the door, she noticed a Rolex graced his left wrist. *Of course.* "I don't have any customers for the rest of the afternoon," he explained. "Please follow me to the back office, and I can take a closer look at the watch."

"Thank you."

This smaller room was no less stamped with luxury. Off to one side stood a desk with an expensive laptop and two plush leather office chairs.

"Please sit down." Mr. Vogel took the chair facing the laptop. "Could you show me what you've brought?"

Cynthia pulled the plastic evidence bag containing the watch out of her satchel and placed it on the dark green cloth lying on the table between them.

Mr. Vogel's pained expression amused her. "What manner of human being would do this to a Rolex?" He pointed at the item. "May I examine it?"

"That's why I'm here."

"Thank you." The manager pulled on a pair of thin white gloves and opened the bag to retrieve the damaged watch. He carefully turned it with his fingers. "Where's the strap?"

"Burned in the fire."

He frowned. "That's unfortunate. It would have helped narrow down what type of Rolex this is." Mr. Vogel rested it on the cloth and retrieved a leather case.

When he opened it, Cynthia let out a low whistle of appreciation. "Those are some impressive instruments. If I might ask a favor?"

He held the watch in one hand, a thin instrument in the other, a questioning expression on his face.

Cynthia leaned forward. "I need you to remove the front of the watch first. I need to see what time it stopped."

"Ah." Mr. Vogel switched his instruments, and she admired his steady hands as he pried the glass cover off with a soft *pop* of vacuumed air.

"The glass didn't shatter all the way through. Impressive."

"A testament to the watch's design." He placed everything on the cloth. "This is a Cellini Moonphase," he told her. "Distinctive for this blue enameled disc at the six o'clock position, which displays a full and new moon. The watch also displays the date on the outer part of the dial, with the time on the inner circumference."

Cynthia saw that the hands had stopped at nine thirty-three on the morning of the explosion. "I'll have to assume that the watch stopped at this time when the bomb went off."

"What?" Mr. Vogel lost some of his refined composure.

"Someone used this watch as a timer."

"Dear God." He touched the watch delicately, treating it like an injured bird.

"I need to know if you can find the owner."

"Of course. Your investigation is mystifying if a Rolex was used for such a crude method."

"This crude method, as you call it, killed several people." She hadn't meant to shock him, but she thought if she mentioned the word *bomb*, he'd get the hint that lives had been at stake.

Mr. Vogel was visibly shaken. "Ms. Cornwall, I…" He stopped. "I hope that I haven't come across as flippant or unconcerned. I didn't think—no, I wasn't thinking. My sincerest apologies." He straightened his shoulders. "Let's discover who this demon is."

She remained quiet as Mr. Vogel turned the watch over and removed its backing.

"This is the registration number," he said, pointing to a series of gold digits. "We can discover who the owner is, and I'm also going to check our records to see if the watch was reported as stolen." He turned to the laptop and tapped the keyboard several times.

"Here we are." He ran his finger across the screen. "Mr. Alberto Creatura. He owns three of our pieces, but he hasn't reported this one as missing."

Weird. "I'll need Mr. Creatura's contact information so that I can talk to him."

"Of course."

As Mr. Vogel printed off Mr. Creatura's details, Cynthia stared at the watch piece. It seemed truly odd that someone would sacrifice a Rolex for a bombing.

"Here you are." He handed her a piece of paper.

"Thank you. If you could put the watch back together, I'd appreciate it."

"Yes, certainly." Mr. Vogel quickly attached the front and back coverings and placed it back in the evidence bag.

She tucked it into her satchel, then pulled out an envelope. "While I can tell you that our conversation was strictly confidential, I'm afraid I have to present you with this as well."

"What is it?" Mr. Vogel took the sheet of paper out and read it quickly. His face blanched.

"That's just the official way of telling you not to discuss our meeting with anyone. Including your boss. I would hate to see you dragged into the police station to explain how an ongoing and important investigation got into the newspapers." She rose.

"I—I completely understand, Ms. Cornwall. I won't say a word."

"Ms. Cornwall, I need to ask you a question," Adam demanded. They were at her favorite coffee shop.

She paused, her cappuccino a hair's breadth from her lips. "Yes?"

He placed his phone in front of her, and watched her expression as she read the short text from Captain Boucher.

"Hmm. *'Report to me tomorrow morning.'*" She sipped her drink. "It looks like the captain has come to his senses."

"He never lost them." Her reaction told Adam what he needed to know—she had something to do with his return. Ah, Ms. Cornwall. Mysterious, beautiful and smart as hell, going behind the captain's back to keep Adam in the loop. "Boucher wouldn't ask me to come back unless it was urgent, or it was requested." He placed his phone in his pants pocket and sat back, waiting.

"I agree."

"Do you know which?"

"Me?" She put her cup down with an audible clink and

stared at him with an innocent look that almost fooled him, because the ghost of a smirk played around her lips.

"Yes." He smiled.

She laced her fingers together and rested her chin on them. "It's a bit of both, actually. We're overwhelmed at the station. Hawthorne and Timmins are good at their jobs, but they can only do so much. They're working on the serial killer case as well as the bombing. I was worried the captain might have called for outside assistance, so…"

"So you managed to convince Boucher to have me back, if only temporarily. Nice."

"Keeping you on ice when you could finish your big case didn't make sense. That could be done in, say, another week?"

"Give or take."

She nodded. "You really do have the makings of a first-class detective."

His parents, and particularly his dad, had always praised his hard work and dedication to the police force. But hearing it from someone like Cynthia just added that big cherry on top. "Thank you."

"Now, the case." She stopped and looked at him with concern in her eyes. "How are your friends, by the way?"

"Surviving." Literally and figuratively. "It's going to be a long road to recovery."

"I'm sorry." She reached out and covered his clenched fist with her hand—warm, soft, comforting. "And how are you holding up?" she asked quietly.

He nodded, because he couldn't trust himself to speak. Being home meant seeing Dad wherever he looked—pictures, books, anything that caught his eye. He had slept in the guest bedroom because it held nothing of Dad's that could upset the thin balance of his sanity. Today was spent outside as much as possible until he had to head back home. Thankfully, Cynthia's call this afternoon gave him a reason to get away, if only for a while.

Her touch offered the small piece of solace he needed to hold himself together—support, understanding and the willpower to solve the case. With nothing else holding him up, Adam clung to what Cynthia provided.

"Are you okay to talk about the case?"

"Yeah," he managed. "Keep me distracted."

"Okay, let me tell you what I've found out so far." She was back to business. "The bomb had a watch wrapped around it as a timer, meaning it was meant to go off at a specific time."

"Like when Dad and the others would all be in the clubhouse." Adam ruminated on that. "I know the guys had regular meetings, but they weren't every day."

"Which meant whoever planted the device had an idea of when most, if not all, of the MC members would be in the building."

Adam knew his expression held disbelief. "You're saying this was an inside job."

"No, I'm saying it's one of two possibilities."

"What's the other one?"

"That your dad's enemies have been casing the club, recording your friends' movements until they found an opportunity. Larry talked about a second drug gang during the interview I showed you, remember?"

"Larry could be a damn mafia gangster and I wouldn't know." His temper threatened to boil. "The Desperados are smart. I couldn't nail them on anything more than weed possession, but I knew they were dealing in harder stuff. Just couldn't prove it."

"I see. Let me show you the bomb remnants…" she paused, biting her bottom lip. "If that's okay?"

Adam nodded. He needed to stay strong—it was the only way to nail the son of a bitch who attacked Dad and his friends.

"Swing your chair around over here."

He did so, being more careful not to brush against Cynthia's body, but he still managed to touch her thigh with his as he settled in. Something else caught his attention—a faint hint of perfume when he inhaled. He didn't notice it when sitting across from her, but now, at such close range, he picked up on it. The scent of roses filled him with a longing he hadn't felt in a long time. They were his favorite flowers, and he bought them for the ones he truly loved—the women in his family. Roses grew prolifically in his grandmother's garden in Mtein, Lebanon, where he'd first seen and appreciated them as a boy. Mom had followed *Teta*'s tradition and had several rosebushes in their backyard as he grew up. As he thought about this petaled wonder of natural art, Adam suddenly realized he never bought any for his ex-fiancée. That mind-awakening bit of news should have been an obvious hint.

"Adam? Are you all right?"

"Yeah, sorry. Was just thinking of something."

Cynthia stared at him a moment longer before turning back to the screen. "You're sure you're up for this?"

"I said I was fine." *Damn emotions.*

She clicked a few keys until several pictures of items appeared, including a bunch of ball bearings and a busted watch. "The timepiece is a Rolex that belongs to an Alberto Creatura. Ring any bells?"

Wow, sacrificing a multithousand-dollar watch to blow up a motorcycle club was more than a bit much. "The name isn't familiar."

"I looked him up on the internet. Multimillionaire, lives in the Bridle Path area, CEO and majority owner of a pharmaceutical company. Donates to charity, all-round good guy, blah, blah."

"Has he been brought in for questioning?"

"He'll be at the precinct the day after tomorrow—I heard he's traveling on business. From what I heard, he was surprised at the call."

Adam frowned. "So he didn't know his watch had been stolen? Sounds off to me."

"Right? I doubt Boucher will let me question him."

"But since it's his watch, it's possible he assembled the bomb."

She had a spoon in her hand and waved it for emphasis. "I couldn't find any fingerprints on it, which was annoying. I have to place my hopes on the other evidence I found."

"I've seen how you work, and one thing that's struck me is, you never give up on a lead, no matter how obscure." The compliment came out of nowhere. Adam pressed his lips together and turned his head slightly away, embarrassed.

"Why, Detective Solberg, what a kind and observant thing to say. Thank you."

He let his mind wander for a moment on other, more interesting offers he'd like to make, then shut down the thought—quick. "Anything else?" he asked in a gruff voice.

"The amount of damage done to the clubhouse revealed that this was not a small device. How the hell did someone sneak it in there?"

"That's what you'll hopefully find out." He swung his chair back—reluctantly—and finished his coffee. "I suggest we call it a night. Since I've been asked to come back to the station, I'll need my beauty rest."

She chuckled. "Like you need it."

Was that a compliment? Adam watched her discreetly as she packed up her things. "Then I guess I'll see you tomorrow."

"But only about the serial killer case." She stood up, a determined look on her face.

Cynthia knew the second she stepped into her apartment that something wasn't right. As the front door swung open, Cynthia remembered that pest control had come by earlier, but that wasn't what bothered her.

She took a few steps into the living room, looking around as she placed her satchel on the floor. Several items were moved out of place, her living room curtains crooked, and the items in her meditation space disturbed, which set off her anger. Aunt Ki loved to tease Cynthia about her obsessive-compulsiveness, but it never bothered her. Organization was her middle name, and now it was missing in her apartment.

Someone—other than pest control—had been here.

She eased into the kitchen, where she picked up a large chef knife. Adrenaline pumped through every part of her body, heightening her senses as she did a methodical sweep of the kitchen and living room—checking the closet and other hiding spots, behind furniture, under tables. The curtains were whipped aside, but revealed nothing. The windows were locked.

She made her way down the hall toward the bathroom and bedroom, flicking the switch to bathe the area in bright light, her weapon held in front of her. Fear, which Cynthia had fought to hold tight, now wormed with insinuating glee through her limbs. Cold sweat drenched her neck and back, and her hands trembled. She jumped at every noise, her gaze darting back and forth, searching. If someone was in here, they had the advantage of watching her movements, while she had to guess where they hid.

The hallway closet door was thrown open and clothes shoved and thrown to the ground while she held the knife ready—nothing.

That left the bedroom and bathroom.

Cynthia had been trained in dealing with situations like this. But no matter how many times she'd been through it, it never got easier.

The bathroom was at the end of the hall before reaching the bedroom. It was clear, and she had closed all the doors before reaching the last room.

When Cynthia flipped the light switch, her fear slowly morphed into red-hot anger.

In the center of her bed rested a sheet of paper, with a photograph of her taped to it.

She needed to finish her sweep. She went for the bedroom closet first. She stood half-turned in order to watch the dark space beneath the mattress, swung the door and pulled all of her clothes out of the way. No one was here. As she moved away, Cynthia grabbed a flashlight sitting on the top shelf before standing in front of the bed.

The final hiding spot scared her the most. If someone was underneath the bed, they could watch her feet as she worked out the best plan of action for taking down the stranger.

After a few seconds, she decided just to go for it. She clicked on the flashlight with the knife held in front of her, then dropped to the floor, holding the light steady before her. If she could blind her intruder, she'd have a chance...

No one was there.

Cynthia sat back on her haunches, fighting to control her breathing, every part of her shaking with relief. Her heart thumped so hard she was scared it would jump out of her mouth. She finally got up and checked the bedroom window—that was locked as well.

When she turned around, the note taunted her, as if laughing at her antics. Dammit, she wanted to shred it and throw it into the toilet, but she left everything untouched as she made her way back to the kitchen.

She picked up her phone, ready to call the precinct. But as the other end rang, Cynthia suddenly realized she had dialed Adam's number.

Chapter 5

Adam sat down heavily on the couch and rubbed his face with his hands. He'd just gotten off the phone with Bruiser, and the news was so-so. Everyone had pulled through with varying degrees of success. Jeffrey was the worst off—broken bones, internal bleeding, possible brain damage, and he'd been put into an induced coma. But Bruiser said the doctors involved were the best in the province, and if Jeffrey and the others made it through the night, they stood a good chance.

It was going to be difficult for Adam to concentrate on his serial killer case while Timmins and Hawthorne figured out who attacked his dad and friends. And next to impossible to keep his mind on his work while Cynthia roamed through the police building.

This was why he didn't like office relationships. Police work was his focus, his life. His body craved the adrenaline rush of discovering solid clues, pinpointing a suspect and then swooping down on them like a falcon spying its prey. He lived for his job, breathed and slept with it like an intimate lover.

But now...a woman stood in his peripheral vision, an intelligent person who also seemed to care so much about her work, whose gaze could cut a man in half or fill them with teasing laughter. A beautiful woman who didn't seem to realize how gorgeous she was.

He thought about grabbing dinner when his cell phone rang—his work phone. He dug it out of his jacket pocket and looked at the number. It was Cynthia. He clicked it on. "Hey, what's—"

"I—I need you to come over to my place."

O-kay. Her words were a potential threat to keeping their relationship strictly business. He swallowed against the lump in his throat and adjusted his jeans. Of course his mind went right to the gutter. "Is that a demand?" he asked, with a slight tease in his voice.

"What? No! I didn't mean it—" He heard her swearing under her breath.

Adam tried not to snicker.

"I want you here because someone broke into my apartment."

"What?" All traces of humor disappeared.

"There's a note with a photo of me sitting on my bedroom pillow." A faint tremor shook in her voice.

"Don't touch anything." He was all business. "Get pictures of it and anything else that looks suspicious. I'll put a call in and have a police cruiser out there. In the meantime, pack a small bag and bring your office stuff. You're staying at my place."

* * *

"Now, hang on!" Cynthia's anxiety at having her personal space violated by a stranger instantly morphed to anger when Adam assumed he needed to protect her. "Please explain why I have to stay with you."

"I can think of a few reasons." His voice had changed when she told him about the break-in. It became more gruff, more demanding. Normally, hearing a man talk to her like that raised the hackles on her neck, but this time she didn't argue and, even more intriguing, she didn't mind.

She'd have to mull over this unusual feeling. "Which are?"

"Do you want to sit in a safe house, twiddling your thumbs? Or be shipped out of province? Even better, how about 24-7 security watching your every move?"

Damn. "You have a point," she admitted somewhat grudgingly.

"Excellent. What's your address?"

She gave him the information, then indulged in a fleeting moment of other reasons he could be coming over. She sighed, feeling almost regretful.

"I know where that is. I'll come get you in about fifteen minutes after I've talked to the officer on duty at the precinct."

"No, I'll do that." Cynthia needed some control of her situation. "I'll be ready when you get here."

A short pause. "Fine." He hung up.

The irresistible urge to yell obscenities into the phone almost overcame her. Who the hell did Adam think he was anyway?

Cynthia had no time to dwell on that. She had the sneaking suspicion that if she was late by one second,

Adam would drag her out of her apartment like some damned caveman, and that would not do.

With time against her, she carefully moved around the apartment, getting photos of the suspicious letter, misplaced items and the layout of each room. The fact that she was treating her apartment like a crime scene bothered her. When—not if—the intruder was apprehended, she would promise them a world of hurt.

She dug out her travel backpack, grabbed what she needed for a two-night stay and placed it by the front door along with the satchel that held her personal and work phones, her work tablet and trusty laptop. After triple-checking that the remaining windows were locked and appliances turned off, she went back to her bedroom to grab the last critical item.

The idea itself was as cliché as they came, but in the end, it worked out for the best. Her police-issued weapon lay hidden within a small box, painted and shaped like a book. It sat on her night table, an innocent-looking thing that no one would bother giving a second glance.

Cynthia picked it up and looked inside. The Browning Hi-Power 9mm handgun was the weapon she'd been given in her earlier days of combat training. She took the pistol and spare cartridges and placed the hollowed book back on the table. After securing her gun within its holster, she pulled on a leather jacket to conceal it. When she turned around, the piece of paper taunted her, lying smugly against a cushion her aunt had made for her birthday.

One more thing to do. She dialed her landlord. "Mrs. McCarthy, I'm sorry I'm bothering you, but I've had a problem."

"What is it, dear?"

"Someone broke into my apartment. Pest control came here today, and they're the only ones I can think of who could have done this. I've called the police to check it out, so I won't be here for a couple of days. I didn't want you to worry about me."

"What the hell? I've never had any problems with this company! I should call them and give them a piece of my mind."

"Mrs. McCarthy, that's what I don't want you to do. Let the police handle it, and please cooperate with everything they ask."

"Yes, yes, of course. Are you sure you're all right?"

"I'm angry as hell, but I'm fine. I'll be staying at a friend's tonight. You can always reach me on my cell."

Three minutes to spare. She'd call the precinct when she got to Adam's place. Next to being organized, self-sufficiency was a close second character trait of hers. She understood his concerns, but treating her like a damsel in distress was going to rub her the wrong way.

When she got to the lobby, the sound of a loud, rumbling engine caught her attention. The large, distinctive motorcycle cruised down the street toward her. A pair of saddlebags, along with the bike's recognizable orange and black logo emblazoned on the gas tank, completed its distinguished style. By the time the driver pulled up in front of her building, she had a sneaking suspicion who it was.

"Ready?" Adam called out as he kicked down the stand and swung out of his seat in one long, feline move.

Cynthia swallowed as two thoughts came to mind—she would be riding behind a colleague who she liked, but needed to remain a work partner. The second thought—*damn, change his clothes into armor and he'd be a regu-*

lar shining knight. This wasn't going to be easy. "I wish you'd told me that you were riding a chopper."

He smiled as he walked toward her. "Don't tell me you're scared."

Was he deliberately trying to rile her? "I'm not scared of the bike, just the driver's experience."

That got to him. Adam stopped directly in front of her. His wide chest was at the same height as her nose, and as much as she hated it, Cynthia took a step back to give herself room to stare up at him. She hadn't picked up on how tall he was. Wearing a plain black leather jacket, white T-shirt, jeans and his helmet, he managed to come across as intimidating. It must be the scowl that marred his face. "Don't worry. I've been riding since I was a teenager. Dad taught me." His expression shifted slightly, as if remembering.

Dammit, she hadn't meant to upset him. "Then I trust you." She held up her backpack and satchel. "Do you have room for these?"

He grabbed her backpack. "You'll need to carry your satchel." He tilted his head to one side. "You're carrying a piece?"

"Yep. Don't worry, it's not loaded."

He nodded, his gaze remaining on her a moment more before turning away.

After storing her things, he turned around with a second helmet.

"Thanks." Cynthia tied her hair back into a ponytail, then secured the strap. She adjusted her satchel so that it rode on the back of her hip.

She hadn't realized Adam's legs were so long until he settled into the seat. He displayed such ease, like he was born to it. "Climb on."

Cynthia, however, wasn't as comfortable. In order to get on, she would have to use Adam for balance. Huffing out a frustrated sigh, she grabbed his broad shoulders and got on quickly.

"Cynthia, you'll have to get closer than that." He looked over his shoulder.

Yeah, she knew she had to sit right behind him. *Well, I have no choice.* She scooted closer until her thighs were alongside his, then wrapped her arms around his waist. She heard him say something. "What was that?"

"Nothing." He shifted in his seat. "Make sure you move with me when I take the turns."

"I've been on a bike, so not to worry."

He gunned the motor, and Cynthia held her breath as the vibrations shook her in her seat. They drove off, the motorcycle feeling like a pent-up animal waiting to be released. The road was busy as usual, with cars darting within traffic. A horn suddenly blared behind them and she flinched, her arms instinctively wrapping tighter around Adam's waist. "Sorry," she called out.

He nodded, understanding, then shifted gears and moved to the far-right lane for the highway. He eased into the fast-moving traffic with no problem, shifting gears, and the engine growled in response. The warm summer wind blew into her face, and she leaned forward, almost resting her chin against his back. She'd forgotten to ask for goggles.

Adam's body shifted in tune with his chopper, small adjustments that he seemed to do without thinking. However, as she felt his muscles flex beneath her arms and legs, Cynthia's body wanted to respond—not to the bike's movements, but to his. She bit her lip when her thighs squeezed his as he leaned into a turn, and her heart raced when he inched backward. She found her fingers moving slowly across the smooth leather of his jacket, and she had to stop by clenching her hands into the material.

God, she hoped this would be over soon.

Bringing the motorcycle was the wrong thing to do.

Adam knew Cynthia would be close and personal—that *was* the plan after all, and it seemed like a good idea. She would have to hold on to him while he drove.

She seemed to have picked up on his idea as well. Her reluctance stung more than he realized, and his attempt at easing the tension with a joke unfortunately backfired. He should have backed off, realized that she put up a wall to keep him out of her personal space. But something made him push back against her resistance. He understood where she came from—he was just as cautious around women, maybe more so. She was the first lady in a long time to attract his attention, but he didn't want to scare her off, either.

His light flirtations were neither brushed off nor accepted, which confused him. The only thing he did know was Cynthia refused to be taken advantage of, and he respected that.

Her mild yet snarky comment on his driving skills got under his skin, however. Dad had taught him how to ride before he was old enough for his driver's license. Any hint of criticism would turn Adam into an unkind person. He was glad Cynthia got the hint fast and retreated.

He also noticed the gun holstered beneath her jacket. The weapon wasn't small, but she carried it like it was a part of her, and damn, if that wasn't sexy as hell. His jeans became suddenly uncomfortable. When her arms wrapped around his waist after she got on, he fought not to squirm in his seat. Thank God his chopper demanded all his attention as he maneuvered around honking cars. Cynthia shifted her body at his subtle prompts, making the ride that much smoother.

He drove around an eighteen-wheeler, keeping as much distance between them and the huge vehicle as he could. When he glanced at the irritated driver, Adam knew he would blare his horn and readied himself to keep the motorcycle straight. When it happened, Cynthia jerked and held him tighter. Her strength surprised him, and he was forced to move a bit in his seat until she relaxed her grip.

On the highway, Cynthia moved in closer, her thighs encasing his. He'd never had a lady ride with him before—he'd never let his ex-fiancée on his bike, for some reason—and this would be something he'd have to carefully think on the next time.

Next time?

The chopper swerved slightly, and he fought to get the wheel straight. Dammit. Distraction was the devil's name on a bike.

"Are you okay?" Cynthia shouted.

"Yeah, sorry about that." He was more than sorry—he had scared himself. If there was ever another chance to have Cynthia ride with him, he'd have to do a whole lot better than be damned *sorry*.

He turned off and headed down several side streets before arriving at the condo. It was an older building, more concrete than glass and well-kept. Adam cut the engine after parking in his spot and sat there for a moment, more shaken than he realized.

"Hey." Cynthia grabbed his shoulder and squeezed it. "You sure you're okay?"

Couldn't she tell he wasn't? He yanked off his helmet and threw it to the ground. "That shouldn't have happened," he muttered through clenched teeth.

She got off the bike, picked it up and handed it back to him. "It happens to everyone."

"Not to me." Dad would be pissed if he'd seen it. He dismounted, grabbed her backpack and strode toward the elevator, Cynthia's quick steps keeping pace. "You could have been hurt. I'd never forgive myself."

"Adam. It's a choice I made. If I didn't want to get on, I would have told you."

He twisted his mouth. Yeah, she would have.

They stood facing each other as the elevator headed to the top floor.

"Have you lived here long?" she asked.

"About four years," he said.

Cynthia was faster in starting the small talk. "The condo was one of my picks for a place to live. I couldn't get in because they had no rentals available. Do you like living in this area?"

"Yeah. Dad—" He stopped, almost choking with the sudden rush of grief, then tried again. "Dad bought the penthouse about twenty years ago. He and Mom loved it."

"Oh!" Her surprised look caught him off guard. "Is your mom living with you?"

Jeez, Adam, get it together. "No. She and Dad got divorced a while back." He sighed. "I can't seem to get my thoughts straight."

"You've been through a lot." Cynthia laid her hand on his arm. "Try not to take it out on yourself."

This close, Adam saw the gold flecks in her brown eyes. Her dark brown skin held its own glow—she wore no makeup, and in his opinion, she didn't need any. Her full lips enticed him to lean down and discover what they tasted like. The thought traveled from his brain to his body in record time, and his mouth hovered over hers, waiting.

Cynthia didn't move away, but her gaze didn't miss a thing. She blinked once, twice, then parted those luscious wide lips. "Are you attempting to do something inappropriate, Detective Solberg?" she asked quietly.

He froze. Using his title and last name could only mean one thing—she was angry. However, she remained where she stood, an odd thing to do if she didn't want him to kiss her. "Only if you want me to, Forensic Investigator Cornwall," he whispered.

She had one hell of a poker face. The only change he caught was the widening of her eyes.

The loud ping of the elevator arriving at the top floor startled both of them. Cynthia immediately backed away, and he mentally kicked himself for missing out on his chance. Would she have allowed him to kiss her? He'd never know. Maybe it was best that way—they'd have to see each other at work, and *awkward* would be an understatement.

Of course, it didn't help that he had figuratively manhandled her into staying at his place until the investigation at her apartment was finished. He hadn't felt right after hanging up the phone with her, but his protective instinct kicked in before he had the opportunity to think through his decision.

He opened the door and stepped aside to let her go in first. With a small smile of thanks, she moved past him into the large foyer. "Wow," she breathed. "This is nice."

"Thanks. Mom loves decorating. There used to be a lot more stuff in here." He hung their jackets and placed the helmets on the bench by the closet door. "Did you want to hang your holster with your jacket?" he asked.

"I—um, I have a habit of keeping it in the bedroom with me. I was told it was the best place to keep it," she added, seeming almost defiant.

"It is. I do the same thing." He didn't want her to feel embarrassed. He shook off his shoes and grabbed her backpack. "Come on—I'll give you the quick tour."

Adam loved this place. In the ten years he'd spent here, from a teenager until he moved out at twenty-three, his parents' love had infused these four walls. Mom's eclectic choice in her native Lebanese art, combined with Dad's Nordic love of the bare necessities, made their home so unique it had been featured in a popular Canadian home magazine.

Cynthia was the second woman to visit—Else, his ex, was the first. "Here you are. Make yourself at home." He placed her backpack by the bedroom door.

"Thanks." She turned a slow circle before facing him. He caught the questioning look in her eyes.

Instead, he headed for his own room. Adam wasn't going to mess this up. He sensed the attraction between them, but one wrong move, and he'd lose his chance to…

He stopped, suddenly realizing that he needed something more than a passive working relationship.

Chapter 6

"What do you mean the break-in has something to do with the bombing case?" Daniel demanded.

Cynthia sighed. "Instead of asking all the questions that I don't have the answers to," she said, trying to control her frustration, "how about you get a couple of officers, go to my apartment building, get the key from the landlady and, you know—investigate?"

He sputtered. "Yeah, sure. Sorry about that."

"Call me as soon as you find anything on the letter." Her anger grew as she remembered part of the message. *I'll be watching you, Cornwall.*

"You bet. Where are you staying?"

"At a friend's house. Only for a couple of days."

She hung up the phone and blew out a sigh. She hoped Daniel found something.

A knock. "Cynthia? Are you okay?"

"Yes." She scrambled to her feet. "Give me a minute."

Damn, she needed more than a minute. "Oh man." She grabbed her hair and gently pulled. How the hell did she get into this situation? Oh yeah, by calling Adam to rescue her instead of heading straight to the police station and staying at a hotel.

Was she getting too close? Memories of her own similar tragedy, and solving it when no one else could, had dragged her into Adam's world of pain. She wanted to be the one to help ease it, but she wasn't doing a very good job of it.

Being in his apartment should have been the last thing on her mind, and yet, here she was. She hadn't refused his demand to stay with him. Why not?

"Argh." Cynthia didn't have time to figure this out— Adam was on the other side of the door waiting for her. She grabbed her laptop and phone, put on her "officially at work" face and walked out to brave the unknown.

She observed the clean lines of the condo, noticed how the rooms flowed into one another in an open concept plan, and how big it was—maybe too big for one person. Beyond the cozy dining room was the large kitchen, with Adam moving about. The delicious smells she inhaled caused her stomach to growl loudly. She approached slowly, not wanting to startle him.

Cynthia already knew Adam was tall, but she was again surprised by how broad his shoulders were, and how his upper body tapered to a trim waist. He wore a T-shirt, and his muscles flexed with a will of their own as he worked. Studying a body in motion was a whole new ball game.

"There I go again," she mumbled. She'd never get any work done. This was why relationships were a serious no-no in her books.

Adam turned—he must have heard her. "Hey," he called out. "I'm just throwing something together for us to eat. You can wait in the living room if you want."

She should have taken him up on that offer and studied the photos she'd taken of the crime at her apartment until he finished. Instead, she walked over to the breakfast nook adjoining the kitchen and placed her stuff on it. "I don't want to be rude," she said by way of explanation when she saw his surprised expression. "Plus, we can talk."

His boyish, impulsive smile made her stomach feel weird. *Damn emotions, getting in the way of work.* Cynthia made a show of opening her office laptop, before plugging it and her phone into the handy outlet behind her and transferring the photos so that she could study them better on the larger screen.

"You're not allergic to anything, are you?"

"Sorry?" She glanced up, and her breath caught in her throat. Adam wore a pair of khaki cargo pants that looked tailored. They were a snug fit, showing off the definition in his thighs and backside.

Lord have Mercy. Cynthia kept her gaze glued to her laptop screen, fiddling with buttons. "Did you ask me something?"

"Allergies." He said this slowly. "Do you have any food allergies?"

"Nope, none, I'm good." She sensed him standing there a moment longer before moving away. Damn, that was close. No more looking at Adam for now. She pulled up the first picture—the letter that was discovered on her bed. The words were written in block letters to try and disguise any personality traits. "I should hear from Daniel in a couple of hours," she started.

"What the hell does the letter say?"

Cynthia had read it, but in the heat of the moment, the meaning never registered. Now as she stared at her screen, the words angered her even more. "*'Be a good girl and back off. Don't want to see a pretty thing like you get hurt. I'll be watching you, Cornwall.'*"

"It's a bit vague, isn't it? I mean, how does it relate to Dad and what happened at the clubhouse?"

She turned the laptop around for him to see the photo taped beneath the words. "That's a picture of me conducting my investigation after the explosion."

He moved closer and bent down to look at the screen. He frowned. "The perp was there."

"Probably hiding in the crowd." It was a close-up shot of her, standing to the side of the clubhouse wearing her hazmat suit. "I think this was taken just before I went into the building to start my investigation." She shivered. "I hope Daniel finds something."

"He will. He was trained by you, wasn't he?" Adam had two plates on the counter beside him.

"Let me help you." Cynthia put her stuff on the floor behind her and got up.

"If you can grab the cutlery and place mats in that drawer and lay them out on the dining room table, that'd be great."

She stared at the multitude of utensils before her. Adam must do a lot of entertaining. "We're keeping this simple, right? I mean, we're not having a four-course meal or anything like that?"

"We're having a three course one—salad, main and dessert." He glanced over his shoulder.

"Gotcha." He didn't have to do all of that. She picked up the required pieces and got to work setting things up. "Um, listen, I'd rather not have any alcohol, if that's okay." She needed Adam to understand that this was not a dinner date. The fact that he even went through all this trouble of cooking a meal that made her mouth water was already awkward.

"That makes two of us. Water glasses are in that cupboard." He pointed with a spatula.

Cynthia just finished putting the glasses on the table when Adam came over with two bowls. "*Fattoush* salad," he announced, setting them down. "Do you want anything else besides water? I have soda and juice as well. Oh, and I'll be brewing cappuccinos for dessert."

Wow, who is this man? If she had pursued a different career, she wouldn't hesitate to be all over this guy—handsome, a cook, a good listener. Along with his excellent work ethics, she was surprised he was single. "Just water for now, thanks." He sat down opposite her.

"This looks delicious." She spied cucumbers, radishes, tomatoes and what looked like pieces of fried pita bread. "This is a Middle Eastern salad?"

"Lebanese. One of Mom's specialties. That's where she's from."

Intriguing. That explained the paintings and his knowledge of them. She took a bite, and let the flavors do a dance in her mouth. "Adam, this is really good." Her stomach agreed as well, growling in response. She paused, glancing at him.

He gave her a small smile. "Displays your appreciation of the food."

"I'm sorry—that was embarrassing."

"Don't apologize. It's a compliment." He got up. "Let me take that for you."

Cynthia hadn't realized she finished the salad so fast.

She gave him the bowl, their fingers brushing against each other. A warm tingle of heightened awareness had Cynthia watching Adam's every move as he went into the kitchen to get the main meal. Oh, this was bad—in so many good ways.

She rubbed her sweaty hands across her thighs as he returned. "And what's this?" she asked, savoring the smells of the meal before her.

"These are called *arayes*, basically meat-stuffed pitas."

She looked at it, curious. "I think I smell…cinnamon?"

"Got it in one." He slid a couple onto her plate before attending to his. "They're hot, so fork and knife is best at first. But I like to use my hands." He demonstrated by cutting his into quarters, grabbing a piece and dipping it into the small bowl beside him. "The yogurt gives it an extra level of flavor. One of the best family meals my grandma taught me to make," he said, licking his fingers.

So in this short time frame he'd mentioned a few important family members. His love for them was obvious. "How are your friends doing in the hospital?" she started, mimicking his movements and managing to get dinner into her mouth without making too much of a mess.

"Bruiser said they did well through surgery, but not out of the woods yet. There's going to be a lot of healing and physical rehab for the next few months." He kept eating, but the sadness in his eyes tore at her.

"Have you visited them?"

"No."

Something in that one word raised a red flag. Cynthia wouldn't push it. "I'll analyze as much as I can tomorrow, and find out if Mr. Creatura knows anything."

"Hey, you don't think…" He hesitated. "Will Boucher

try to take you off the case after the break-in at your apartment?"

"Like that's going to happen." She almost spat out the words.

Adam nodded and went back to eating. "I figured you'd say something like that."

They ate in silence for several minutes. "Adam," she said, then stopped.

He glanced at her.

"I'm sorry—I didn't mean to upset you earlier, asking about your friends." She rubbed her arms, thinking of an all-too-similar story in her life, with similar results.

"Cyn, I'm not mad at you. It's been a rough couple of days." He got up to take her plate.

Hearing him use her nickname sent a shiver of goose bumps across her arms. *Oh boy, I am going to go downhill fast.* "No, please—let me." She jumped up, grabbed his stuff and hurried into the kitchen before he could protest. She put everything down, then looked around, feeling bewildered. "Do you have everything hiding behind a panel?" she demanded. "Where the hell is the garbage can?"

Adam leaned against the wall, his arms crossed. He didn't say anything, but his amused expression spoke volumes. He pointed at the door beneath the sink.

She scraped off the remnants of dinner, put everything in the sink, then turned and gave him a look. "Dishwasher?"

Another damn panel. "How do you know where everything is?" she asked, then regretted that question. She turned her attention to the dishes, rinsing them off and placing them in the machine.

He laughed. "Practice, Ms. Cornwall. Now if you're

done, let me get the cappuccino machine going. In case you've forgotten, you are my guest, after all."

He had taken several steps into the kitchen, and in order to get out, she had to pass him with almost no room to spare. "Excuse me," she said softly, leaning back. Adam didn't move. "I need to get by," she added.

"I know." His voice held a low timbre, and the grin that slowly spread across his face was the teasing kind that made Cynthia shiver in her socks.

Lord. Undaunted, she put her hands against his chest and pushed. No luck. She tried using her hip to shove him out of the way. Nope. "Adam, come on," she implored.

"There might be a toll you'll have to pay in order to pass."

"Oh, you mean like a gold coin?" Sarcasm usually worked to help get her out of sticky situations. If that didn't work, she'd have no choice but to put on her "office" attitude.

"Something a lot more fascinating than that." He lowered his head.

"Detective Adam Solberg."

He stopped—that got his attention.

"May I ask what you're doing?" Cynthia didn't know how she kept her voice from trembling.

He stared into her eyes. His blue gaze was so intense it could put the sky to shame. "Flirting with you."

It wasn't even a question on his part. His honest response left her speechless for a few seconds before she finally found her voice. "Office relationships are a no-go for me."

"Have you ever wondered what would happen if you met someone at work who, I don't know, ticked all of your boxes?"

"I haven't met any man who's completed my list." Although Adam hit almost everything she wanted in a guy, damn him.

"That's a shame." He shifted just enough for her to squeeze by, but not without touching a part of him. She sat at the dining table and glared at his muscular back while he prepared dessert.

Maybe coming to Adam's place was a mistake. Despite keeping her distance as much as she could, she couldn't deny the attraction that seemed to be growing between them. Thankfully, Adam hadn't overstepped any boundaries, but how long would that last? His truthful admission of flirting was cutting it awful close. *Maybe he'll back off now that I've put my foot down.*

As for herself? Well, she wasn't knew what she was doing. Touching his unmoving pecs like that was somewhat deliberate and using her hips to bump him out of the way was sheer madness. She stifled a laugh. Yeah, she sort of did that on purpose too—no need for Adam to know that, though.

Cappuccinos arrived first, along with dessert that she knew was complicated to put together. "Did you make the baklava?" she asked in awe, staring at the delicate pastry.

"All from scratch."

"Holy crap." The first bite melted in her mouth. Cynthia made the second bite last to enjoy the flavors. Sweet, flaky, nutty and utterly delicious. "Where have you been all my life?" she asked, chewing on another mouthful. If she wasn't careful, she'd eat the whole pan. "This is just… I don't know what to say. It's amazing."

"Thanks." He sipped his drink, watching her.

She carefully swallowed, then picked up her cappuccino.

"So…" He placed his cup down with a clink. "Have you heard anything from your colleague?"

She glanced at her watch. "It's ten o'clock. Daniel should have something by now. I'll give him a call after I help you clean up."

His smile was almost shy. "No, I'll clean up while you talk to him. Might be better that way."

Adam listened to Cynthia's muted conversation while he kept himself busy. Occasionally, he also gave himself a good mental talking-to for daring to push against her personal space. She had given him a stern reminder about office relationships, a rule that he normally followed, but with her, it was getting difficult. Especially when she did things that contradicted her cardinal rule. Shoving against his chest to make him move was one thing—pushing her hip against his to try to slip past him was a whole other level of damn sexy. How could he resist teasing her?

He'd been nervous when she walked into his home, knowing her gaze would miss nothing. When he left her so she could call Daniel after their meal, the thought of waiting for her had set his nerves on edge. The next thing he knew, Adam found himself in the kitchen, replaying the dinner and their conversation while he cleaned. He hadn't expected her questions that teased out information about his family. It felt natural, like longtime friends finally seeing each other after several years, and picking up where they left off.

He loved being with his female family members while they enjoyed each other's company and cooked. The feeling of closeness and love filled him with such good vibes. When he finally had the courage to ask if he could help, at the ripe age of seven, *Teta* had practically squealed with delight. She had shown him her secret recipes that even

Mom never laid eyes on. The summer vacations spent with Grandma, Mom and their relatives in Lebanon had been the best part of his life.

He had made a promise to talk to her every day, even if it was only for five minutes, and the past two days were the first times he hadn't followed up.

He finished cleaning, and glanced over at Cynthia. She was still on the phone, her voice quiet. With the dishwasher running, he turned off the lights and headed into the living room to switch on the television. He rarely used it, preferring to read a book before bed, but he needed the distraction until she finished. He kept the volume low as he flipped through the channels, hesitated when he saw the nightly news, then finally settled on a documentary.

His phone pinged. He got up and retrieved his personal one, and read the short text from Bruiser.

Thought I'd let you know. Your uncle has been on the warpath. He did a short interview with one of the news channels, demanding justice. Check it out on channel 24.

Adam changed the channel, and watched with pride as Uncle Henrik laid it out to the reporter. If that didn't get Boucher moving, he didn't know what would. He texted back.

Thanks, B. I'll let you know how it's going. Give my love to everyone.

He spied Cynthia out of the corner of his eye as she approached him, catching the last bit of Uncle Henrik's interview. "Man, I hope he doesn't try to storm the station," she said. "He looks like a Viking. We wouldn't stand a chance."

He laughed out loud—he couldn't help it. "That's Uncle Henrik and, as my father's side is Nordic, yes, he has Viking blood in his veins."

"Oh!" She looked cute when she was surprised. "I didn't mean to be insulting."

"Far from it." Adam put the television on Mute and tossed the phone and remote on the low wooden table in front of him. "What's the news from Daniel?"

She sat down on the leather couch, but her expression had him on alert. "What's wrong?"

Cynthia glanced at her phone, then made a motion as if to throw it.

"Hey!" He grabbed her arm and sat beside her. "What is it?"

Her hands clenched and unclenched, as if she wanted to strangle someone. "Daniel said he did a complete sweep of my apartment. He managed to find some blond hairs that weren't mine, but there were no fingerprints around the windows or interior doors. The front door had three sets of fingerprints—mine, pest control and my landlady. He found no other hits."

He could see the wheels turning in Cyn's head. "The letter and the picture attached to it—that is a mystery, and one I'll be glad to sink my teeth into."

"Did Daniel find any prints on the letter and photo?"

"He said he found a faint smudge of a fingerprint on the edge of the photo, and is working on trying to lift a good impression of it. He didn't discover anything on the letter, but I'll make him double-check."

"You don't trust him?" It seemed weird that Cynthia would look into her colleague's work.

The question had an odd effect on her—she sank back into the cushions. "I sound so ungrateful, don't I?"

"Hey, it wasn't meant as an insult—" he started.

She held up a hand. "I know, I know. Daniel's great and he does his job well, but he can be a bit arrogant about his skills. He needs to work on his empathy."

Interesting. Adam admired this side of her—assertive and not playing around when doing her job—but she did have a soft spot for wanting to help others.

"I'm sorry about this. I honestly thought I'd have more answers for you."

"Hey, I know you're doing your best." He ran his fingers through his hair. "The fact that this smells like a professional cover-up is especially a pain in the ass."

"You think so too?" She looked at her hands. "Tomorrow, I'm going to have to pull out all the stops. It's not something I'd normally do. If I had my meditation space, I could calm my nerves and be better focused. But as it stands, let's just say no one had better get in my way."

Oh boy. He sat back. "And what exactly does that mean?"

"It means no more Miss Nice Investigator. If there's any hint of this being a cat-and-mouse game, they're playing with the wrong kitty."

"Kitty? Try a saber-tooth tiger." Cynthia was being too modest. He'd seen her anger and respected it.

She laughed, a sound joyous with mirth. "Thanks." She quieted suddenly, as if thinking. "I also want to thank you for…" She waved her hand.

Adam knew what she meant. "It's the least I could do. Stay as long as you need."

Her questioning look set off a warning bell.

"Maybe that wasn't the right thing to say," he murmured.

She offered a small smile. "I wasn't offended if that's what you're worried about. You helped me out, and I'm grateful. I'll make sure to return the favor."

He frowned—that was not his intention. "This isn't a favor," he retorted. "You don't owe me anything. I did this because you needed help."

He rose and strode to the kitchen, fighting to keep his annoyance in check. He had a habit of letting his emotions speak first before allowing logic to intervene. Cynthia was a very independent woman—he got that, and she made sure that everyone knew it. But sometimes, like now, it became too much, like shoving a hand into his face.

The dishwasher was still running, so he retrieved a clean cloth and a bottle of kitchen cleanser, then proceeded to wipe down everything around him. The fact that he'd already done this didn't matter. He needed to keep himself busy until his frustration died down.

"Hey."

He paused, then continued cleaning.

"Adam?"

"What?" he growled. It wasn't meant to be polite. She ticked him off.

Silence. "I'm sorry."

He sighed, loud enough for her to hear, then half threw the kitchen stuff into the sink. Seriously, he didn't want to stay mad—he'd been there and done it with the ex-fiancée, which made for tense conversations and regretful evenings. "I have to apologize too," he said, turning to face her. "My anger sometimes—"

He stopped, watching her. The look on Cynthia's face

was contrite. It was so unexpected he clenched his hands as his heart did a funny flip-flop.

"I've been trying to…" She looked up at the ceiling, her hands, everywhere except at him. "I'm not very good at this."

"What? Accepting help?" It wasn't a guess—she'd provided all the clues.

Cynthia nodded. "Working in law enforcement revealed certain people's views on things—I'm sure you know that. Women are seen as weak and getting in the way. I always have to show that I can take on the worst without acting like a woman." She shook her head and swiped at her face with her fingers.

Was she crying? He grabbed a napkin and passed it to her.

"Usually I'm okay. Put up a thick mental wall and deal with whatever is thrown at me for the day. Sometimes, it catches up with me. I'm usually at home dealing with it, then pull on my big girl pants and next morning, I'm Ms. Cornwall."

She blew her nose and crumpled the napkin in her fist. "But I hadn't realized how arrogant I'd been until you got angry."

He was wrong—she wasn't crying, but it was close. "I didn't mean to upset you," he apologized again.

"It's all right. It was an unexpected wake-up call." He spied a faint smile tease around her mouth. "You reminded me that not all men are jerks, that there are nice guys out there."

A compliment. From Ms. Cornwall. He tendered her a modified bow.

She giggled, the sound humorous and sweet at the same time.

"How about some ice cream?" he asked. He turned to the freezer and swung it open. The soft whoosh of cold air helped to calm his heated skin. Adam had no clue that his reactions to her moods would be so strong, and it made him nervous. He knew he liked her, but hadn't realized how much when he stared at her remorseful expression. And to listen to Cynthia talk about her fears in the police workforce and how she dealt with them had shown a surprising amount of trust to confide in him. He wasn't sure how to handle it. "I've got French vanilla, double chocolate chip..."

"Whoa, the chocolate please."

He grinned. "Coming right up."

On the couch, he turned the television volume back on. He would have preferred music, but as Cynthia kept reminding him, this wasn't a date. Too bad. He found a movie and turned down the volume.

"This is so good." She licked her lips. "This isn't a double chocolate chip that I know of."

"It's made in Mexico. Nutmeg, chilies and nuts."

"And not as sweet." She scooped some more onto her spoon. "Seriously, did you cook before joining law enforcement?"

"I worked as an assistant chef at a fancy seafood restaurant while living in Nova Scotia."

The spoon stopped halfway to her mouth. "No."

He nodded. "Gave me the experience and courage to try different things." He shrugged. "I didn't think cooking would be something I enjoyed."

"But you do—I saw that when you were in the kitchen."

Trust Cynthia to pick up on that. He dived into the vanilla ice cream, half wishing he had chocolate sauce on top of it.

"Could I try some of yours?"

He almost dropped the spoon. How could she not know that she was flirting right now? He was going to take her up on the offer. He scooped up a small amount on his spoon and presented it to her, but held the utensil.

Her knowing glance told him she knew what he was up to, and he waited, wondering what she would do.

Cynthia stared at him, her brown gaze unwavering as she slowly leaned forward and surrounded his spoon with her lips. He held his breath as she gently tugged on the spoon, her mouth taking in the sweet treat. She remained close, her face inches from his as she swallowed and licked her lips. "Mmm, that was delicious," she whispered.

His breath stopped. This close, her brown skin was smooth, flawless. Long lashes accented the slight tilt to her eyes, and black hair cascaded around her face in soft-looking curls he ached to touch.

She raised her eyebrows. "So?"

He blinked, knocked out of his stupor of staring at her. "So?" he echoed.

"Did you want to try my ice cream?"

He huffed out a laugh as she moved away. "Dammit, Cynthia. I didn't realize you were a tease."

She shrugged. "I can be if I want something." She scooped ice cream into her mouth, watching him.

What the hell was going on? One minute, she was coming on to him and making him hot and heavy, and then the next thing he knew, she acted like nothing happened. He didn't like games like these. "Teasing is more fun when both parties are involved."

That got her. Cynthia's eyes widened in surprise.

"What, you didn't know that? It's an unstated rule. It's not fair to the other half. At least, not in my books."

She gulped, then her face contorted in pain as she raised her hand to her face. "Brain freeze."

Adam really wanted to laugh, but it wouldn't be fair—he had distracted her. "Let me help you with that." He had planned on kissing her tonight, but needed the right moment—this was it.

He put his bowl down and scooted closer, their thighs touching. She raised a brow. "What are you going to do?"

He didn't answer. In one smooth move, he gently grasped her chin and molded his lips to hers. The taste of chocolate on her mouth was tantalizing, and he was hard in seconds. But when she swiped his lower lip with her tongue, all thoughts of being a gentleman went out the window. He deepened the connection, gently nudging her lips with his tongue until she parted them. God, the taste of her, mingled with double chocolate…

Adam angled his body toward her so that he could get closer, feeling her breasts brush against him. Cynthia was tentative at first, but at his encouragement, her tongue slid along his, filling his mouth with so many emotions he almost backed away from the sensation, it was so much.

Her hand brushed against his chest, and she retreated a little. "Adam, I want to be up-front with you."

He managed to get his brain to listen to her. "What is it?"

"I—I want this. I honestly never thought I'd admit to something like that, but I do." She stared at him, her expression concerned.

He would have stripped her in seconds flat if it wasn't for the odd look on her face. "But?"

"I don't think we should do it again."

Chapter 7

"You're suggesting a one-night stand?" She had gone through a hellish day, only to end it with a violation of her home. To come here, even though she didn't have to, spoke volumes. And her admission to wanting sex…well, he never thought he'd hear that coming from her. Cynthia, a woman who didn't need help and who stood up to the most arrogant of macho men.

She nodded, looking almost sad.

Adam didn't feel any better about it, either. There was something about her…taking advantage of her situation would be all kinds of wrong. Not that he would ever do it—he wanted his partner willing and enjoying it as much as he, or else what was the point? "Look, sometimes one night is all that's needed." He smiled. "Who knows? You might enjoy it enough to come back for more."

She cocked a brow.

"What? You scared now?" He hadn't meant to tease, but his ego had deflated a bit at her look.

"Not scared. Intrigued." She smiled back. "You've always come across as the kind of man who loved his work as well."

"Not sure what my job and hoping to get you naked have in common."

Her eyes widened in shock for a moment before she burst into laughter. "I guess I just thought...well, that you didn't make time for things like relationships."

Ah, if she only knew. "You make time for what you want." He leaned in close. "I always make time for play."

Her gaze cast downward, embarrassed. It was adorable.

"Please tell me you want to play," he said, clasping his hands together and giving her his best "take pity on me" smile.

She laughed again. "Oh my God, you're something else!"

"Thank you." He let his gaze fall to her lips as his thumb brushed her bottom lip. Cynthia's mouth parted on a breath, and he closed the distance. This time, his hand did the talking, stroking her thigh until her breaths became faster. She squeezed her legs together, but not before he got his hand in between them. She gasped in surprise as he gently massaged her inner thigh with his fingers. "This would feel better if we didn't have clothes between us."

Cynthia smirked. "Persistent, aren't you?"

"Yep." He wasn't going to lie—he wanted her naked and lying beneath him.

Her squirming kept him laser focused. When her legs parted, he zeroed in on the area between her thighs, stroking gently with his thumb.

"Adam?" she whispered. She was shifting her body as if to get off the couch, but he wrapped his other arm around her shoulders to keep her in place. "Oh no, that won't work," he told her, his voice gruff with desire. "If you're getting up, that means we're heading to my bedroom."

She stilled, her gaze curious. "But if I can't get up that means I can't take my clothes off, either."

Whoa. Nice move. "You can take your clothes off on the way to the bedroom," he compromised. He liked that they were making a game of this—it helped to make her more comfortable.

She took that as her cue. Grinning, she pushed him away, stood and took a few steps back. She slowly undid her jeans, her gaze on him as she shimmied the material down curvy, toned legs.

She wasn't shy, and as his gaze narrowed, catching hints of a pair of green panties beneath the hem of her T-shirt, he couldn't help wondering if she was just as confident fully naked in front of a man. He knew nothing of her past, which made Cynthia all the more alluring.

He rose and in one movement, stripped off his own shirt.

She didn't move, but her eyes had a will all their own as they checked him out. She waved a hand in his general direction. "I see that you take care of yourself." Her voice held a hint of admiration.

Years of working in various labor-intensive jobs had chiseled his body into large, sculpted muscle. He remained active by playing sports when he could all year, since he never liked the gym. "I hate the detective stereotype of eating doughnuts and drinking pots of bad coffee." He approached her, watching carefully to see if she became skittish until his body touched hers. He rubbed his hands along her arms, savoring the warm, smooth skin.

She hadn't moved, just looked at him with a steady gaze.

"Don't you want to touch?" he whispered. "You don't need permission."

Cynthia blinked and looked to where his hands rested on her shoulders. She placed her hands over his own, then mirrored his gesture, stroking his arms. Her fingers teased along the definition of muscle, curving over his biceps, sending tingles of sharp awareness through him. She skimmed beneath his arms and placed her palms on his chest. "You have a strong heartbeat," she whispered. Out of nowhere, she placed a kiss between his pecs.

Damn, if that didn't make his erection stand at attention. He sucked in a breath as she caressed his chest.

"Sorry, I couldn't help it."

"I already told you, you don't need permission." His voice was rough. On impulse, he gently grasped her wrists and directed her hands lower, pausing to let her touch his abdomen. "Well?" he said, cocking a brow. "What's it going to be?" Adam couldn't hide his erection if he tried. There was no way Cynthia could miss it.

A soft gasp, but when she looked up at him, a hint of a smile played around her lips. "How could I say no to that?"

He caught her hand just before she brushed it against the front of his jeans. "If you do that, it's game over. Control is not my best trait."

"You could have fooled me. You come across as the epitome of calm, cool and collected at work."

"That's different." He raised her hands and kissed both palms. "When I make love, I give my all to my partner."

She bit her lip. "Good to know."

He massaged her hands, trying to get a better read on her emotions. She wasn't frightened, just hesitant. "Tell me what you want, Cyn," he murmured.

Her eyes widened. "Well, I did say I wanted you."

"I know, but you've got to tell me more." His thumb stroked her wrist, and he caught the racing beat of her heart beneath the skin.

"I—I don't know what to tell you."

He frowned, confused.

Cynthia saw his expression and looked away. "The few times I've had sex, no one ever asked what I'd like."

"Excuse me?" Did she just admit that men had their way with her?

"I mean, I enjoyed it, but…" She shrugged.

If her past sex life had been less than satisfying, Adam could understand why men were off her list while letting her job be her life. So why did she come on to him with the ice cream?

He wouldn't think about that now. Adam wanted to show her how enjoyable sex can be, and now that he heard this nugget of vital information, he would change his tactics. "That's not cool. I'll have to do something about it."

"Um, look, I'm not asking you to do anything."

"Hey. Look at me."

She turned, her expression conflicted.

"That's not what I meant. You and I will have a fun time tonight. That's what sex should be—a fun time between two adults." He put on his best smile. "So, what do you say?"

Her gaze traveled over his body again, then back up to stare at him. She swallowed, then nodded, a gesture he barely caught.

Thank the gods, Cynthia was still on board. Adam bent down and gave her a thorough kiss, using his tongue to swipe softly across her lips. He pulled her slowly toward him until their bodies touched, chest to thigh, his fingers clasped with hers.

He walked backward toward the guest bedroom, pulling Cynthia along with him, not taking his eyes off her until they stood in front of the bed. Now he needed to follow his instincts, paying close attention to Cynthia's reactions and moods. He kissed her again and released his grasp on her fingers, letting his hands trail up from her hips to the hem of her shirt. Adam was encouraged when her arms slipped around his neck, her mouth opening slightly, and responded by caressing the soft skin of her stomach. He touched her belly button, which got a muffled bout of laughter from her. He broke the kiss. "Are you ticklish?"

Her straight face dissolved into an impish smile.

"Glad to hear it." He licked his lips as he slowly drew her T-shirt up, watching her. She didn't stop him as he pulled the material over her head and dropped it to the floor behind him.

She wasn't wearing skimpy lingerie, which suited him just fine. But the low-cut boy shorts and fitted tank top that barely covered her large breasts were a serious turn-on. "I like the color," he managed to say. *Jeez, that sounded pitiful.*

She glanced down. "Green is my favorite." She stuck her thumb in the waistband and snapped the elastic. "And the shorts are more practical than wearing a thong."

Judging by the view of her round and toned backside, the thought of thongs almost had him salivating. "Whatever you say."

"Isn't it true for guys too? Aren't boxers more comfortable than briefs?"

He held out his arms. "Why don't you find out?" Adam wanted her to enjoy their time together, which meant letting her take the lead when an opening occurred. He wanted her to direct the way the rest of this night would go.

She wagged her index finger at him. "Ooh, that sounds like a challenge."

He grinned. "Challenges are your specialty."

"Damn you." She laughed, a naughty twinkle in those deep brown eyes. But a moment later, her smile faltered and he was surprised that her hands shook. Cynthia's confidence in her work was rock-solid, but now he wondered if, in this particular instance, she thought she was taking on too much.

He grasped her hands—no harm in encouraging her—and positioned them at his waist. "Go for it," he told her. "I won't stop you."

She bit her lower lip, then, taking a breath, she quickly unbuttoned his pants and pulled down the zipper. She took a step back.

He took that as his cue, and shimmied his pants down to his ankles. In one smooth move, they were off and joined Cynthia's T-shirt. Her expression caught him off guard—surprise, curiosity, and as he watched, her gaze lingered on his crotch. "Like what you see?" he asked, smiling.

She nodded. "So you do wear boxers."

Not the answer he was expecting. Adam opened his mouth to protest, but remained quiet as Cynthia stepped closer. He tensed as her fingers brushed against his thigh. "I like the color."

He huffed out a laugh. "God, Cyn, you really are a tease."

"Just being honest." She reached around him and squeezed his ass.

"Right. Turnabout…" He reached for her and deftly whipped off her tank top. He caught a tantalizing glimpse of dark, satiny skin before Cynthia stepped back, covering her chest with her hands.

"You little stinker," she accused.

"Now we're even." Well, almost. Her hands couldn't cover all of that delectable flesh, and he wanted to see everything.

"Hmm, I must get my revenge," she said in a cartoonish evil voice.

Adam was seriously enjoying the banter between them. His plan to put Cynthia at ease was going better than he ever dreamed of. She even had the evil grin down.

"Now I know what I must do."

He placed his hands on his hips and cocked a brow. "There's nothing you can do to surprise me."

Well, he got that wrong. She reached up to take a clip out of her bound hair, exposing the drool-worthy view of soft breasts she had tried to hide from him. She fluffed her hair, curls framing her face, then moved in close, her body brushing against him, and reached up to wrap her arms around his neck. He bit his tongue as she ground her hips against his, then forgot all logic when she wrapped a long firm leg around his hip.

Thoughts fled him, and all he could do was react. He reached down and grabbed her butt with both hands, then lifted her. Cynthia ensnared him with both legs, then wriggled, which made him grunt in surprise. She kissed his neck, trailing hot pricks of desire wherever her mouth touched. And then she bit his shoulder.

That pushed Adam over the edge. He marched to the bed and climbed on, Cynthia still clinging to him. He eased his weight onto her, propping himself up on his elbows, and gave her a good grinding of his own. Her mouth parted, enticing him to kiss and flick his tongue over her lips. She moaned and kissed back with an urgency that set fire to his blood. When he finally raised his head, the view was glorious—Cynthia's brown skin glowing in the semidarkness, her eyes closed and her mouth making noises that set his heart racing. He gently bit her neck, then licked the spot. "Earth to Cynthia," he crooned.

"Mmm." She half opened her eyes and gave him a smile that made his heart race, but not from lust. It was a weird sensation, almost like…it wasn't love, he felt sure about that. Caring, maybe? That made more sense. He certainly liked Cynthia, or he wouldn't be in bed with her right now.

"How are you doing?"

"Good. More than good." Her hands slid down his back, a warmth that made him squirm until she stuck her hands beneath the boxers. "Let's remove these." She yanked down the material, then used her feet to push them off the rest of the way.

He sucked in an unsteady breath when her hand slipped between their bodies and caressed him. *Holy crap.*

"You certainly have a lot of control," she murmured.

He shifted and kissed the delicate skin of her breast. She grasped his shoulders, arching her head back and making these little mewling cries that had him gripping the bedsheets. He gave the same loving attention to its twin, then started to ease down the curvy length of gleaming, soft skin. She rubbed her hands up her body and writhed beneath him, making Adam momentarily forget what he was doing. It was difficult to keep his promise to go slow.

He kissed every bit of skin his mouth could reach, his hands all over her and feeling like he wasn't getting enough. When he reached the top of her panties, he planted a firm kiss between her belly button and the sweet spot, inhaling her tangy scent and gripping her hips as Cynthia twisted beneath him. He slid his tongue beneath the fabric and groaned. She tasted amazing. He snagged her underwear with trembling fingers and slipped them down her legs. She kicked them off, and Adam slowly let his hands slide up her thighs, amazed at the softness of her skin. He leaned in and rubbed his cheek against one thigh, then trailed kisses across the satiny skin until he reached the pink perfection between her legs.

He gently probed, listening to Cynthia's soft cries and stuttered breathing. She wasn't making it any easier by wriggling on the bed like that, which almost drove him over the brink. With a low growl of desire, he eased his tongue into her, tasting her incredible sweetness until Cynthia's body arched off the bed, her cries music to his ears as she shook with the force of her orgasm. Ah, Cynthia— so proper at work, a powerhouse with all things analytical—now a sexy kitten beneath his caresses.

When she finally fell back on the bed, he crawled over her. Her eyes were open, but she looked unfocused. "Hey," he whispered, kissing her nose. "Doing okay?"

"Mmm." She stretched beneath him, all taut muscle and soft flesh.

"Don't go away." Adam jumped up and raced to his bedroom to grab a condom, rolled it on and ran back in under a minute.

Cynthia lay on her side, her head propped up with a hand, and a sexy smile just for him. "What took you so long?" she asked, arching a brow.

This woman. He eased himself onto her, positioning their bodies. He wasn't in the mood for talking, instead, planting a firm, long kiss on her mouth as he parted her legs with one knee. She wrapped her legs around his waist as he slowly pushed into her, surprised at how tight she was. Her startled gasp caught his attention, and he immediately stopped, afraid that he hurt her.

"Hey, what are you doing?" she demanded. Cynthia thrust her hips up, and Adam's vision became hazy as he entered her.

Going slow was not in the cards. He rocked his hips, listening to her soft whimpers that drew a veil of primal lust over his eyes. He kissed her again, harder, determined to hear her scream, his fingers digging into her butt for leverage. Cynthia matched his frenzied pace, her gasps mirroring his own until her voice filled the room with the sounds of her desire. Adam wanted to make this last, but it wasn't going to happen. His whole body tightened, and he groaned and bit her shoulder hard as his orgasm took over, leaving him helpless in its grip.

He rolled to the side, dragging Cynthia with him. He smoothed his fingers over her cheek, then kissed her more gently this time—it felt so natural. He wanted to ask how she was, concerned he might have been too fast, too demanding, but the expression on her face didn't reflect any kind of disappointment.

"Thank you."

That caught Adam unawares. He expected her to say something different. "For what?"

She rested her hand on his chest. "For showing me that anything is possible."

Chapter 8

Last night had felt surreal. It had been better than any dream she could have imagined. She never thought—never would have believed—that making love to Adam would feel so good. Her body ached in places she couldn't name, and after cuddling for a bit, he had been ready for seconds, while she was still in awe from the afterglow.

They moved slower the second time, exploring, teasing. He somehow discovered her ticklish spots which he mercilessly took advantage of until she couldn't breathe from laughing so hard. The kisses were more sweet than lustful. If they talked, she couldn't remember what was said—all that she saw, that she marveled in, was this guy who made her toes curl when he looked at her in a certain way, who was attentive and made her feel so comfortable that enjoying sex felt so natural.

She had fallen asleep with his arms around her, the nightmare of her apartment invasion fading away beneath a blissful veil of contentment. She woke up several hours later to the sound of gentle snoring. He had shifted onto his back, an arm flung over his head.

Cynthia quietly turned over to watch him. She couldn't see his face in the semidarkness, but could imagine his relaxed expression. Without thinking, she reached up and brushed the hair out of his eyes. This odd emotion—satisfaction, peacefulness, she wasn't sure— felt like a favorite quilt she could enfold herself in, reveling in its warmth and coziness.

She had drifted off again while watching him.

When she woke up a second time, she shivered as if a patch of cold air had hit her, and when she turned toward Adam, he wasn't there. *Damn, he's gone back to his room.* But she couldn't be surprised. Still, the thought of not having his warm body beside her left her feeling a little down. It was a feeling she wasn't quite ready to accept.

She heard Adam moving around the apartment, and glanced at her watch—she had an hour and a half to get ready and make it to work on time.

The guest bedroom had its own en suite, and she showered, thinking how to approach him, until she came to the conclusion to just act like herself. There was no use trying to put on an air of false cheerfulness. *It had been a one-night stand, nothing more, and today they would go back to how things were.*

Somehow that statement didn't ring true to her.

The awkwardness she had worried about didn't make an appearance when she approached him in the kitchen. Adam had a filling breakfast laid out—eggs, toast, fruit, coffee. They ate mostly in silence, helping her keep her vow to view their relationship as all work. They finally talked about the investigation and what to expect, until it was time to go.

"You'd better give me a half-hour start," she told him as he cleaned up. "I don't want us showing up at the precinct together."

He nodded his agreement and kept cleaning. Feeling guilty and not sure why, Cynthia walked for a couple of blocks before hailing a cab. She had left her backpack at Adam's place because she had no idea if she would need to stay another night while her apartment continued to be processed. When she got to work, she would have a long, detailed talk with Daniel.

"Hey!" Daniel hurried around the large counter toward her. "Good morning. Everything okay? How are you?"

"I'm fine, Daniel, thanks." She angled around him and headed for her desk. "I hope you have some answers for me."

"I found a couple of things." He grabbed a clipboard. "The printed letter showed some distinct personality traits. Aggressiveness and confidence stood out due to how hard the marker was pressed onto the paper. The letters themselves were neat, but I found certain strokes, like completing the *A* and *E*, gave me the impression the perp was writing in a hurry."

"Excellent." Daniel had come through—she chided herself for worrying about his experience. "Any prints?"

"I finally managed to lift one from the back of the photo. With so many people taking pictures at the crime scene, we'd never have seen the photographer, and if we did, we wouldn't have thought twice about it."

"I know." Cynthia got her laptop and phone out and charging on the desk. "Did you get an ID on the print?"

Daniel gave her a strange look. "Yeah."

"What's wrong?" Why did the hairs on the back of her neck rise?

"Let me show you." He walked to the table in the corner. On it was the machine that plotted certain points on fingerprint images until it resulted in a complete print. "I ran it through the analysis. When it gave me a hit, I decided to run it again just to be sure." He paused.

"And?" Why did Daniel look nervous?

"It belonged to that teenager you interviewed a couple of days ago. Larry."

"What?" Cynthia shouted. She shut her eyes tight and breathed deeply a couple of times. "Are you sure?" she asked in a calmer voice.

"Yeah, that's why I ran the print twice."

There had been a remote possibility that Larry or one of his Desperados buddies was involved—Cynthia hadn't ignored that. But it pissed her off that she hadn't caught the bastard in his lie. "Does Captain Boucher know?"

Daniel shook his head. "I only got the results around six this morning. Constable Grant's the officer in charge. He's gone to pick Larry up. Should be back in an hour or so."

Cynthia needed to know firsthand why Larry did this, because damn if anything in this case made sense. "Did you find anything else?"

"There were some hairs by the front door that weren't yours, but no hits." He went through his notes. "Because you had the kitchen and bathroom cupboards open, pest control wouldn't have touched them. And I think they wear gloves while spraying. There were three sets of prints on the front doorknob."

"Hmm. Those would be mine, pest control and Mrs. McCarthy." She glanced over his shoulder at his notes.

"The blond hair must be Mrs. McCarthy's. She would have let pest control in."

"Does she also hang around while pest control is spraying?"

Cynthia nodded. "Liability issues in case something happens."

"Then how could Larry get into your apartment?"

"One of the Desperados' MOs is breaking and entering. But what I need to know is why I'm being targeted." There was only one way to find out.

"Good morning. I'm here to observe the interrogation." Luck was with Cynthia today—Constable Sandra Turnbull had been on duty when Cynthia first questioned Larry with Captain Boucher.

"Oh. Grant didn't say anything about that."

"He wouldn't know." She thought fast. "I don't believe Captain Boucher informed him that we interviewed Larry a couple of days ago. When I found out from my lab colleague that Larry had been brought back for further questioning, I wanted to be here to see if he had other evidence I needed for the MC bombing case I'm working on."

"As far as I know, Grant's questioning him on the B&E of your apartment. Detective Solberg is his backup." Turnbull tapped a pen against her chin.

Adam was in there? "I thought Solberg had only returned to the precinct to finish his serial killer case."

"That's right, but when Grant brought the teenager in, Timmins and Hawthorne weren't here." She tilted her head at Adam. "Just Solberg. Grant's okay with it so long as Solberg doesn't dig too deep with the questioning."

Several tense moments passed before Turnbull stepped

to one side. "Wouldn't want you to miss out on firsthand evidence, Cornwall. But you know I can get into big trouble with Boucher for doing this."

"Thanks. I won't breathe a word, I promise." Cynthia walked into the well-lit room, where four computers sat on a wide table, each one hooked up via video and audio link to the interview rooms.

"Number Three." Turnbull sat in front of the computer and hit several keys. "Recording," she said into the microphone.

Cynthia pulled up a chair and saw Grant raise his hand in acknowledgment on the computer screen. Larry, on the other side of the metal table, sat slouched in the chair, fingers linked across his chest. His expression was rebellious, and ready to do battle. Adam sat in a corner, arms crossed, his gaze not missing anything.

"Well, Larry, I understand you're paying us another visit. Welcome back."

Larry looked him up and down. "Who the hell are you?"

"Constable Edward Grant."

"What am I doing here?"

"You were brought in to answer some additional questions."

"Like what?" Larry seemed more defensive than usual.

Grant flipped through several sheets of paper. "Last night, someone broke into Forensic Investigator Cynthia Cornwall's apartment."

Larry jerked in his seat, then sat up straighter. "Who's that?"

"Come on, Larry. She's the lady who questioned you with Captain Boucher."

"Okay, yeah, I remember. She backed me up when your captain got snarky with me."

Constable Turnbull looked over her shoulder, her eye-brow cocked.

Cynthia shrugged. "Larry wasn't going to talk if Boucher kept threatening him. I intervened and dialed it down."

"You're gutsy for a forensics analyst. I like that."

In the interrogation room, Larry propped his arms on the table. "So someone jacked the lady's home?"

"Larry, we know it was you."

The teenager didn't move, but his expression was angry. "I told your captain that I don't do that anymore."

"Well, that's hard to believe, since we have evidence to the contrary."

"Now wait up!" Larry slammed his hand on the table. "You all trying to set me up, is that it? Can't believe that a guy wants to go straight?"

Out of the corner of her eye, Cynthia noticed Adam sliding to the edge of his chair. He leaned forward and clasped his hands—an innocent enough move.

"That's not the point, Larry. The point is, we found something with your fingerprint on it." Constable Grant shuffled through his papers and pulled out two plastic bags—one containing the letter, while the second held the photo. He placed them on the table. "These were found in Ms. Cornwall's apartment."

Larry looked sick. His dark brown skin turned ashen. "Hey, man, I didn't break into anyone's place."

"Well someone sure did, and did a damn good job too." Grant jabbed the evidence with a finger.

Larry got up and paced the small room. "This ain't right, man." His hands gestured with each word he uttered. "I didn't do shit!"

"Larry, take it easy." Grant pushed his chair back,

keeping an eye on the teenager. "All I'm asking is for your side of the story."

"Are you going to believe me, huh? How do I know you won't lock my ass up?"

Larry was scared—really scared. Did he know something?

"Because my dad believed in you," Adam said.

Startled, Cynthia watched as Adam rose and approached Larry, who had finally stopped pacing.

"My dad agreed to help you get straight because he saw something in you," Adam continued. "Something that mattered. And in return you helped him by being his informant. Dad wouldn't have done that unless he felt in his gut that you were trying to clean yourself up."

Larry tilted his head. "Hey, I know you—"

"No, you know my dad. The guy who ran the Chariots of Chrome."

"Mr. Solberg? He's your old man?" Larry's demeanor changed suddenly. His body relaxed, and he actually had a smile on his face. "He was one cool dude. Nobody tried anything with him."

Cynthia was sure no one else noticed, but she did— the sad, but proud expression on Adam's face when the teenager praised his father. "Yeah, he was my dad."

"Look, man, I'm sorry about what happened to him. That was some serious stuff."

"Yes, it was. And we need your help." He pointed at the photo. "That picture of Ms. Cornwall was taken when she arrived at the MC clubhouse, after the explosion. Your fingerprint is on it. You need to tell us how that happened."

Larry started pacing again, but it wasn't the frantic movements of an agitated young man. He seemed more relaxed, arms hanging at his sides.

Adam backed off and sat down. "Whenever you're ready."

Another minute went by before Larry took a seat. "First, I'm telling you straight up I had nothing to do with the bombing."

"We're not talking about that, Larry," Grant intervened. "We're just discussing the picture and the letter. Did you do this?"

"No, man. When I was with the gang, the Desperados cased houses, but we never left letters. Are you kidding? That's a whole other level of creepy."

Cynthia breathed a sigh of relief. She had hoped Larry had nothing to do with that part of the crime.

"I did take the picture, though."

She gasped. "The little bastard."

Grant leaned forward. "Why?"

Larry shrugged. "For money, what else? Look, I wasn't there when the place blew up, all right? Yeah, I was there talking to Mr. Solberg, but that was to give him the lowdown on a drug deal. Ms. Cornwall and Captain Boucher questioned me on that.

"Anyhow, when I heard the explosion and came back to check it out, I saw it was Mr. Solberg's place." He glanced at Adam. "There was already a pretty big crowd of people checking it out, so I hung around to watch. A lady came up to me, asking what was going on, and we talked for a bit. She told me she was a reporter, but her partner wasn't with her, and asked if I could help in taking photos. Showed me her ID and gave me her business card, one of those disposable cameras and cash on the spot—two hundred and fifty bucks. She said she wanted pictures of the building and the emergency crews when they arrived. Said she'd give me another two hundred and fifty if I got the photos developed and delivered them to her in person."

Cynthia nodded—that explained her picture in particular.

"I finished the roll and went to one of those places that got photos ready in one hour and called her while I waited. When she showed up, I took the pictures out and showed her. She said I did a great job and paid me the other half. That's it."

Grant was taking notes while Adam tapped the floor with his foot. "What did she look like?" Grant asked.

"Reached my shoulder, blond hair, sort of fat. Looked like the grandmother type."

"Did she touch the photos?" Adam asked.

Larry looked at him. "What?"

"Did you notice if the woman touched the pictures when you gave them to her?" Adam asked again.

"Man, I don't remember. I only wanted the money—easiest five hundred bucks I ever made."

"Except you're here." Adam stood and paced the small room like a lion in a cage. "Do you still have that business card?"

"Yeah, I think so." Larry pointed at the small plastic container beside Grant that held a wallet, cell phone and a set of keys. "It should be in the wallet."

Grant pulled on a pair of gloves and opened the wallet. He rummaged through it until he found a couple of business cards. "Which one?"

"That one, the blue and pink. I thought those were weird colors for a reporter, but hey, however she wants to roll, man."

Adam looked over Grant's shoulder. "'M. McCarthy,

Reporter.' There's nothing else except a phone number. Odd."

The air around Cynthia suddenly grew cold. McCarthy—her landlady's name. When her home had been violated, she knew she couldn't leave the older woman out of the equation, but she had hoped…

"Thanks for letting me listen in," she told Turnbull as she gathered her things.

"Cornwall, I don't think Grant's finished."

"I am. Thanks for your help."

The elevator to the laboratory floor couldn't move fast enough. Her landlady. The woman who helped Cynthia move in, watched out for her when she came home late at night, the landlady who offered the comfort and humor that she missed when she moved out of her aunt's house. That woman. She was part of all this.

Cynthia pulled the gloves off and carefully rubbed her eyes. She had managed to pry open the small portable safe she had found at the clubhouse. It was fire-resistant, and the items inside hadn't been damaged—small bills, a couple of keys, the lease to the clubhouse and insurance papers. The fingerprints she had carefully managed to lift all belonged to Adam's father, and the insurance stated that his friend Bruiser would inherit the clubhouse.

She hadn't expected much from the metal box, but it was still disappointing. Her hope for answers now lay with Mr. Creatura's upcoming interview about his Rolex, and the remaining pieces of evidence—the wires and the strange white dust. If she couldn't find any clues with them, she'd have to head back to the burned-out building and pray she'd find something else.

Man, she was tired, and the emotional toll felt greater

because of Adam. She was determined though, both for him and herself, to solve this case. She wasn't going to give up by a long shot.

Her cell phone pinged with a text.

Hey, it's Adam, are you still here?

Yeah, just trying to figure out something. What's up?

Getting ready to leave and now I just realized you don't have a way to get in if you get back before me. I'll have to find my extra keys.

Wow, she hadn't expected that. It made sense, but getting a set of keys to his condo screamed another kind of trust. Um, okay.

What are you up to? You said you're figuring something out. Need a hand?

His last question sent a warm, fuzzy feeling through her insides. An honest, innocent inquiry about her progress. Adam was up to his eyeballs with his own work, yet he asked if she wanted help.

While work had been busy, Adam was constantly at the back of her mind. What surprised Cynthia was that it wasn't intrusive or bothersome. It was almost like…

Her heart clenched at what she thought. He was like her Buddha in her meditation space—always present, but never in the way, a fixed point she could turn to if she felt emotionally vulnerable. She started typing without thinking, and it wasn't to give him her typical *"I'm fine"* spiel.

Actually, I do need you. Would you mind coming down to the lab?

This was so unlike her, and she didn't care in the least. Cynthia wanted to see Adam before he went back to the condo, even though she knew she'd see him later tonight. Anticipation made her heart race.

Footsteps in the hallway, then the door opened to reveal Adam's strong form. "Hey," he called out, walking in. "What's up? You said you needed me?"

Too late to turn back now. She took a deep breath, rose from her desk and walked toward him, never hesitating while she wrapped her arms around his neck and gave him a thorough kiss. Adam's eyes widened in surprise before he embraced her, returning the kiss with such fervor she thought she might pass out.

Cynthia lost track of time, and finally stopped, although she didn't want to. She held his face with her hands.

He tucked a finger under her chin and caressed her cheek with a thumb. "Did you want to go home now?"

"I—I have a bit more work to do, but I'll see you later?"

"You bet." He kissed her nose and walked out.

His words—they tugged at her, made her feel like she was a part of something. She let this heady feeling fill her with a happiness that maybe—just maybe—would let her take the next step, if Adam gave an indication he wanted to do the same thing.

Chapter 9

Adam read Bruiser's text again, guilt and grief warring for attention. While he had thought constantly about his cousin and friends, and was praying for their recovery, he hadn't been back to the hospital to see them. His friend said Jeffrey was still in a coma, but everyone else was out of immediate danger and recovering—thank God for that. But he should be there too, if only for a little bit to show his support.

Right, decision made. As soon as Cynthia returned he'd head out. She could keep herself occupied for a couple of hours. He hadn't eaten, so he'd have to grab a sandwich along the way. For her, he threw together a salad and arranged fixings for a quick meal—it was the best he could do on short notice, and he knew she'd be back soon.

Her surprise text and their discreet make-out session in the lab had been a serious turn-on and cheered him up immensely—it was the last thing he'd expected. What surprised and pleased him was that she'd forgotten her important rule of no precinct shenanigans, and it didn't seem to bother her. Adam knew they had something special, and sure, he could gently try to convince her, but Cynthia needed to convince herself.

His phone pinged. Hey, I'm at the condo, be up in five.

He grabbed his jacket and helmet, and opened the door at her knock. "Sorry, I wanted to get back earlier—" She stopped, frowning. "Is everything okay? What's going on?"

"I'm just heading to the hospital—I won't be long." He gestured toward the kitchen. "I've put together dinner for you. I'll eat something on the way back."

She was silent for a moment. "Thanks." She stepped inside and dropped her satchel on the floor.

Not quite the reaction he'd expected. She seemed disappointed, which was sort of a good thing, right? It meant she wanted him here to have dinner together.

He shrugged into his jacket, reached for his keys…

"I'm coming with you."

He turned around. She had reached for her own jacket, and was rummaging through her satchel until she found her phone and shoved it into a pocket. His surprise must have been evident, because she offered up a small smile. "What?"

He shook his head, because he didn't have the words. "You don't have to do this," he blurted.

"You're right, I don't." Cynthia reached out her hand and clasped his fingers within her own. "But I want to."

Adam was feeling restless, edgy. The thought of going back home after that hospital visit filled him with dread. Jeffrey was unconscious, the other officers in various stages of healing. Bruiser, the rock who had held everyone together, was close to an emotional breakdown. To walk into the condo and face everything attached to Dad would push him over the edge. He needed to get away, if only for a couple of hours, and he had the perfect companion. "Do you want to go out?" he asked Cynthia, strapping on his helmet.

"Sure. Anything particular in mind?"

"A friend of mine owns a *tapas* bar about twenty minutes from here."

"That sounds like a great idea." She climbed on behind him. "We could do with a break."

Parking wasn't a problem, but the sidewalks were filled with pedestrians. "There must have been a baseball game tonight," Cynthia said. She dodged around a group of guys hollering their admiration of Toronto's favorite baseball team.

He grabbed her hand and pulled her close. The crowd's excitement for the team winning a major game lifted his spirits. Having his arm around Cynthia's shoulders was even better. They navigated the boisterous men and women, with Adam having to play linebacker against a few guys who got too close. "Good grief," he muttered.

"Hey!" Cynthia yelled.

He turned, and watched with escalating fury as a guy dragged Cynthia out of his grasp. Before Adam could get his hands on him, Cynthia had leveled an accurate and deadly kick to the man's crotch. His groan was loud enough for everyone nearby to hear as he sank to the pavement, clutching his manhood.

"One of the reasons I wanted to live someplace a bit quieter," she said, pointing at the guy as he struggled painfully to get to his feet. "I'm tired of city life. It has its perks, but…" She shook her head.

There was nothing hotter than a woman defending herself, and Cynthia had plenty of that.

Nuevo Comienzo Tapas and Bar was off the main street. Inside, it was a lot quieter, but it looked like all of the tables were taken.

"Adam, *mi amigo*!" Luis Garcia was in his early forties, fit, smiling and always welcoming. "*Bienvenido*, welcome! It's been too long. Where the hell have you been?"

"Working mostly." He shook Luis's hand.

"You need to slow down, young man, enjoy life. I've always told you that." Luis looked over at Cynthia. "And who is your beautiful friend?"

Adam smiled. "Luis, meet Cynthia." He thought it best not to say more than that, and it looked like she took it in stride, shaking Luis's hand. "A pleasure to meet you."

"Please come in. It's busy, but I have a table upstairs with an amazing view of downtown and the CN Tower." Luis looked up. "And a lovely evening. The moon should make her appearance as well."

Luis started to sing an old love song as he led them upstairs. Adam had brought his ex-fiancé here as well, once upon a long time ago, and he silently thanked Luis for not asking any questions.

The small table sat on its own away from the others, and at this angle, the downtown view was filled with people, lights and music. The CN tower was framed between two condo buildings, and lit with red-and-white lights that strobed a swirling pattern from bottom to peak.

He pulled out the chair for her, and when she sat down, he brought his around so that he could sit closer to her.

"This is a nice place." He felt her thigh brush his. "How do you know the owner?"

"I helped nail the bastard who was robbing Luis."

Man, that was six years ago. "I wasn't a detective yet, but wanted to help with the case for practice. The detective in charge kept insisting it was an outside job until I decided to case the premises and discovered the manager sneaking out the back and talking to a Mafia criminal I recognized. The detective gave the manager another chance to talk, and that's when we found out he owed money for a favor."

"So he used your friend's sales to fund it." Cynthia shook her head.

"Luis has been thanking me ever since. It gets a little embarrassing."

"You saved his business, Adam, and that's always a good thing." She rested her hand on his.

He linked their fingers. He loved how natural it felt, and Cynthia had been suspiciously quiet about the "not dating a colleague" scenario, which suited him just fine.

"So, what shall we get?" She picked up a menu. "I've never had *tapas* before."

"Really? Then you're in for a treat. Luis will surprise us. And before you say it," he added as she opened her mouth. "No alcohol. I'm driving anyway."

Damn, Cynthia had a gorgeous smile. "And we have a long day tomorrow."

He groaned. "You had to say that, didn't you?"

"I've got a lot to do. I need to finish analyzing the bomb evidence, then hope that Mr. Creatura's and Mrs. McCarthy's interviews provide additional information, and…"

"Whoa, time out." Adam made a T with his hands. "How do you know about Mrs. McCarthy?"

She wrapped a lock of hair around her fingers and actually looked away. "I might have eavesdropped on you and Constable Grant's interview with Larry."

"What?" He laughed hard enough to hurt his stomach. "Here I was, getting ready to tell you the latest, and you'd already beaten me to it."

"Um, sorry?"

"Oh no, I won't make it easy for you." The cautious expression on Cynthia's face was priceless.

Luis reappeared with a tray filled with small plates. "Are you working tomorrow, or do you have the day off?" he asked.

Adam shrugged. "I gotta work, man. I can't play hooky."

"That is too bad." The owner placed several plates on the table. "A beautiful woman enjoying dinner with you, both of you should skip work."

"It's tempting," Cynthia agreed, and squeezed his hand.

If he wasn't so much of a gentleman, he would keep Cynthia in the condo and make up any excuse to get out of work tomorrow. But he knew that wouldn't fly with her—there was too much at stake.

As if she read his mind, she added, "We—I mean Adam—is working on a big case right now that needs all of his attention."

"I completely understand. Did he tell you how he assisted me?"

"Yes, he did." Squeezed his hand again.

"Since you will be working tomorrow, I'll bring you alcohol-free sangrias."

When Luis left, Adam leaned close. "Cyn, I need to ask you something."

She frowned, picking up on the change in his voice. "Go for it."

"When I first met you at the coffee shop, and asked

why you were risking your job, you didn't give me an answer." Her lack of response had raised his suspicions, but as he got to know her, he didn't think she was doing this for the wrong reasons.

She sighed. "I figured you'd ask me again sooner or later."

"Don't get me wrong—I've appreciated everything you've done. It's just... I haven't met anyone who'd stick their neck out like this for me. If you're ever found out, you'd lose your job and the reputation you've built. Is it really worth it?"

They were briefly interrupted when a waitress brought their drinks. When she left, Cynthia picked hers up. "To success," she cheered. They clinked glasses, and she drank half of hers before setting it down.

"Personally, I don't see a problem if a relative in law enforcement has the experience to solve a complicated crime. But having said that, I also understand the emotional toll wears a person down as time drags on. Despite years of solving horrendous crimes, someone who's involved in a relative's murder can—and usually does— lose perspective." She gestured at him. "Case in point during your argument with Captain Boucher at the crime scene."

He nodded, remembering. That had not been a pretty sight.

"But to your question. Is it worth it? Most would say no. For me, it's a resounding yes."

A pause. She still hadn't answered the question. "Because?"

"Because...I can relate." She stared at him. "I was in a house fire when I was fourteen."

Hell, he hadn't expected this. "Cyn," he said softly. "If you don't want to—"

"No, it's okay. You'll understand why I'm doing this." She released his hand and rubbed her arms. "Short version, I lost my mom and brother in that fire. The police couldn't solve it, and it became a cold case. As soon as I graduated from forensics science, I found the report, solved it and had the asshole arrested for arson."

Wow. He stared at her, not able to fathom how she handled her grief. "How long?"

"Ten years? I remember like it was yesterday, though." She grabbed a couple of pieces of fried calamari and popped them into her mouth. "I promised myself I wouldn't have the same thing happen to another family— the waiting, the lack of answers. It isn't fair to them." She looked at him, her eyes dark. "It's not fair to you."

And just like that, Adam felt himself falling for Cynthia a little bit more.

They managed to get back to the condo before ten o'clock. While Adam was ready to call it a night, Cynthia grabbed her satchel and spread her paperwork and laptop across the dining table. The scene reminded him of another time—his ex-fiancée Else planning their wedding. There had been magazines, pictures and brochures scattered around the condo, and everywhere he turned, he'd spy another wedding dress photo or venue or tropical island to spend their honeymoon. Frantic, colorful and exciting—at first.

"Adam, what's wrong?"

She caught him staring off into space. He closed his eyes, willing the vision to get out of his head. "Nothing." He wasn't ready to open up that history of his life—it was still too fresh, too painful. "I'm good." He waved his hand at the table. "What's all this?"

"I just want to take another look at everything. I keep thinking I've missed something obvious."

"Have you analyzed everything?"

She chuckled. "No, and I think I'm working myself into a stressful frenzy. I have a habit of doing that when an investigation stumps me."

He knew she wasn't being flippant when she said that, but it stung. Those pictures in front of her represented the death of his dad and the attack on his friends. People he loved who had been killed in cold blood. Cynthia had turned in her chair, and her sympathetic expression tugged at him. "We'll get the bastard, Adam."

She sounded so convinced, so sure of herself, and he loved the sound of it.

"Are you thinking of listening in on Mrs. McCarthy's interview?" he asked.

"I don't think that's a good idea. I might get nasty." She waved at her laptop. "I have plenty to keep me busy tomorrow."

"Fair enough." He sat down opposite her. "I wanted to know if you could give me some intel on your landlady."

"Mrs. McCarthy?" She frowned. "She was always helpful. Polite, liked small talk, organized. Nothing out of the ordinary."

"It figures. So, two things—I don't know how, but Daniel managed to find a very faint partial print on the letter and matched it to McCarthy's in the database."

"Thank God he found something concrete." She paused, then raised a finger. "Wait a minute—her fingerprints were in the police database?"

He nodded.

"One Minute" Survey

You get up to **FOUR** books <u>and</u> a Mystery Gift...

ABSOLUTELY FREE!

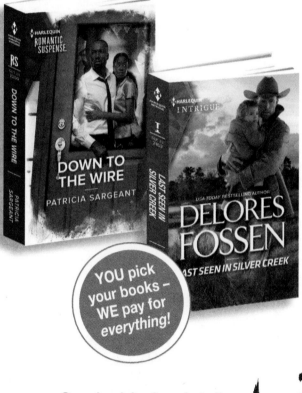

YOU pick your books – WE pay for everything!

See inside for details.

Dear Reader,

Your opinions are important to us. So if you'll participate in our fast
and free "One Minute" Survey, YOU can pick up to four wonderful
books that WE pay for when you try the Harlequin Reader Service!

As a leading publisher of women's fiction, we'd love to hear from you.
That's why we promise to reward you for completing our survey.

IMPORTANT: Please complete the survey and return it. We'll send
your Free Books and a Free Mystery Gift right away. And we pay for
shipping and handling too! ← *We pay for EVERYTHING!*

Try **Harlequin® Romantic Suspense** and get 2 books featuring
heart-racing page-turners with unexpected plot twists and irresistible
chemistry that will keep you guessing to the very end.

Try **Harlequin Intrigue® Larger-Print** and get 2 books featuring
action-packed stories that will keep you on the edge of your seat. Solve
the crime and deliver justice at all costs.

Or TRY BOTH!

Thank you again for participating in our "One Minute" Survey. It
really takes just a minute (or less) to complete the survey... and your
free books and gift will be well worth it!

If you continue with your subscription, you can look forward to
curated monthly shipments of brand-new books from your selected
series, always at a discount off the cover price! Plus you can cancel
any time. So don't miss out, return your One Minute Survey today to
get your Free books.

Pam Powers

"One Minute" Survey

GET YOUR FREE BOOKS AND A FREE GIFT!
✓ Complete this Survey   ✓ Return this survey

1 Do you try to find time to read every day?
☐ YES   ☐ NO

2 Do you prefer stories with suspensful storylines?
☐ YES   ☐ NO

3 Do you enjoy having books delivered to your home?
☐ YES   ☐ NO

4 Do you share your favorite books with friends?
☐ YES   ☐ NO

YES! I have completed the above "One Minute" Survey. Please send me my Free Books and a Free Mystery Gift (worth over $20 retail). I understand that I am under no obligation to buy anything, as explained on the back of this card.

☐ **Harlequin® Romantic Suspense**
240/340 CTI G2AD

☐ **Harlequin Intrigue® Larger-Print**
199/399 CTI G2AD

☐ **BOTH**
240/340 & 199/399 CTI G2AE

FIRST NAME

LAST NAME

ADDRESS

APT.#

CITY

STATE/PROV.

ZIP/POSTAL CODE

EMAIL ☐ Please check this box if you would like to receive newsletters and promotional emails from Harlequin Enterprises ULC and its affiliates. You can unsubscribe anytime.

HI/HRS-1123-OM

HARLEQUIN Reader Service —**Here's how it works:**

Accepting your 2 free books and free gift (gift valued at approximately $10.00 retail) places you under no obligation to buy anything. You may keep the books and gift and return the shipping statement marked "cancel." If you do not cancel, approximately one month later we'll send you more books from the series you have chosen, and bill you at our low, subscribers-only discount price. Harlequin® Romantic Suspense books consist of 4 books each month and cost just $5.99 each in the U.S. or $6.74 each in Canada, a savings of at least 8% off the cover price. Harlequin Intrigue® Larger-Print books consist of 6 books each month and cost just $6.99 each in the U.S. or $7.49 each in Canada, a savings of at least 10% off the cover price. It's quite a bargain! Shipping and handling is just 50¢ per book in the U.S. and $1.25 per book in Canada*. You may return any shipment at our expense and cancel at any time by contacting customer service — or you may continue to receive monthly shipments at our low, subscribers-only discount price plus shipping and handling.

"Right, I'm waiting for the other shoe to drop. What's the second thing?"

"I did some investigating into her background. It seems McCarthy had a rap sheet. Burglary, assault and a second-degree murder charge. She killed her husband."

"What the *what*?" He'd caught her completely by surprise.

"Sorry, I shouldn't have shocked you like that."

"Mrs. McCarthy is a murderer?" Cynthia rubbed her face with both hands.

"She said in her trial it was self-defense. I have my doubts."

"Why?" she demanded.

"Because the evidence they found pointed to premeditated murder. Maybe at one point, she believed she was defending herself, but not when rat poison was discovered in her husband's dinner."

She shook her head. "You just never know what a person is like."

"You got that right."

"I'm not sure I want to know the real reason why she trespassed into my apartment." She looked at her laptop and sighed. "Forget it—I can't concentrate. It's late too." She rose and started packing her satchel.

"Hey listen, I'm going to give you my extra set of keys."

She eyed him suspiciously.

"What's that look for? I'm sparing you the trouble of sitting in the hallway waiting for me."

She propped a hand on her ample hip. "Damn it, how long will it take before I can go home?"

He shook his head. "Not until I find out what the hell McCarthy knows. If this was an elaborate setup, there's no telling if someone else is watching you and your place if the landlady screwed up."

"You have a point." Cynthia frowned suddenly. "You know, I just thought of something. Did your dad live here with you before the explosion?"

"No. He moved out, about two weeks before. Said I wouldn't have a chance of dating if he was still around." He almost choked, saying that.

"Where's his place? Is it close by?"

"He was living at our family cottage, about a couple of hours away from here. The guys helped him move most of his stuff out." Adam looked at her. "Why?"

"I was wondering if someone might have been keeping tabs on your dad, like they did with me." Cynthia smacked her forehead. "I hope I'm wrong, but it's stuff like this that gives me nightmares."

Cynthia's taxi crawled through early morning traffic toward the precinct. She had almost pulled out her work phone out of habit, but suddenly changed her mind when she realized she hadn't talked to Aunt Ki in almost two weeks.

The other line rang twice before it picked up. "Cynthia Cornwall, how come I haven't heard from you until now?" Aunt Ki's irritated voice greeted her.

"I'm sorry, it's been busy at work." But not so busy Cynthia couldn't make a five-minute phone call, like now.

"I've told you—that's no excuse. We promised each other, remember? A call every day, two minutes or two hours, I don't mind."

"I know, and you're right, it's no excuse." She sighed, knowing she'd need to do better. "How are you? Anything new?"

"I joined a walking club."

She smiled at the news. "That's amazing! You'll meet new people, get your exercise. I'll even join you."

Her aunt chuckled. "It gets me out of the house, that's the important thing. I've been trying, Cyn."

Cynthia closed her eyes to fight back the tears. Aunt Ki had become a shell of her former self after the fire and tragic loss of her sister and nephew. But during the past couple of years her aunt was slowly regaining her life back. "I know you have, and I'm so proud of you."

"Speaking of life…" Aunt Ki paused.

Cynthia tried not to groan. *Here it comes.*

"Are you still working that job where you touch gross stuff?"

"It's called forensic evidence, Auntie."

"Uh-huh. And what about you? Are you letting that job of yours take over your personal life? Please tell me you've tried to meet a nice, handsome man since our last call."

Cynthia remained quiet because she couldn't in all honesty deny her aunt's question.

"Wait, you haven't chewed me out. Does that mean…?"

"Aunt Ki, I don't know yet…"

A loud, high-pitched squeal came through the phone. "About damn time! When do I meet him?"

What could she say? "When I'm sure, Auntie, not before."

"You've just made my day, Cyn. The next time you come around, I expect to see a *fine* man beside you."

She laughed—she couldn't help it. "If it works out, then yes, I'll bring Adam with me."

"Adam, huh? A strong name. I think I like him already."

"Aunt Ki!" Cynthia couldn't get frustrated with her aunt if she tried. And the funny thing is, she knew Auntie would love him.

"Is he tall? Handsome? Good kisser? Good at more than kissing? Talk to me."

"I can't, I'm actually pulling into the precinct."

"Hmph. Your job getting in the way again. All right, but I want updates, do you understand?"

Cynthia couldn't be annoyed with her—this was the Aunt Ki she remembered and loved. "I'll call when I can, but I'm in the middle of a big case right now."

"Fine, sweetie. Just—don't forget to call, all right?"

Her heart clenched with guilt. "I promise, I'll call you the first chance I get. I love you, Auntie."

Cynthia was very conscious of Adam's keys sitting in a side pocket of her satchel. They didn't feel like a burden—more like they developed another connection, one of trust and friendship. And she realized that she liked it.

Last night had been a big step for her. Opening up about her past had been hard, but Adam had every right to know her reasons for working on the sly. In a way, it'd felt like a huge weight had come off her shoulders. She'd been keeping her grief inside for so long, it had started to fester, turning her into a shell of her former self. Other than Aunt Ki, no one else knew of the pain and anguish she'd gone through. Talking to Adam had opened her up to the possibility that she might get through this, and be allowed to live a life her mom would have wanted her to obtain.

Cynthia felt herself blossom in his company. Adam had found every opportunity to touch her last night at the restaurant, every reason to be close. They talked about anything that came to mind, and she didn't want last night to end. Judging how Adam was toward her, she believed—she knew—they could have more nights like that. If she was willing and ready to knock down her rule of no office relationships.

"A penny for your thoughts, pretty dreamer?"

Cynthia mentally jolted herself back to the present, and into the company of Detective Walter Timmins as they walked to their respective offices. "The name's Cornwall," she said in her professional "don't piss me off" voice. "But you can call me Ms. Cornwall."

"Okay, okay. Jeez, can't even give you a compliment."

"You know that wasn't a compliment." As she watched him trying to hold in his laughter, she added, "You think Mrs. Timmins would appreciate that kind of compliment directed at a female colleague?"

That shut him up fast.

"I'm glad you agree. Let's keep it that way." After a mental fist pump she continued. "Mr. Creatura should be here by now. I know you're very good at this, but don't give him any leeway. We need answers."

"Yes, ma'am."

Daniel hadn't arrived yet. She spent the next peaceful hour analyzing the white residue found near the blast site. Cynthia had a couple of ideas as to what it might be, and after obtaining the chemical breakdown of the material, she went through a list of common explosive compounds until she found a match—Tannerite.

This opened up a new can of worms. This stuff could only be detonated by a high-velocity weapon at a minimum one-hundred-yard distance.

Which meant a sniper had set the bomb off. What the hell was going on?

This was getting ridiculous. First being stalked by her landlady, and now this. Cynthia ruminated through the evidence, sorting through clues, trying to find plausible theories. There was only one problem—she needed to prove these ideas, but didn't have the means.

However, one friend did.

She dialed his number on her personal cell and he picked up on the second ring. "Maverick's Mighty Locksmith."

"Mav, it's Cyn." It was good to hear his voice.

"Hey, how are you, sugar? What's happening in the world of forensics?"

She sighed. "Things that don't make sense right now. Did you hear about the Chariots of Chrome MC bombing?"

"Yeah." His voice became serious. "The boys and I knew one of the members. Are you working that investigation?"

"Trying to. I've got few clues and fewer leads." She paused and bit her lower lip, trying to decide if asking Mav for help was the best idea.

He beat her to it. "Let's hear what you've got."

She sighed, thankful. "I found something that doesn't make sense," she started. "Tannerite at the scene of the blast."

"Tannerite?" Cynthia could almost hear the wheels turning in Mav's head. "That's used for target practice. And the only way it could cause an explosion is if it's hit with a high-velocity bullet." He paused. "Are you thinking sniper?"

She shrugged. "It's possible. There was a watch attached to the bomb. I thought it was a timer…"

"No way. The only thing to set off Tannerite is a bullet."

She swore under her breath. "Then I need to find bullet fragments or the casing."

"I'll do a discreet sweep around the MC club for you. Where was the bomb located?"

"Just inside the back door."

"I'll take a look for the best sniper nests in the area and text you. I gotta be honest, I'm not happy. You'd better watch your back like we've taught you. You want me to let Hammer and the guys know about this?"

There was nothing Cynthia would love more than having her former team watch her back. Mav, Hammer and the others were members of the Emergency Response Team, part of the Royal Canadian Mounted Police. Highly skilled in SWAT tactics, her friends were a tight-knit bunch, and when she had trained with them several years ago before joining the Forensic Identification Services, they accepted her as one of their own.

"No, let's keep this between ourselves. The less they know, the better. I hate to think what Hammer would do to me if I messed up."

"That makes two of us. Keep me in the loop, and no playing superhero, okay? If you need me, call."

"Morning," Adam called out.

Hawthorne's brows went up in surprise. "Hey, Adam. What are you doing here?"

He poured himself a cup of coffee and took a healthy sip. It wasn't great, but it'd have to do. "I'm interviewing Mrs. McCarthy in about…" He checked his watch. "Fifteen minutes."

"You are?" Hawthorne sat forward. "I thought the captain kept you off the bombing investigation."

"He did."

Hawthorne shook his head. "I'm confused."

"About what?" Adam used his mug for emphasis.

"We don't know if there's a link between the break-in at Cornwall's apartment and the explosion. That's what I'll establish. If there is, then I guess the case will fall in your lap."

"Yippee." Hawthorne eyed the stack of paper sitting on the corner of his desk.

"I'd help, but…" Adam shrugged. "The investigation is getting a lot of media coverage. I heard families are yelling for answers." *Great job, Uncle Henrik.* "If you and Timmins need an extra pair of hands, get the captain to agree to me coming on board."

Adam mentally went through his checklist as he walked down to the interview room and nodded at the female officer who would be his backup while talking to Mrs. McCarthy. As for the landlady, she sat quietly at the metal table, a Styrofoam cup in front of her and her hands clasped in her lap.

"Mrs. McCarthy, I'm Detective Adam Solberg. The officer behind you is Sergeant Tanya Windfield."

No answer. He glanced at the officer, who shrugged and made a motion across her mouth with two fingers— a zipped lip, meaning the landlady hadn't talked at all.

He sat down opposite her. "Mrs. McCarthy, I need to talk to you about what happened at Ms. Cynthia Cornwall's apartment two days ago."

The landlady picked up her cup and took a noisy sip. "What about it?"

"I want to know why you left that threatening note and photo on her bed."

"What makes you think I did it?"

"We have evidence, Mrs. McCarthy. Your print was on the letter." Daniel had pulled a miracle out of his hat with that find.

"I doubt it."

Adam opened his folder and pulled out a photograph of the letter. "Do you see that? In the lower corner? That's a fingerprint. Not a full one, but enough to get a hit. Your fingerprints were already in the police database. It didn't take long to put two and two together."

She sipped her drink, louder this time. It was an irritating noise, but Adam kept his expression calm.

"Maybe I found that letter."

"And went into Ms. Cornwall's apartment without permission and placed it on her bed?"

"Maybe someone threatened me to take it into her apartment." She nodded. "Yes, that's right."

The woman was a few cards short of a full deck. "Why?" he demanded.

"How the hell would I know? Maybe they didn't like her?"

"Look, along with that fingerprint, we have video surveillance."

She stilled at that.

"The security cameras don't just feed to your office. They also feed to the security company that installed them." He watched her. "What? You didn't know that? You do now." He pointed at the photo. "Why did you put this in Ms. Cornwall's apartment?"

She looked away. "I can't tell you."

"Can't, or won't?"

"I can't tell you," she repeated. "He'll find out."

"He? Who?" Adam demanded as he watched her. A tic developed around her jawline—she was nervous about something. "Give me a name."

"I can't! He'll find out and kill me!"

"He won't know."

"Yes, he will! The story's in the newspapers!" She squeezed the cup between her hands. "He'll know I screwed up."

Adam glanced at the female officer, then leaned in close. "Do you want to know why he won't know?"

Mrs. McCarthy looked at him out of the corner of her eye.

"Because the story hasn't been released to the press. While it's part of the investigation, we couldn't afford a mass panic that the criminal was threatening police officers. He doesn't know you're here. Now, can you give me a name?"

"Don't Screw With Me."

He sat back, pissed. "Fine. If you don't want to talk—"

"I just told you his name, his nickname."

Adam hesitated, then started tapping his fingers on the table, growing impatient.

The landlady nodded. "He says that just before he kills someone. That's what I call him."

He wasn't sure who was the more outrageous one— her, or this mystery perp. "Can you tell me *why* he threatened Ms. Cornwall?"

"He said she was getting too close."

"Too close to what?"

"The answer."

Adam continued tapping, but remained quiet as his mind took in what was just said. *The answer.* "Do you mean the bombing?"

Mrs. McCarthy nodded. "Ms. Cornwall's a smart girl."

She certainly is, he thought. "Anything else you'd like to discuss, Mrs. McCarthy? Are you sure you don't want to identify the criminal who put you up to this?"

She shook her head. "I didn't want to scare Ms. Cornwall, you know. She's always been kind to me."

Interesting. "And you don't want to return the favor? Help her out?"

The landlady shook her head again.

"All right. You'll be transferred to Vanier Centre either tonight or tomorrow morning. If you think of anything else or want to talk, let the officer in charge of the jail cells know."

"I don't want to go there." Mrs. McCarthy leaned across the table. "Please."

"Oh, I know you hate it there. Saw it in your report. But if you don't want to come clean with me, that's where you're going." He stood. "Maybe a couple of nights there will jog your memory."

"I don't want to go there!" The landlady came around the table so fast that Adam barely had time to take on a defensive stance. She grabbed his arm. "Please, take me to another prison, but not Vanier, please!"

Windfield was on her in moments. Mrs. McCarthy struggled, but the officer clinked the cuffs together and locked the woman in a tight grip. "That was an assault on an officer," Windfield hissed into the landlady's ear.

Adam waved a hand. "It's okay. Get her ready for transport. I'll get the paperwork filled out."

"If I could talk, I would!" Mrs. McCarthy jerked her arms against the handcuffs.

Adam shrugged. "It doesn't help me. Windfield, can you escort her back to her cell?"

"With pleasure." The officer was stronger than she looked, and got the landlady moving.

"What about my phone call? You know I have rights to that," she exclaimed.

"According to my notes, you were read your rights and you refused to acknowledge them. You'll get your damn phone call."

He waited for the next elevator, and as he rode up to his floor, his frustration got the better of him. He slammed his fist into the wall several times and resisted the urge to add an animalistic yell to the mix.

There were too many hidden secrets, too much vagueness surrounding this. A murder case engulfed with mysterious witnesses and too little to go on.

He hoped Cynthia got better results.

Chapter 10

Cynthia glanced at her watch and frowned. More than two hours had passed and Timmins still hadn't called to tell her about his interview with Mr. Creatura. Weird.

She had scrutinized several videos about Tannerite—how it was mixed to create a bomb, and several ways it could be detonated. She had even found an old newspaper article about a bombing in downtown Toronto that had Tannerite as the key element. She had written her notes, and cleaned her lab area before continuing work on the other evidence. If the wiring they'd found had even the slightest print on it, she was going to find it no matter what.

She had everything lined up neatly and ready to go when her phone rang. "Cornwall. It's Boucher. I need to see you in my office, and bring everything you've got on the bombing investigation. Now."

"Yes, sir, five minutes."

When she opened Boucher's door, she stopped dead in her tracks. Timmins, Hawthorne and Daniel were missing. However, Adam sat at the meeting table. "Sir, where are the others?" she questioned.

"They were called out to a major drug bust and explosion at Kootenay Ridge, north of us off of Dufferin Street." The captain's expression could cut through stone, he was that angry.

"Another explosion?" That explained Timmins not calling her. But it didn't explain Adam's presence.

"I want a rundown of everything you've got. Solberg is here to update on his interview with Mrs. McCarthy. I'm sure you've seen the news the last couple of nights. Relatives of the dead Chariots of Chrome MC members are screaming for justice."

"They have every right to be upset," she said.

"I'm more concerned they might take justice into their own hands, and that can't happen. Give me an update, Cornwall."

"Sir." Cynthia took a breath to get her thoughts in order. "We have little to go on. This was planned meticulously. The Rolex gave me nothing to work with. However, the white residue I found near the blast site was Tannerite."

"Tannerite?" Boucher frowned. "It's an explosive, but it can't be used in bombing materials."

"Actually, sir, it can if enough ammonium nitrate and aluminum powder are used, or if it's mixed with other incendiary materials. I believe the watch was a ruse. That bomb could only explode if a high-velocity bullet struck it." Cynthia had to take another breath because her conclusions seemed so far-fetched, but what else could they be? "Either someone inside the club fired into the bomb package, or there was a sniper who fired a shot at the bomb from a distance."

The captain rubbed his face. "And the safe?"

"Clean, sir. All the prints belong to Mr. Magnus Solberg. There are items that Detective Solberg should have once the case is closed." Cynthia would let him know what she found later. "Captain, did Timmins provide any critical information on his interview with Mr. Creatura before he left?"

"He doesn't think Mr. Creatura is a suspect." The captain wandered to his favorite spot by the window. "His house is built like Fort Knox, he says. The only time Mr. Creatura thinks his Rolex could have been stolen was during a party a couple of weeks ago. He promised to send security footage from that night."

"Well, that's something at least."

"But probably has nothing to do with the bombing," Adam interjected.

She nodded. "We won't know until we see that footage."

"Solberg, what did you get out of the interview with Mrs. McCarthy?" Boucher asked.

"I think she knows who it is."

Cynthia stared at him. "But?"

"She refuses to talk. Even though she likes Cornwall, Mrs. McCarthy's too scared to help." Beneath his calm demeanor, Cynthia felt his barely controlled rage. "She's going to Vanier to think about it."

"Did you know that your landlady was convicted for murder?" Boucher asked her.

"I do now." Hearing it again gave her the heebie-jeebies.

"Dammit, we could possibly seal this case, but our one good suspect won't give us answers!" Captain Boucher smacked his hand against the glass pane. It shivered violently, but didn't break, thank goodness. "Cornwall, keep at it," he told her, turning around. "Solberg, thanks for your help, but you're still off the bombing case. The both of you get out of here."

Adam paused in the middle of stirring the sauce. Cynthia's voice was filled with anger, accompanied by tossed papers and punctuated with colorful cursing that earned admirable respect from him. "What's on your agenda?"

"I have to solve all the clues, don't I?" She started ticking off on her fingers. "Why did Mrs. McCarthy leave that note and photo in my apartment and who does she work for? Who bombed the clubhouse? How did Mr. Creatura lose one of the most expensive watches in the world, and *not know about it*?" She let off more swear words.

Adam brought the dinner dishes as she cleared away her mess, then hurried back into the kitchen to keep an eye on dinner. Cynthia sounded pretty stressed, and in some ways, so was he. Her lack of progress weighed on his mind, and he worried that he and his mom, along with Dad's friends, wouldn't get closure. But he had to have faith in her. As much as he never liked discussing work while eating, maybe being her soundboard might help in jogging loose some ideas. He returned his attention into presenting dinner—pan-seared steak with garlic butter, mashed potatoes and carrots, with a salad.

"You know, this meal deserves a nice wine," she said.

"Now you're talking." Adam had a bottle chilling in the fridge. He opened it with a satisfying pop and grabbed two glasses.

"Just half a glass, please," she pleaded, as he started pouring. "We have to be at work tomorrow."

"I know." He sat down, then raised his glass. "To success."

"In all that we hope and dream for." She clinked glasses.

Cynthia's statement gave him the chills, and he figured this was a good time to talk about her comment. "What do you hope and dream for, Cyn?"

"Hmm?" She placed her glass down, her beautiful eyes wide with surprise.

He knew he had caught her off guard, which, according to her, was a rare thing. "What do you want?"

She started cutting into her steak. "You mean like world peace, save the oceans, that kind of thing?" She took a bite. "Adam, this is…" She kissed her fingers.

He smiled. "Thanks." If she was trying to change the subject, it wasn't going to work. "I mean, what do *you* want?"

"Oh." She placed her elbows on the table and leaned forward. "You mean, like what I wanted a couple of nights ago?"

Adam knew his brow shot up at that, but in truth, it didn't faze him. Well…yeah, he was aching to know what Cyn loved in her sex life. But this wasn't the time and place to talk about it. He had the feeling Cynthia wanted to throw him a curveball to see how he'd react. He remained silent.

After a few seconds, her expression became serious. "I'm sorry—that was uncalled for."

"Oh no, Ms. Cornwall, you're not getting away from that so easily." He started eating, but didn't take his eyes off her. "That particular question? I want an answer when the time is right."

Her look confused him. She seemed annoyed, and yet, it was tempered with a quick smile she tried to hide behind her fork. Cynthia was a mystery Adam wanted to solve. He wanted to take his time, peel away the intriguing layers to discover the core of what made her tick.

His fork stopped halfway to his mouth. This was something he hadn't quite expected. Sure, to have Cynthia here in his condo, work related or otherwise, was an achievement any man would brag about. But this... wanting to know more about her, to understand how she felt about her work, her life, her everything...

A very distinct chill raced up his back.

"Is that a demand, Detective Solberg?"

Ah, her "in the office" voice and look. It wasn't going to work this time. "No, it's not. I don't demand things from people, unless they're suspects." He continued eating. "You can answer it whenever you want to. Or not."

She wiped her mouth with the napkin and pushed her plate back, then had a sip of wine. "What I wanted was to be the best at my job."

"Everyone wants that, Cynthia," he said, but she held up her hand.

"To be the best. Do you understand what that means? To have a case in front of me, and with all the expertise at my fingertips, solve it and give families closure." She stared at him. "I made sure to graduate at the top of all my classes to get to this point."

He understood. Adam had wanted to be at the top of his game, to follow in his dad's footsteps and aim higher. He loved his job, and at the time, didn't want anything else.

"But my aunt..." She shrugged. "She keeps asking when I would settle down, start a family. She likes to remind me that there's more than just a job to fulfill my life."

"She's right."

Cynthia smiled. "You're on her side."

"There's a balance to everything. I love my job too, but I remember when my parents were together, and the love they shared." His chest tightened as he said the words. "I wanted to find something like that. Almost did."

Silence for a few moments. He took a breath and said, "And then I didn't."

She rubbed her forehead. "Hell, Adam, I'm sorry to hear that."

"Don't be. I'm not." *Not anymore*, he thought, finishing his meal. He thought he'd been ready to talk about what happened, but the wound was still deep, even though it had been close to a year since he called off the engagement.

"That's one of the reasons I'm afraid of getting involved with someone. You learn to start trusting, to fall for someone so hard you're barely breathing. And when you think you've found the person of your dreams…" She snapped her fingers. "Reality hits you like a ten-ton truck."

"It's not always like that." Adam thought of Uncle Henrik and Aunt Michelle, almost at their thirtieth anniversary. He stood. "But it sounds like you went through some crap yourself."

"That was a long time ago in a city far, far away." She drained the rest of her wine in one gulp.

"Wait, you're referencing *Star Wars* now?"

"I loved that movie."

Well, hot damn. Cynthia was looking better and better in his eyes. His ex-fiancée refused to watch any type of sci-fi movies—her loss. "I have two surprises for you. The second one is dessert, but the first one is more…personal." He grabbed her hand and pulled her to her feet.

"A surprise?" Cyn's expression was cautious. "What kind of surprise? Should I be worried?"

"Of what?" He led her down to the end of the hallway and stopped in front of a door. If anyone should be worried, it was him. Adam had left the precinct yesterday after their secret kiss in her lab to set up this impromptu meditation space for her. He hoped it would help, especially since she couldn't use hers at her apartment.

He opened the door and stepped to one side. "I hope you like it."

Cynthia's reaction was priceless. She stood still, her jaw hanging open with surprise.

He had remembered her mentioning that she missed her meditation space back home. He couldn't find a Buddha, but he located a small wooden table and a piece of multicolored carpet, which had been rolled up and sitting in the master bedroom closet. He dug out the box of candles on a kitchen shelf and arranged them on the table. Hell, he even had time to buy a yoga mat, incense and a small palm tree.

"Adam." She managed to say his name, then went all quiet again. She finally stepped into the small space, her gaze missing nothing, before turning back to him.

"This was Mom's little studio. It was also her hiding spot if Dad pissed her off." He touched the door frame. "I never used the space because it felt like I was trespassing her domain, you know?

"But I've seen how stressed you've been getting, and I thought…" He hesitated, now feeling embarrassed at his efforts. "Well, it's here if you ever need to use it."

Her eyes were suspiciously shiny, but it was the huge smile that caught and held his attention. "You really know how to push my buttons, don't you?" she whispered.

He wasn't sure how to take that, but in the next second, she threw herself into his arms. "This means a lot," she said before crushing that beautiful mouth to his.

He wrapped her in his embrace, before picking her up and laughing against her mouth as she squealed with surprise and delight. "Are you sure it's okay?" he asked, a bit anxious.

"It's more than perfect." Cynthia kissed him again.

Adam breathed a mental sigh of relief. Overstepping boundaries was a thing he feared. "Did you want to get acquainted with it?" he asked.

She frowned. "It feels rude sitting in here while you're cleaning up."

"Nope, don't have a problem with it." He released her slowly, feeling every inch of her body brush against him. "You've had a stressful day. Take your time."

He cleaned the dining room and got the dishes into the dishwasher. Yes, that went so much better than expected. Hell, he might even use it himself.

Adam finished cleaning the kitchen when Cynthia appeared, her expression almost tranquil. "That was exactly what I needed," she said.

"Glad to hear it."

She sat at the breakfast nook, chin propped on her hands. "I believe you said you had two surprises for me?"

He laughed. "I have more ice cream for dessert."

She smiled. "Yes! Bring it on!"

"Which ice cream would you like? I have rum and raisin or chocolate chip mint."

"Jeez, you're making this hard, aren't you? I'm going to close my eyes and point, so whatever I choose, I'll take."

"Fair enough." He turned around. "When you're ready, I'll switch the containers around."

"Deal." She closed her eyes, a slight smile on her face.

He placed the ice cream on the counter, making enough noise to fool her into thinking he was playing along, then leaned over the counter toward her, his eyes fixed on her full lips. "Ready to choose?" he whispered.

She jerked in surprise, but didn't open her eyes. "Yeah."

"What do you want, Cyn?" He loved saying her nickname, and right now it felt kind of poetic.

She licked her lips, a very small gesture that screamed all kinds of dirty thoughts. "I want to know if there's a third choice."

So, she wanted to play. He'd have to keep his mind focused, or the urge to feel her up would take over. "I only have two flavors of ice cream in the freezer," he reminded her.

"Maybe the third choice doesn't involve that kind of dessert."

Damn. "You're making this interesting." Adam brushed her shoulder with his fingers and felt her tremble. "What are you thinking of?"

Cynthia slowly opened one eye, its brown gaze unwavering. "Well, it could be considered dessert. I'd have to use my lips and tongue to taste it."

He inhaled the sweet scent that surrounded her. "And what is this new treat I haven't heard of?" he teased.

Her other eye opened, and the look on her face gave him goose bumps. "Adam à la mode." She rose and touched her lips to his with the whisper of a kiss.

Why does it feel so natural to flirt with Adam?

Lord, this was supposed to be a strictly professional relationship—instead, she had allowed it to dissolve into a situation where getting too close and personal with a colleague was almost as easy as breathing itself.

How had she let herself drift so far off the mark? When she had called him after discovering the break-in of her apartment, her plan had been only to advise Adam of the situation, and *her* plans on how to deal with it.

And why did you call him first? Why didn't you call the precinct?

She tried to justify the question that Adam needed to know her predicament, that it was connected to the bombing case—anything really, to tell her that she'd done the right thing, but it wasn't working. She knew better.

And what was really odd? Her girlish delight when he insisted that she stay with him instead of being cooped up in a safehouse. Which, dammit, was so unlike her.

Cynthia liked him—as in, really liked him. But she needed to think of her next move very carefully. She had to weigh the pros and cons of a possible relationship, had to decide that if it didn't work out, could they continue working as colleagues.

This is why staying single was so much damned easier!

He cocked a brow. "Are you saying that I should lie on the bed, naked, with ice cream on top?"

Now that was a mental vision to behold, and more of a turn-on than she expected. Dangerous too. If she didn't put a dead stop to her wild fantasies with Detective Solberg, she was worried she'd find herself in too deep to pull herself out. At the moment, she was cutting it close.

Space—she needed to put space between them, mentally and physically. Cynthia sat back on the stool, using the counter as a barrier. "Sorry, I let my imagination get the best of me." She shrugged, her go-to defense to put up a wall between them. That wall was shaking, though.

His icy gaze dragged over her body, and she fought not to squirm. How could a look make her so hot and bothered? "I like the way you think."

Damn, he was making this harder. "What I like and what I do are two very different things," she told him, keeping her voice as neutral and steady as possible. She had no reason—actually, no right—to continue their flirtation. She had told him during their first night together she'd only wanted a one-night stand, and she got that, but had no idea that Adam would offer her a hell of a lot more. Adam had been so attentive, and her body—her soul—had craved what he'd freely given. Add the little touches, such as the improvised meditation space—and well, she had some serious thinking to do. But she couldn't do it while still being around him.

"Adam," she started, then stopped, fighting to find the right way to say what she didn't feel. "I think you and I need to slow down a bit."

"Why?" He propped his arms on the counter and leaned closer, which wasn't helping to keep her mind on task.

Her go-to answer—avoiding office relationships—didn't sound convincing anymore, but that's all she had to work with. Cynthia could say she was unsure about how their budding relationship would progress, but that made her feel vulnerable. "Because this shouldn't have happened in the first place between us."

His stare hadn't wavered. "I know you don't mean that."

She didn't feel convinced either, but it was true. "I only wanted to keep you up to date on the investigation. This…" She waved her hand. "This wasn't part of it."

Adam stood away from the counter, increasing the

gap that she didn't want between them, but for God's sake, what else could she do? "So you're saying you led me on? That the one-night stand meant nothing to you?" he asked, frowning.

"No, and I'm pissed as hell that you'd even think that." *Focus, Cyn.* "I like what we have. I'm just saying that I want take it easy, be sure that it's what we both want. I can't afford to have rumors spreading through the precinct."

"Oh yeah, I forgot. You need to be taken seriously."

Why did he make that sound so wrong? "Is there a problem with that, Detective?" she demanded.

Adam's expression was unreadable, but he remained silent.

"I just want to be sure, is that asking for too much?" Being here with Adam had set her emotions on a roller-coaster ride she wanted to stop. Cynthia needed to be in control, but her heart had other ideas.

"Have you ever thought that maybe, you should just go with the flow?" he said quietly. "To discover what makes that other person tick as you enjoy being with them?"

"Opportunities like that were rare, to say the least." How did he make it so easy to talk?

"They're supposed to be." He grabbed the ice cream containers and put them back in the freezer, then shut the door with more force than necessary. "And I believe you and I have that."

Oh my God, did he just admit we have a good thing going? Cynthia wanted to turn her brain off, wanted to shove her "no office relationship" rule down the toilet. But it had been so ingrained into her, it was almost impossible to shut it down. "I love my job," she said, her hands balled into fists on her lap. "Please, I just want some time to think this over."

"I'm not stopping you from doing that, Cyn. It's just…" He hesitated. "I don't want you to automatically think we can't work it out because we're in the same precinct."

Even after her half-hearted refusal to go on, Adam was still giving her hope. Cynthia refused to cry as she fiddled with the hem of her shirt. "Daniel told me that they finished processing my apartment and I can go back home tomorrow."

"I see."

She didn't want to look at his face, but she had to. Cynthia needed him to see how grateful she was. "Thank you for letting me stay at your place," she murmured. "It was gracious of you to offer your home when I needed help."

His expression changed. "No problem. Do you need anything else for tonight?" he asked. Cynthia almost choked at the look on his face—it was the same look she gave when she needed someone to leave her alone.

She shook her head, too sad to say anything.

"Then I'll see you in the morning. Sleep well." He checked the front door, then turned off most of the lights on his way to his bedroom, leaving her at the dining room table, a lone lamp the only illumination against the darkness.

Chapter 11

Cynthia had risen early and packed her few things, and set her backpack and satchel by the front door. When she turned, Adam was making his way to the kitchen, his hair mussed up, and looking damn sexy in his sweatpants. His chest was bare, giving her a front-row view. The shadow of a beard highlighted his jaw. "Morning."

"Morning." He released a loud yawn, then slowly got things together to make a pot of coffee. "At least have something to eat before you leave."

"Thanks." She sat at the breakfast counter and watched him. Well, observed, which was more satisfying. Thank God he was being civil—it made today a little easier to deal with. However, the lazy lull of morning had to be put aside for more businesslike thoughts, and she resented the interruption.

He turned to her, coffeepot in one hand, two mugs in

the other. He set them down, poured the hot liquid and got the sugar and cream.

She fixed her drink and took a sip. Just the way she liked it—hot and strong. "I'd better check my phone. It didn't ping all night." Cynthia slid off the stool and dug for her phone in her satchel. It hadn't made any noise because she had deliberately turned it off—an action she would have never considered before meeting Adam. The romantic evening that could have happened last night had shocked her back to reality, and in that turnaround moment, she'd forgotten to turn her phone back on. Funny how work, which was something she thought about as her life's priority, now felt intrusive. As soon as she entered her password, her phone lit up with alarms and messages. "Dammit."

"What is it?" Adam came around to stand beside her.

"Daniel's coming in around eleven. Looks like the guys didn't get back until really late last night." Cynthia sifted through her emails. "Daniel's catalogued most of the evidence. He's left me a few things to finish up." She looked up at him. "Don't worry—I'm going to examine the wiring I found at the clubhouse first before I work on Daniel's stuff."

He nodded. "Thank you."

Cynthia walked into the laboratory and tucked her satchel into her desk drawer. She noticed the plain white envelope sitting on her desk, and when she picked it up, her name had been typed across the front. It would have to wait—the anticipation of discovering a print on the wire overrode everything else.

She made sure everything had been sterilized and organized before pulling on a pair of latex gloves and retrieving the small pieces of wiring found at the clubhouse. A few of them were bare metal, while one piece still retained its rubber insulation. This one she hoped to find a fingerprint on.

She sat down in front of the large LED device she used for more difficult evidence, and carefully arranged the wire on its glass surface. Since the wire's casing was a dark blue, she grabbed the orange fluorescent powder and gently sprinkled it over the wire. When she was satisfied, she retrieved an orange camera filter and fitted it to the instrument.

She then put on the special goggles, dimmed the lights in the lab and turned on the LED camera. A print revealed itself in a clear, defined pattern. She examined it carefully, turning the wire. The print wrapped around the evidence, and it looked like a whole pattern. This was a very lucky break.

She took and labeled several pictures, then worked to lift the print from the evidence with a piece of adhesive tape. It was tricky, and she had to be careful not to overlap the tape. The small and very narrow surface was not making this any easier.

Cynthia breathed slowly, keeping her concentration and nerves sharp as she peeled the tape off. She immediately placed it on a dark latent lift card and sighed with relief—the fingerprint remained clear, so the Automated Fingerprint Identification System database should get a hit. She took additional pictures, including some with her tablet, and got the database set up to start finding print comparisons.

After sanitizing the lab equipment and tidying up, Cynthia checked the evidence Daniel had brought back with him. Everything was laid out in neat lines on the main laboratory table, clearly labeled. She took pictures, then paused in front of a unique piece of jewelry. A multilinked chain ended with two wolf heads biting onto a ring with a hammer—she recognized it as Mjolnir, the weapon of Thor. When she turned it over, Cynthia discovered a short inscription on the hammer—*Lancelot, Strong and True. Dad.*

She catalogued Daniel's remaining evidence. The bomb residue from this second explosion also contained Tannerite. There was no way this was a coincidence—there had to be a connection between the Chariot of Chrome clubhouse and the drug bust at Kootenay Ridge.

Cynthia stored everything away and sat at her desk to finalize Daniel's work. It didn't take long, and the database was still running, so she picked up the envelope and pulled out a sheet of paper.

You're next, Cornwall.

Everything went still as she stared at the threat. A black cloud of terror enveloped her until all Cynthia saw in her vision were those three words. Her body shook as her heart beat frantically as if trying to escape.

The perp had upped their game, and she was next on the list.

A sharp beep startled her so badly she actually let out a frightened scream, until Cynthia realized she got a hit on the fingerprint lifted from the wire.

When Cynthia read the result, she had to rub her eyes, believing her sight was playing tricks on her. She looked at the screen again, then leaned closer, confirming that the words in front of her were right. "Lord have Mercy," she whispered, then called Timmins. "I—I got a hit on a print from the MC clubhouse," she said in a hushed voice.

"Cornwall, what's wrong?"

"I—" Her throat closed, and she coughed to clear it. If the AFIS database was correct, then the threatening letter must have come from the same person. "Something must be wrong. It doesn't make sense."

"Cornwall, talk to me."

Timmins's demanding voice snapped her out of it. "The fingerprint belongs to Boucher. It belongs to the captain."

"Are you positive?"

Before she could answer, banging sounds echoed through the line. "Solberg! Get back here!"

"What is it?" she shouted. "Where's Adam going?"

"I had my phone on Speaker." She heard Timmins's running footsteps. "Solberg's gone to the captain's office."

"Dammit!" She ran out and headed straight for Boucher's office and Adam.

Adam stood in front of Captain Boucher's closed door, hands knotted into fists, his breathing slow and labored. His heart thumped so hard against his chest he was afraid he'd pass out. Voices and footsteps as someone walked through the precinct's hallways buzzed his ears. He couldn't just stand here and risk an officer finding him, or worse, Boucher opening the door to find him standing there with the look of death written all over his face. How could an officer of the law, sworn to uphold the peace and fight crime, do something so heinous? Boucher was Dad's friend, a colleague, a brother.

There had to be some mistake. But instead of remaining calm, he had allowed his anger to take over. It was time to shake the truth out of Boucher once and for all.

Adam closed his eyes and gritted his teeth as rage warred with reason, forcing his raw emotions to under-

stand that one wrong move could spell the end of everything for him

And that's when he heard her voice. "Adam."

How did she have this effect on him? To describe it
as soothing was an understatement. It was similar to the
exhilarating feeling he'd get when he used to sail in Nova
Scotia. The cold, salt spray stinging his face, his shouts
of absolute joy when he would spot a right whale, dol-
phins swimming beside his boat, so close that he could
touch their smooth, gleaming skin.

Cynthia somehow tapped into the calm, happy memories and made him remember something positive, something good.

He opened his eyes as her hand grabbed his. "What the
hell are you doing here?" she whispered fiercely. "This
is a bad, bad idea. Come on."

She tugged on his fingers, and he obediently followed,
the anger and disappointment temporarily muted. Back
in his office, Adam fell into his chair and sounded off
with choice swear words before eventually coming to a
stuttering halt.

"Thank God you didn't do something ignorant enough
to get your ass thrown in jail," Timmins admonished.
"What the hell were you thinking?"

"I wasn't." Adam wasn't sure what would have happened if Cynthia hadn't shown up.

"Let's just take a breath," she told them, grabbing a
chair and sitting across from him. Timmins stood, arms
crossed.

"Should we run the fingerprint scan again, just to be
sure?" Timmins asked.

"There's no need. The database's accuracy is top-notch."
She tapped her folder. "The reason the captain's print is

in the database is the same as the rest of us—getting a job with law enforcement. Is the piece of wire part of the bomb? Possibly, but it's not enough. We need more."

"Mr. Creatura's security footage should be here within the hour," Timmins said. "If we recognize anyone at the party, we can narrow things down."

"What if Captain Boucher's at that party?" Adam demanded. "He's in big trouble if we see him in the footage."

"And if Mr. Creatura covered up for him." Timmins turned and smacked the wall with a fist. "I hate being played."

"We still have to be careful," Cynthia cautioned. "Because if—*if*—the captain is guilty and we accuse him, he could make up any kind of story to hide the truth. He'll also be on his guard and we'll lose our chance to nail him."

Trust Cynthia to prevail with a cool, logical head. "What do you suggest?" Adam asked.

"If we're going to accuse a police captain, we need to be ready for anything."

"I guess that's my cue to leave." He stood. "I shouldn't even be listening to this, since I'm not on the case."

"I'm sorry, Solberg. I wasn't paying attention. I automatically set my phone to Speaker…" Timmins paused.

"Don't worry about it." He glanced at Cynthia. "I'll finish the report on Mrs. McCarthy at home, and stay out of everyone's way. I'm too worked up as it is."

Once inside the condo, Adam took one look at his kitchen and nixed the idea of cooking—he had plenty to do writing up his findings, and he was damn tired. It also felt lonely without Cyn—she had moved back to her apart-

ment today, and he didn't know how to feel about it. He
dug through a kitchen drawer and found the sushi bro-
chure. After placing his order, he brought out his office
laptop and sat down at the dining room table to think.
He started typing, his thoughts and observations flow-
ing onto the screen until he took a short break and ran his
hand through his hair, aggravated. Too many questions,
not enough answers.

He filed the report and securely emailed a copy to
Boucher, then shut the laptop with a bang that could have
broken the screen. He also wanted to throw it across the
room, but that wasn't the best idea in the world, so he
shoved it to one side, rose and stood by the window. The
clear night sky was illuminated by faint stars and an almost full moon.

He vividly remembered another night like this—he
and Dad had gone for a walk after dinner, because he
needed to talk to him about his decision to marry. The
old man had been supportive as always, but advised that
Adam had to make that fateful choice.

The video intercom startled him—dinner was here.

He grabbed a drink and was halfway through eating
when his work phone pinged. As Adam read Cynthia's
text, goose bumps prickled his arms.

Hey there, sorry to bother you. Still at the precinct. Saw
Mr. Creatura's security footage—not looking good. Listen, is it okay if I come over to talk to you instead of calling? If not, no worries, I'll ring you later.

Adam typed YES so fast he was worried he'd broken
the phone. He slowed down and added, I have sushi if
you're hungry.

He waited while she answered. OMG yes, thank you! I've barely eaten all day. I should be there in twenty.

Which meant he needed to order more sushi, since he knew how much she enjoyed food.

The solid three taps on his door, along with her beautiful face through the peephole, reminded him that she still had his spare keys—she hadn't returned them when she announced her apartment was clear. He opened the door just enough to peek through. "May I ask who's calling?" he inquired in a serious voice.

Her dark eyes widened in surprise for a moment before she caught on. "Why, it's your friendly neighborhood forensic investigator."

"I believe you still have my spare keys."

"You're right, sorry." She dug them out of her satchel and stared at them nestled in her hand. "I forgot to give them back."

"And you could have used them to come in, you know."

"I didn't want to just walk in." She smirked. "What if you were naked and dancing in the living room?"

That caught him off guard, and he laughed—it felt good to do that. "Excellent point," he agreed, opening the door wider to let her in. "My dancing skills suck."

Her own chuckle was low and amusing. She headed straight for the dining table, then stopped. "Did I bother you while you were eating? I'm sorry."

"Don't apologize. I'm glad you came over. I ordered more sushi though, since I finished this." He cleared off the dirty plates. "It should be here soon."

"Hey, I didn't mean to have you order extra."

"I told you, it's okay. Besides, it's nice having you around." *That slipped out without a second thought.*

"Wow, I'm touched." She dropped her ever-present

satchel on the floor, along with a backpack, then sat down. "And I have to say, being around you has been…" She paused. "Surprisingly pleasant."

That was good enough for him—for now. "I'll take that as a compliment."

She offered a small smile. "It's a rare one, believe me."

Cynthia seemed a little sad, and as much as he would have liked to discuss what bothered her, he'd also learned that she could be intensely private. He decided to give it a shot and sat down opposite her. "Is everything okay?" Adam watched her carefully, and noticed a shift in her gaze, the slight rise of her eyebrows, as if something came back to her. "What is it?"

Her stare haunted him—a mixture of grief and anger that took away the easy smile and laughter from earlier. "Hawthorne finally came in and told us to watch the news of the drug bust and bombing. Someone had sent videos of the explosion to the media, and seeing it…" She paused. "I saw my home and family, Adam, and I don't know how I kept it together while the guys talked about the case in front of me."

Cynthia was trembling, and before he knew it, he stood behind her, wrapping his arms around her shoulders. Her body jerked from a sob that she fought to hide. "Hey, it's okay," he whispered. He kissed the top of her head.

"You know that's not true," her voice cracked.

"No, but it's the hazard of the job. The risks we take to protect others." The words sounded hollow. This job that Adam loved had its downsides too. If he wasn't doing it, someone else would. He had come to the conclusion long ago that if he could solve some of the madness that criminals created, he was on the right track. If he delved too deep, he was afraid his sanity would be lost. "We do what we can, Cyn."

"Yeah." She sniffed. "Doesn't make it any easier."

"No, it doesn't." He grabbed the tissue box and handed it to her. In the precinct, Cynthia always kept her cool, so it was a relief—in an odd way—to see that cases got to her too. It made her more human, more endearing, to his eyes.

Adam bit the inside of his cheek. Man, he was falling hard. He needed to distract himself from that, and work was always the best go-to. "So, what happened at the office after I left?"

The question caught her attention. "Oh my God." She wiped her face, then grabbed her satchel and pulled out her laptop. "You're not going to believe this."

He moved to sit beside her, constantly aware of her body movements, her scent. She tapped a few keys on the laptop to get into the precinct database, then pulled up a video. She paused. "Promise me you won't freak out again," she cautioned, looking at him.

What the hell was he going to see? "I won't."

"I mean it."

"What are you going to show me?" he demanded.

After a moment, Cynthia started playing the video. The footage showed people coming through a front door. "Timmins received three CDs of security footage from Mr. Creatura, focusing on different parts of the house and grounds," she said. "I'm showing you this part of the video for a reason."

Adam heard her, but his gaze was locked on the arriving guests. "Is that Creatura?" he asked, pointing at a well-built older man with black hair. He stood near the entrance, greeting people.

"Yeah. His wife is just behind him."

She was a good-looking woman. She seemed to be staying out of the way, and would talk to the ladies as they greeted her. But her gaze would occasionally dart to her husband, almost like she was asking permission to speak. "She seems a bit skittish."

The intercom buzzed. "Pause that, will you? The rest of dinner is here."

Ten minutes later, Cynthia dug into the meal. "I'm so glad you ordered this. Thank you."

"My pleasure." She'd finished the miso soup, salad and dumplings in five minutes. "You didn't eat at all at the precinct?"

"Too busy." She placed several pieces of spicy salmon, vegetable and dragon roll sushi on her plate, then popped a piece into her mouth. "This is delicious," she mumbled while chewing.

Despite his enjoyment in watching her take pleasure in the food, Adam was impatient to continue. "You want to start up the video?"

"Hmm, sorry." She hit Play.

A few more minutes passed before Adam sat straighter in his chair. "Is that who I think it is?" Captain Boucher had walked in, along with his wife.

Cynthia remained quiet, but put her plate down and hit a few keys. The next video displayed a different section of Mr. Creatura's home. "This camera is located toward the back of the house."

The captain and Mr. Creatura looked like they were in a deep discussion. They both held drinks, their heads close together as they talked. The men walked several feet away before Mr. Creatura reached into his pocket, pulled out a key and opened a door. Captain Boucher followed him inside.

"What I'd give to be a fly on a wall," he grumbled. "Did you or Timmins find out how they know each other?"

"No." She tapped the keys several times. "This is security footage from inside the locked room."

The room was filled with shelves and display cases, filled with what looked like antique pieces. One case in particular held several different timepieces, and Adam immediately noticed the one bare spot. A large desk and leather chair commanded one end of the room where Mr. Creatura stood, talking to four men. Captain Boucher was amongst them.

"As I understand from Timmins," Cynthia explained, "Mr. Creatura is the only one with a key. He mentioned there's extra security besides the camera and alarm system, but he didn't explain what it was."

"It doesn't matter, does it? Boucher's in there. How did he make off with a Rolex without Creatura noticing?"

"We can't be sure that the captain took it—there are three other men in the room. But maybe Mr. Creatura gave it to him?" Cyn suggested.

"That doesn't make sense."

"I think it's the only theory that *does* make sense. Mr. Creatura told us he didn't know his watch was missing, and I think he's lying. Mr. Creatura kept the only key on his person. There's no way anyone can get in that room unless he lets them in."

"Or someone managed to get the key," Adam added.

"I doubt that. Timmins said that key is on a chain in his pocket."

"Okay, so let's say the captain had this Rolex. Are we supposed to go to him with a watch that has no fingerprints, these videos, his print on a piece of wire, and theoretically accuse him of murder?" This couldn't be Cynthia's plan.

"We have another problem."

He opened his mouth to make a sarcastic comment, and paused. Cynthia's expression had changed, as if thinking of something, and his gut roiled with worry. "Cyn, what is it?"

She fiddled with the laptop keys. "I—I need to show you something," she whispered.

He watched as her body started to tremble. Something— or someone—had terrified her, and it was the same reaction when she had told him about the threatening note and photo left in her apartment. He fisted his hands; impatient, scared and sympathetic.

Finally, she turned to her laptop and pulled up a picture. As he read the short note, his fury threatened to overcome him. "This is real?" he gritted through clenched teeth.

She nodded. "It was in an envelope on my desk when I arrived at work this morning, but I ignored it. When I finally—" She stopped and tilted her chin at the screen.

"You think the captain left that note, don't you?" Adam wasn't sure what to believe. "Did you scan it for prints?"

"There's nothing on the note or envelope. Trust me, I checked."

"But you think Boucher's responsible because you found his print on a piece of wire." This was getting too outrageous, even for him. "You know this is thin, right? I can't even call this circumstantial evidence. All we have are bit and pieces and theories."

She blew out a breath. "Timmins and I are going to

talk to Boucher tomorrow morning. Not to accuse," she added as he opened his mouth. "Just to ask why he was at the party."

"And what do you think he's going to say?" *This was a bad plan.*

"I honestly don't know. But since he's up-to-date on our investigation, he must know that this was inevitable."

"If Boucher is responsible for any of this, don't you think he'll have a plan, too? He knows he's up against you and Timmins, who's a bulldog when it comes to digging for the truth." Adam was liking this scenario less and less.

"I know, and I've thought of something, but wanted to be sure you're okay with it." She turned in her seat and faced him head-on. "You're our ace. The captain and the guys don't know I've kept you updated on the Chariots of Chrome bombing case. If things go south in any way, you're the backup."

"Backup to what? Cyn, you and the others need to come up with a better idea." Adam had worked with the captain long enough to know what the man was capable of. "Boucher's ruthless and doesn't give up."

"Neither do I. Neither do you, for that matter." She played with the laptop keys.

"This is a bad plan, Cornwall."

"Do you have any other suggestions?" Her voice trembled, with fear or anger, he couldn't tell. "Do you want to know why I really came over tonight? Besides showing this to you?"

He held his breath, afraid he might move and make her think twice on what she wanted to say.

"I hate my apartment." She shoved the laptop back and reached for the teapot to pour a cup of matcha green tea. She sipped it a couple of times. "I know it sounds irrational, but I refuse to step inside it. Ever since Mrs. McCarthy invaded it, she's ruined what sanctuary I was able to build in there."

Damn. He wanted to touch her, caress her hair— anything. Instead, he waited to see if she'd say more.

"I'd spent months looking for a place when I decided to move closer to York Regional Police." She laughed. "Dammit, I'm so picky."

"Nothing wrong with that. You knew what you wanted. Having it ruined deliberately by your landlady makes it that much worse."

"I had the most amazing view of the park and river. Looking at that kept me calm. Fixing up and arranging everything in my home calmed me. It helped to keep work where it belonged—at the office. And that woman stole it from me." Cynthia finished her tea in one gulp. "I didn't have any other place to go tonight." She sighed. "I'm sorry for barging in like this."

"Will you stop with the apologies? You're not trespassing, and you still have a key, remember?" If there was any way to make her stay, he'd be all over that like a bee on honey.

"I know." Her smile was small but genuine. "Thanks again."

They cleaned the kitchen together. Adam was about to ask if she'd like dessert, and hoping that it would lead to the other type of sweetness which was her delectable body, but she cut that short. "I haven't had time to get my facts down," she said, and grabbed her laptop, satchel and backpack. "I'd like to do that before going to sleep."

Well, if that wasn't a bucket of cold water thrown all over him. "Oh, okay." He stumbled over what to say next.

"You know where the guest bedroom is." He rubbed a hand over his hair. "And the meditation area is still in the studio room."

Cynthia nodded. "Thanks." Without another word, she turned and headed for the second bedroom.

Well, she had warned him they needed to slow down their attraction for each other. Guess she wasn't kidding.

Chapter 12

Cynthia cursed herself. Last night had been the worst.

Keep it all business, Cyn. Don't let Adam distract you, Cyn.

Who the hell was she kidding? As soon as she had shut the bedroom door behind her, she wanted to turn right around and jump his bones. But she couldn't—no, she told him they needed to take things slow, make sure a relationship was what they really wanted. Cynthia had to follow her own advice or she'd look like a hypocrite.

It didn't stop her from thinking what she needed—Adam's caresses, his kisses, his tongue, his… Dammit.

She half hoped to escape the condo this morning without his knowledge. When she came out, dressed and her bags in each hand, Adam was at the breakfast table, sipping on coffee. "Good morning," he called out.

He didn't have to rub it in by sounding so cheerful.

"Morning." She put her things by the front door and accepted a mug of the fresh brew. A little sugar and cream, and her first sip perked her up.

"Sleep okay?"

The coffee almost spewed out of her mouth. Did he really ask her that question? "So-so. I'm worried about my talk with the captain."

"Honestly, Cyn, don't do it. I have a bad feeling about this."

She glanced at him over her mug. "There's not much we can do. The clues lead back to the captain."

Adam sighed.

"Like I said, we're not accusing him. We're going to ask some questions and see what he offers." She looked around—no hot breakfast, and a sharp pang of disappointment hit her. "I'd better get going. Timmins is an early riser."

He stood and took the mug from her, placing it on the table. "Please be careful."

Cynthia put on her best smile, but inside, she wished he was coming with her. "Always am."

"I mean it."

His concerned expression tugged at something a little too close to her heart, and she swallowed. This man…

She couldn't help it. Cynthia grabbed his face and planted a firm kiss on those delicious lips of his, then backed off quickly before he could ensnare her in his unbreakable grip. "I gotta go."

Cynthia checked her phones on the cab ride to work—getting on the bus was not appealing today. On her personal phone, she received an answer from the property manager, who advised of three apartments coming up for rent at the end of the month. This was good news, as she loved the building and the area it resided in.

There was a text from Mav, and she read through it carefully.

Hi, doll. Did a reconnaissance around the MC clubhouse. There are four possible targets you or a colleague can investigate to locate spent shell casings. Details of each one below.
BE CAREFUL.

She had a message from Daniel on her work phone, who apologized for not coming in yesterday, but would be there as early as possible today.

She entered the lab and sat down at her office desk to finalize her report for this morning's meeting when Daniel walked in an hour later, yawning. "Morning."

"Hey, good morning. How are you feeling?"

"Better than yesterday. That crime scene was intense."

Cynthia had everything prepared. She gathered her papers and stuffed them into a large folder. "Timmins and I are having a meeting with the captain this morning."

"About everything we've found so far on the Chariots of Chrome bombing investigation?"

She nodded. The one item she hadn't told Daniel about yet was the print on the wire. "I finally got the results back on the fingerprint I found on that piece of wire."

Daniel frowned. "Why do I have a feeling I'm not going to like this?"

"Trust me, none of us do. It's the captain's."

"Holy crap!" he exclaimed, then immediately quieted down. "Is that wire from the bomb?"

"I—I don't know. Timmins thinks it's too small to belong to any of the electrical setup in the building."

"Wait a sec. So you're basing Captain Boucher's involvement on a theory?"

"We also have possible evidence that Mr. Creatura gave the captain that Rolex."

"Possible?" Daniel asked. "Cynthia, this is thin, even for you. Do you know what the fallout could be?"

"I know the consequences, Daniel, but Timmins is willing to take a chance. It's just a few questions. We're not accusing Boucher of anything, but we need to find out his side, if he's willing to tell us." Cynthia hoped the captain saw it that way too.

Daniel rubbed his face. "Good luck."

"Yeah, we're going to need it."

She was about to mention the threatening letter addressed to her when Timmins walked in. "Cornwall, you ready to go?"

"No, but we have no choice." She tucked her tablet and a manila folder under her arm and followed the detective. Cynthia needed to keep her cool, to display the look of a highly competent forensics investigator. They had no idea how Boucher would react, but they needed to be ready for anything. "Is Hawthorne coming?" she asked.

"No, but he's up to speed on what we're doing." On the elevator, he looked at her. "You're sure you're good?"

She shrugged—what did he expect? "A little nervous but completely on point. We got this."

"Good for you. I know sometimes, I don't treat you as a proper colleague. I say stuff that ticks you off. But you're A-OK in my books. An excellent forensic investigator."

Cynthia tried to speak, but all she got out of her mouth was, "Um, thanks."

Timmins chuckled. "Guess I caught you unawares. Sorry about that." The door opened with a loud ping. "Here we go."

Captain Boucher indicated the large round table near the window. "Have a seat," he said.

Cynthia grabbed a chair and put her report and tablet neatly in front of her. Timmins sat opposite her and plunked down a thicker folder.

Boucher eased into his own seat. "All right then," he said, rubbing his hands together. "Tell me what you've got."

Timmins glanced at her. "Cornwall, you want to start?"

"Sure. First, I wanted to let you know that the survivors will be at the hospital for a while."

"Shit." Boucher hid his face in his hands for a moment.

Eyeing him, she opened the folder and woke up her tablet. "As we mentioned in our last meeting, we found clues, but the obvious ones didn't provide any positive hits. So we had to take a different path.

"The Rolex was our most obvious and best clue, but we didn't discover any prints. I examined everything else with the same result, except for one thing." She paused, watching him. "A small piece of encased wiring with traces of Tannerite on it."

"I still don't get how someone was able to use that in a bomb," Boucher said. "It's so out of place, it's almost unbelievable."

She glanced at Timmins.

"While waiting on Cornwall, I conducted my interview with Mr. Creatura," the older detective continued. "He insisted that he didn't know his watch was stolen, which we didn't believe. We asked for security footage during a party he held. We felt that night would have been the perfect opportunity for the theft to occur."

"This is what we found." Time for the big reveal. Cynthia placed a picture in front of Boucher—the one with the wire and partial print. "Sir, I found one print on this wire." She hesitated, but there was nothing to do but go for it. "It's yours."

"We also discovered that you were at Mr. Creatura's party," Timmins added. "Footage shows you in a secured room with him, filled with display cases, one of which had Rolexes in it."

She waited for the usual levels of denial that all criminals displayed, but it remained quiet in the office. Captain Boucher hadn't reacted at all.

"Sir, we were hoping you could explain this," Timmins said quietly.

She and Timmins waited and watched. The ticking of the captain's old-fashioned clock on his desk accentuated the tension in the air.

Boucher's surprised look almost seemed genuine. "My print is on the wire." He sat back in his chair.

Cynthia's wariness was on high alert—he was too calm. "Yes, sir."

"I'll be damned." Boucher's smile was unsettling.

"Is there anything you'd like to tell us, Captain?" Timmins asked. His hands had bunched into fists on the table.

"What, did you expect me to admit guilt?" Boucher rose and stood behind his chair, sticking his hands in his pockets. Cynthia wondered if it was a defensive maneuver.

"We were hoping for an explanation," she replied. "Sir, your name came up with this print."

His gaze was penetrating, and she fought against flinching.

He started to pace. "So, you found me at a party, and you found my partial print on a piece of wire. Is that it?"

She bit her lip. "Evidence doesn't lie, sir."

"No, it doesn't, but I can provide an explanation for the evidence in question."

She knew this would happen—Boucher would give them plausible reasons, then be on his guard if he was, in fact, the arsonist and killer. In response, she tapped a couple of keys on her tablet to open a document. "What's your alibi, sir?"

He paused and glanced down at her. "I'll start with Mr. Creatura. I was there because he wanted extra security he could trust during the party."

"So you were there in an official capacity?" Timmins asked, his eyes wide in surprise.

"Alberto Creatura and I go way back—college actually. I used to work security intel at his R & D facility when I was an officer." Boucher shrugged. "He calls on me now and again to provide added muscle for his events."

"I didn't think a captain was allowed to do that," she observed.

"Why not? I'm still an officer."

"Sir, you didn't just attend this party as a security guard. You were also allowed access to Mr. Creatura's private treasure room."

He started pacing again. "Creatura and I are old friends. I've been in his private room before to see his babies, as he calls them."

Cynthia kept her face straight as she made a note of his comment—neither she nor Timmins mentioned the fact that Mr. Creatura gave his treasures a nickname. "I find it coincidental though, that you happen to be in this trophy room when a Rolex goes missing."

"Are you insinuating that I stole it, Cornwall?"

"Or Mr. Creatura gave it to you." She tapped her tablet. "As I said, the facts don't lie."

"Well, well." He laughed. "If that's all you have, you'd better get a move on before the public tears us apart."

Timmins started to rise from the table, but she held up her hand. "Hang on, Timmins." Cynthia grabbed another photo and set it out on the table for the captain to look at. "Timmins, Hawthorne and Daniel investigated the second explosion and drug bust on Kootenay Ridge. I assisted Daniel in cataloguing the rest of the evidence. That bomb also had traces of Tannerite in it, but that's not what's bothering me." She was amazed at how she kept her cool, despite the terrified tremors coursing through her body. Her hands shook only a little, a testament to her meditation practice and the iron will to find out why the hell her own boss might be an arsonist and murderer.

She tapped the photo of the threatening note. "This was sitting on my desk yesterday morning. There are no fingerprints on it, but my God, if this is your idea of a sick joke…" Cynthia couldn't continue. Finding out her sweet landlady was a murderer had been horrible enough, but this… Cynthia had mad respect for her boss. "I really want to believe you have nothing to do with this, Captain."

The look on Boucher's face gave her chills. *Was it true? Could he really be responsible for the bombings and murders?*

Boucher rubbed his face with both hands. "Dammit."

"What is it, sir?" Timmins asked.

Boucher didn't answer the question. "Was there anything else at the drug bust? Anything odd?" he demanded.

Cynthia was now sure he knew more than he was letting on. "As a matter of fact, yes." She pulled out a picture from her folder and placed it before him. "This necklace is very distinctive, and was already in a baggie when Daniel found it. I plan on tracing it back to the designer, then hopefully narrow down my investigation to the potential owner."

He looked at her and said, "You need to get away from here."

"Now hold on!" Timmins stood. "What are you saying?"

"I'm saying Cornwall is being stalked and she needs to leave this precinct. Hell, leave the city if you can."

"You've made it very obvious that you know something, sir." Cynthia didn't know how she kept her voice steady—her shock at the captain's words certainly told a different story. "What the hell is going on?"

The captain smiled—she wasn't expecting that. "I've got to tell you, Cornwall. You're one hell of a forensics investigator. Continue staying on track, and I know you'll find the answers to those bombings within a week." He placed his hands on the table. "I'll bet Solberg didn't tell you everything about Mrs. McCarthy's interview."

"Captain, what does that have to—"

"Your former landlady mentioned that her boss knew how smart you are, that you're getting close to finding the answers to the bombings."

She sat still, but her heart raced like an out-of-control train. The bomber knew who she was?

He pointed at the pictures. "I'm surprised you found out as much as you have."

That wasn't exactly a confession, but Boucher was involved somehow. Cynthia had heard of detectives being threatened with bodily harm or families hunted down by a criminal organization when one of their perps was caught. It was part and parcel of the job, but how they handled it, she had no idea. She had never been on the receiving end of such antagonism. Even her previous job with the Emergency Response Team was almost a walk in the park compared to working with the police force.

Now she found herself in the bull's-eye of someone higher up the criminal food chain than Boucher. If the captain feared for her safety, it was possible he was in the same tenuous position. "Sir, you have to give us something more to work with, anything," she insisted. "If I'm as close as you say, then let's finish it."

"I need you to leave as soon as you can," he told her. "Don't tell anyone where you're going."

"Captain, you can't be serious!" Timmins leaned in so that he was almost face-to-face. "If you know something, then tell us. Let's get this resolved. You won't be in the picture if that's what you're worried about. You can stay in the background while Hawthorne and I face the media. Bring Solberg back in if you have to."

Boucher looked resigned. "If I can help you, Cornwall, I will." He said this so quietly that she had to lean in to hear him clearly. "But I need you gone. You can't stay here. The sooner the better."

Cynthia hesitated at the door to her lab, really thinking of the implications she found herself in. She was now on the run, something she only saw in movies.

"Cynthia, you okay?"

Daniel's voice cut through her thoughts. "Yeah, I'm fine." She'd been thinking of how to do what the captain asked—hightailing it out of the city. A safe house seemed the best bet because there was no way she'd get Aunt Ki involved. But safe houses leave a paper trail, and just to be on the safe side, she didn't want Boucher locating her. She'd need to think of a good strategy. "Just trying to figure out something, that's all."

"Need to brainstorm?" he asked, approaching her.

"No thanks. This is more personal."

"I hope it's not bad news or anything."

Oh, if he only knew. "Daniel, I need to take a couple of days off from work. Can you handle the workload while I'm gone?"

He gave her a Boy Scout salute. "The serial killer case is wrapped up, so that's off my plate. I have a good handle on the bombings and drug bust. Piece of cake."

"Thanks, Daniel, I owe you one."

She packed her laptop, tablet and some personal items into her satchel. "If you need anything, you have my work number."

"Cynthia, I hope everything's all right." He followed her to the door.

"Don't worry—I'll be fine."

Once outside, she took a deep breath of cool air, enjoying the breeze that kissed her face. The secrets and lies within the building behind her clouded her thoughts, even made her start second-guessing herself. Out here, there was no judgment—nothing stood in her way. And Cynthia had to do one thing before calling Adam.

The phone picked up on the second ring. "Maverick's Mighty Locksmith."

"Mav, it's Cyn." No matter how much she believed she kept herself calm, Mav would see right through it.

He didn't disappoint. "What's wrong, sugar?"

She sighed. "I might be in trouble." She gave him

the condensed version of her conversation with Captain Boucher.

"Are you sure your captain said he'd help you if he could?" Mav demanded.

"Yeah." Cynthia still wondered about that comment. Boucher was definitely involved, but how much? Or was his comment a possible ruse, a false promise? "I don't know if I can trust him, though."

Mav was quiet for too long on the other end. "Mav, you there?"

"Sorry, doll, I was going over some intel I found on Boucher." Another pause. "Cyn, do you still have my text about those bullet casing locations?"

"Yes, why?"

"Forward that information to Boucher."

She held the cell phone away from her ear as if it stung her. What the heck was Mav talking about? "Did I hear you right?"

"Tell Boucher to have someone he trusts search those targets. If luck holds, he'll find the casing and hopefully a print as well."

"Mav, why would I give my captain that info?"

"Because you *can* trust him."

Mav wasn't telling her the full story—she felt it in her bones. Dammit, she hated secrets. "You know something."

"I know enough that you should believe in your boss. Where are you staying?"

"I—I don't know." Her heart kicked up the pace and she struggled to catch her breath. "I'll think of somewhere to hunker down until this is over."

"What kind of plan is that? You know better, Cyn. Stay at my place."

"No, I don't want to do that. I can look after myself—that's why I'm calling. Can you let Hammer and the rest of our ERT know what's going on? I don't think it'll amount to anything, but just in case."

"Yeah, I'll do that. Do you have your GPS turned on? I'll keep track of you without giving away your location. If something happens, you'd better call, you understand me?"

"Loud and clear." She knew Mav would have her back. "Thanks."

"That's why we're best friends. Listen, I'll be digging through some more intel. I'll text you what I find."

"What's bugging you, Mav? And don't tell me it's nothing." If Mav was sniffing around her investigation, it had to be important.

"The Tannerite. The bomb. To pull off that kind of shot, the sniper must have had lots of practice."

She thought a few moments. "You're thinking a police officer?"

"Or a soldier. It's just a hunch, but…"

Usually, Mav's instincts were dead-on, which unnerved her even more. "I'll let you get to it. Talk to you soon."

Cynthia walked into a nearby coffee shop and bought a tea and a blueberry muffin because her stomach wouldn't stop growling at her. She used the few minutes to copy Mav's text to her work phone, pulled up Boucher's number, and after a moment's hesitation, sent the information.

Locating that bullet casing would be one hell of a long shot. If Mav was wrong about the captain, she had just handed over her best piece of evidence.

Chapter 13

Adam returned to his condo, sweaty and exhilarated, after his long run. He grabbed a towel from the linen closet, then went into the kitchen to quench his raging thirst with a liter of spring water. The exercise felt great—he loved pushing his muscles to their limit, the smooth coordination of a body in motion.

Knowing that Cynthia and Timmins were questioning Boucher about his involvement with the clubhouse bombing set Adam's nerves on edge all morning. Keeping busy was the only good solution, so he had changed and was out the door, hitting the pavement. He had left his phone at home on purpose.

Running usually helped him think. But after a couple of hours on the streets, Adam felt more confused. He wished the questions and the weirdness would stand back for just a moment so he could make sense of everything.

He finally looked at his work phone, and was concerned Cynthia hadn't contacted him yet. The silence only added to his tension. Was she all right? Did something happen at the precinct? Several times he had been this close to calling and asking her what the hell was going on, but he held off. Nagging her like some kind of mother hen would tick her off in a truly epic way.

He kept the phone close by as he showered, shaved and got dressed, and still, nothing from her. Adam looked at his watch—it was close to one in the afternoon. If he didn't hear from her by two...

Ten minutes later, his phone rang. "Hey. I'm glad you—"

Cynthia cut him off. "I have to leave the city, Adam."

It took him a second to register what she'd just said. "Wait, what's going on?"

He could hear movement in the background. "Timmins and I met with Boucher. He didn't come out and say anything concrete, but the captain told me to get away for my own safety."

Her voice was trembling, scared. "Cyn, don't do anything. I'll pick you up."

"I won't be here."

"Please, can you just slow down?" Things were moving too fast. "You're saying that after you and Timmins presented the evidence to the captain and asked for his side of the story, that's what he told you?"

"He seemed anxious, scared even." He heard street noises as she talked—Cyn was outside. "Started swearing, then told me directly I would be in trouble if I got any closer to the truth. Timmins heard it all."

Dammit. "Where are you?"

"Just leaving the precinct."

"Get a cab and come straight here."

"I can't—I need to stop at my place to get clothing."

"Cyn, we can stop at a mall and get clothes for you. If Boucher said to get out, you need to. Now."

She sighed. "Fine. It's on your dime. I should be there in ten minutes." She hung up.

Man, she was stubborn.

If Boucher told her to hide, it meant he couldn't protect her. The captain knew something—something big.

"Ready to go?" Adam had walked up behind her as she was checking her phone.

"Dammit!" When she quickly turned, he caught sight of her wide, frightened eyes before she exhaled a loud sigh. "Don't scare me like that." Cynthia was on edge.

"Sorry. I didn't mean to."

She tossed her phone into her satchel and leaned back. "I'm sorry too. I didn't mean to bite your head off."

He noticed how tense she was, how she couldn't stop fidgeting.

"Are we riding two plus hours on your chopper with all of our stuff?" she asked.

"Nope, got something better. Come on."

In the underground parking lot, Adam rested his hand on the Airstream coach Dad had bought when they used to take trips up to the cottage. Staring at the silver vehicle brought back memories—the excitement of arriving in the countryside, Mom getting the cottage ready while he ran around in total glee, following his dad down to the dock to put their boat in the water. Thinking about those good times, Adam's eyes welled with tears, but he quickly wiped them away.

The interior hadn't changed. The coach felt like a warm, familiar blanket, well-worn and comfortable.

Adam walked the length of the vehicle, his fingers touching everything, memories flooding his consciousness
so fast he thought he'd choke on the emotions. Cynthia
stared at him as he made his way back to the driver's
seat. "Just like old times," he whispered.

"We're taking a trailer?" she asked.

"Damn right, it's more comfortable. We're going to
my family cottage. I'm staying with you until we hear
from Boucher."

"You don't have to do this." She grabbed his arm. "I
can look after myself."

She was trying to be brave, the independent woman who
didn't take crap from any man. But behind her bravado,
Adam saw her trembling hands, the way her eyes widened
in fear when Boucher's name was mentioned. This situation was different, and he refused to ignore it. "Under
any other circumstances, I know I wouldn't need to worry
about you. But we're dealing with someone who scares the
captain. We know Boucher is guilty of something—all the
evidence points to that. But telling you to get out of the city
means he doesn't have control of the situation anymore."
He paused. "And what kind of guy would I be if I didn't
offer to stand by you?"

That got a small smile from her. "You sure are something else."

He grabbed her into a hug and kissed her cheek, sens-
ing she needed it. "Shall we get going in our silver chariot?"

Cynthia settled into the passenger seat, dropped her
satchel on the floor in front of her and strapped on her
seat belt. "So, what's this about your cottage?"

He stuck the key in the ignition and turned over the
engine. It roared to life almost immediately. "We have a

cottage in Muskoka. Dad refused to sell it, and now I'm glad he didn't. It's remote and if I know Dad, there'll be weapons and ammo up there."

She rubbed her hands across her thighs. "I hope we don't need to use them."

"So do I."

Adam said it would be almost three hours to the cottage. Which meant too much time for thinking. Cynthia reached for her satchel to drag out her tablet, then stopped. They had been put through hell and high water with this case, and she needed a break before diving in again, hopefully with a calmer mind.

Damn, I need to get back into my meditation work.

She glanced over, watching Adam as he kept a firm, steady grip on the wheel, his gaze focused on the road ahead. She wondered what he was thinking about.

"Dad loved going up to the cottage," Adam said, as if he knew what she was thinking. "As soon as May arrived, he would start planning his vacation and get everything ready."

Cynthia couldn't remember the last time she took a vacation, which saddened her. "Like what?"

"The fishing gear, camping equipment. He'd check that everything was working and fix up loose ends. He was good like that, always prepared."

"I guess that came from working on the force?"

"Yeah." He glanced at the rearview mirror and pulled into the fast lane.

"Did your dad always want to be an officer?" she asked.

He shrugged. "I honestly don't know. Dad was a private guy. He was always there for me when I needed him, and he and my mom loved each other so much. I always wished…" He paused, but she noticed his hands tighten on the steering wheel.

"What is it?" she asked quietly. One thing she had learned about him was that he didn't hide his emotions, unlike most men she knew, and certainly most cops. Getting to know him these past few days, Cynthia realized that Adam's openness had rubbed off on her. For a gal like her, keeping her private life off-radar had been a successful tactic while doing her job. But after she unexpectedly opened up to him about her own family loss, a core part of her shifted. It felt like being blinded by a shaft of sunlight that sliced through the darkness of her grief. While she'd never forget her family, she hadn't allowed herself to move on. Adam, in a small but crucial way, had started her on her journey.

His gaze flicked to her before returning to the highway. "I was engaged a couple of years ago. I thought I found the love of my life."

Cynthia hadn't realized she was holding her breath. The words twisted around in her mind until her temples started aching. Why did it bother her so much? It wasn't as if she knew Adam back then. But knowing him now, she knew what a great catch he'd be. Her hands twisted her shirt as she suddenly realized what her thought implied.

"Our relationship developed fast, which should have been my first warning. But Else loved that I was a police officer, looking after people. And at the time, my job was steady, no shift work.

"But I also had ambition. I wanted to become a detective, and started work on that goal, which meant being away from home a lot more. She didn't like that."

"She knew you wanted to do this?"

"Of course. One thing I refused to do was keep secrets. I told her my plan and what it entailed. She was on board with it for about six months before things went downhill."

"People really don't understand what it takes to be an officer's spouse." As she listened, Cynthia couldn't help but think how similar their lives were. Her own ambition of being the best forensic investigator took up almost all of her time and energy.

"Yeah. I sometimes wonder if that's why Mom divorced Dad. I think it finally got to her, but she never said so." He smiled. "They still loved each other. Dad never dated after their breakup. I think the divorce shattered him. But he kept working—he loved his job too much."

"Sounds a bit like you."

This time, he turned and gave her a big smile. "I get my stubbornness from him too."

It felt comfortable—talking and getting to know each other a bit more. Cynthia had never opened up to her colleagues, past and present, because she didn't like that feeling of vulnerability. People demanding to know details of her private life set off an instant *stay away* alarm. Aunt Kiara told her that she'd never make friends if she didn't open up, and Cynthia had replied that she had three close friends and Mav, who didn't ask too many questions. Granted, she told them what she wanted them to know, but they never demanded anything from her. Everyone had their secrets, and she'd respected that.

"I had found intimate relationships to be…difficult." She saw him frown. "How so?"

"You mean other than the usual?" She crossed her arms and stared out the front window. "It seems that no matter how 'in touch' men say they are with the world, they have an inherent dislike of women who are more successful than them." One particular date she remembered relived itself in all of its arrogant glory. She shuddered.

Adam made a noise. "We're not all like that."

"Find me a guy who'd accept me as I am, and I'll be all over that."

Silence. Cynthia waited a few moments before turning to him. "What? You know someone who fits the bill?"

He shifted in his seat, as if he was uncomfortable.

She looked away to hide her smile. Adam definitely ticked all of her boxes, a feat that no other guy had come even close to accomplishing. And the fact Adam was a work colleague somehow didn't bother her anymore. Cynthia pursed her lips, remembering Aunt Ki's advice about not letting work become her lover. An odd choice of words, but she understood what they meant. And despite her rules, Cynthia was a human being, not a robot. She wanted love and support, someone to back her up when life took a wrong turn. And Adam had been there for her without question.

She rubbed her lip with a finger, thinking back on the time they spent together. It had been more than just a hot-and-heavy one-night stand. He immediately opened his home to her when she needed a place to stay. He hadn't taken advantage at all, and her cheeks grew hot when she remembered that she had initiated their foreplay. But Adam's scary, but exciting observation still burned in her memory when she half decided to give up...

I don't want you to automatically think a relationship won't work because we're in the same precinct.

He wasn't letting go. He wanted more—he wanted her.

Hot tears threatened to spill as her coiled, tense emotions finally released in a burst of relief and intense happiness. Adam wanted to give them a shot. He believed they had something. And she wanted to explore this new, unknown experience.

"It's obvious you haven't met the right guy for you yet." He flicked on the turn signal and maneuvered the coach to the exit ramp labeled Port Carling. "All work and no play won't give you that chance."

She loved how he chose his words so carefully, implying that he wasn't in the running. So considerate of him. "Well, you might be wrong." She played innocent. "There's this one guy I've met who's pretty hard to ignore."

She caught his hard stare out of the corner of her eye. "Really?"

"Mmm-hmm." She ticked her fingers. "Tall, hot and an amazing butt for starters."

"What else?" Adam's voice held a tint of frustration.

"He loves his job, but doesn't let it get in the way of his personal life." She gave Adam's admirable traits a bit more thought. "He's protective, stubborn, but not overbearing."

Silence from the driver's seat. Oh boy, she'd better let him get the hint she was talking about him. "Loves to cook Lebanese food, great sense of humor…"

"Wait, what?"

He pulled over onto the shoulder, parked the trailer, then turned to her with wide, very blue eyes. "Cyn, are you—" He didn't finish, just stared at her.

His look of surprise made her feel like she gave him the best present ever. "Am I what, in love with him? It's too early to tell, but…" She shrugged. "It wouldn't be hard to fall for him. I just hope he's there to catch me. It's a big leap."

Adam narrowed his eyes, and watching him, Cynthia knew the wheels were turning in his mind.

"Are you up for this mission, should you choose to accept it?" Her nerves were on edge, saying those words. She had no idea what he'd do.

He unbuckled his seat belt and turned to face her, then leaned over and unsnapped hers. With his gaze locked on her, he grabbed her arms and dragged her onto his lap.

Everything faded from view as Cynthia stared into eyes the color of the clear afternoon sky above her. Large, strong arms held her so tight she had no wriggle room. "I take it that's a yes?" she asked, trembling.

His answering kiss was gentle but thorough. Breathing needed to happen soon or she'd pass out from complete bliss.

When he finally moved his lips from hers, he whispered, "I'll catch you. And you won't get away that easy from me, either. The Vikings in my family are excellent hunters."

Chapter 14

Adam had made good time to Port Carling. It was early summer, and the small town was bustling with locals along with seasonal visitors who owned or rented cottage properties. The afternoon was sunny and warm, and Cynthia rolled down the window for fresh air and a better look at the area. She noticed mostly tourist shops, restaurants and lots of boats lined up against the shoreline. "It reminds me of Niagara Falls," she commented.

"Think of it as the neighborhood beyond Niagara Falls, but with more lakes and cottages."

"Gotcha."

"Let's hit the grocery store first, then I'll drive you to a clothing store."

The small gourmet store wasn't busy. She offered to push the cart while he selected produce. It was interesting watching him analyze the different types of lettuce, how to pick the best fruits and veggies and decide on certain cuts of meat.

"Hey, Adam, how's everything?" A large middle-aged man called out, wiping his hands on his apron.

"Hi, John." They shook hands.

"Your dad made his way through here a couple of weeks ago. He came into town one evening and grabbed a beer with me at the pub." He frowned. "Wendy and I saw the news about Magnus's clubhouse, and…" John stopped, his expression flustered.

Cynthia carefully watched Adam as his body tensed. She sensed that John knew Adam and his family—possibly were all good friends. She knew it hurt him to hear the grocer talk about his dad, and she could almost imagine seeing Adam building a wall around himself, because she'd done the same thing once upon a time.

It took him a few moments to compose himself. He pressed his lips together and shook his head.

"Damn." John reached out with one hand, then let it drop to his side. "I'm really sorry, Adam. My deepest condolences."

He rubbed his chest. "Thanks."

John glanced at her, giving her the once-over. "Did you catch the bastard who did it?"

"We're working on it." Adam turned to her. "Cynthia, this is John. He owns the store."

She stuck out her hand. "Pleased to meet you."

"Likewise." The man's grip was firm, solid. "So, are you and Adam…?" He paused.

"We're at the dating stage," Adam answered before she could. She remained quiet, because she knew why he said that. It was much easier than telling John—or anyone else Adam knew in the town—that they were work colleagues. That would have drawn suspicion. Good thinking on Adam's part.

"Ah." John winked at her. "You'll love it up here. Lots to do and explore. Quiet and peaceful. Everyone minds their own business."

Cynthia wasn't sure on that last statement, and bit back a snort of laughter. "Thanks, I'm sure I will."

When they finally left, Adam turned to her. "I hope you didn't mind, but saying we were dating was the easiest answer I could give. My parents are close friends with John and Wendy, and he's almost like an uncle to me."

"I didn't mind at all." Hearing him say it gave her goose bumps, and Aunt Ki was going to squeal with delight. She helped him load the groceries into the back of the coach, and noticed how many bags they had. "We're stocked for a few days."

"I don't want us coming into town unless it's necessary. Let's grab some clothes for ourselves."

Thirty minutes later, he pulled up to a large stone-and-wood cottage. It had a wide wraparound veranda, large chimney and picture windows. She stepped out of the trailer to admire it and the scenery around them. "It's beautiful."

"Mom loved hosting parties, so Dad made sure we had a cottage big enough to do it."

As they carried the various bags to the entrance, their shoes crunching across the gravel driveway, Cynthia noticed the expansive lawn and tall, thick hedge surrounding the property. Beautiful rosebushes grew close to the veranda, and several majestic pine trees were the only other plants decorating the area. The front door was a large, very solid piece of dark mahogany.

Inside, the whitewashed walls and dark wood floors

offered the perfect neutral background to the furniture and paintings. A stone fireplace almost as tall as she was dominated one end of the living space, with a huge flat-screen television above it. A leather sectional sofa and large chairs invited people to sit in them and snuggle with a good book—or significant other.

She instantly recognized a couple of the paintings from her favorite Lebanese artist, along with large black-and-white photographs of a fox, mountain lion and Canada geese. Above her, the peaked roof and supporting beams were made of fragrant cedar. "I thought it was beautiful outside," she whispered, following Adam farther into the house. "But it's cozy too."

"Mom has a knack for taking a few things and making it feel like home."

Cynthia paused at the entrance to the kitchen. The setup in the living room flowed into the long space, with plenty of windows to let in light. This time, an old-fashioned gas range held her attention, with the Sub-Zero fridge coming a close second. Fisherman lanterns were neatly hung in a row high above the granite countertop. "Wow."

"Glad you like it." He dumped the bags on the counter and started emptying them.

She did the same, and put the items he gave her into the fridge. "I'm guessing this is what you'd call a year-round cottage, but man, it's more like a home in the city."

"Mom likes it enough during the warm months, but hated driving out here during the winter. Dad was up here as much as possible, especially after the divorce." He paused. "He loved being out here in the winter. I guess it reminded him of Norway."

Hearing about Adam's parents made her ache for

her own, especially her mom. Her father was a man she couldn't care less about these days. "Speaking of your mom," she said quietly. "Have you talked to her about what happened?"

"Yeah, when I was at the hospital." He leaned on the counter, shoulders hunched.

"Have you updated her about what's going on?"

"You mean how you've kept me in the loop, risking your job and reputation? That you and I are now hiding from our boss?" He huffed out a laugh.

She smacked his arm. "When you put it that way, you make us sound like fugitives."

He looked at her. "Sorry. It sounds like we're actors in a movie, and yet..."

"It's all too real. I get it." Cynthia wanted to touch him, but wasn't sure how he'd feel. Her body made the decision for her—she reached for his hand and squeezed it.

His expression. She couldn't put a finger on it. A mixture of grief, anger and what she thought was happiness played across his features. His bright gaze focused on her, so blue that she imagined being swept into it, like a small boat being tossed by an unsettled, emotional ocean.

He raised her hand to his lips and turned it over, kissing the pulse in her wrist. She gasped at the small gesture, which sent her heartbeat racing.

"You know," he whispered, caressing her with gentle strokes of his thumb. "I never would have guessed this investigation would have resulted in us falling for each other."

She laughed. "You think?" Fate had a strange sense of humor.

"But I'm glad you made the stubborn decision to let me know how the case was progressing."

"So am I." Cynthia turned her hand around and linked her fingers with his. Damn, it felt good. "You know, if you want to call your mom, I'll hang around, if you want. For support."

He pulled her into an engulfing hug and kissed her. "I'll take you up on that offer."

Half an hour later, Adam had finally calmed down. His mom's emotions affected him, and while she couldn't hear the woman speak, Cynthia only needed to look at his face to understand the conversation. When he'd finally hung up, he was shaking so badly she was worried he would collapse.

Dealing with any kind of grief, whether in the family or trying to console a stranger who lost a relative to violence, always took a toll. Cynthia got him on the couch, then rushed into the kitchen to make tea. It took her a few minutes to find everything while the water boiled, then she returned with two mugs. "Here," she said, pushing one of them into his hand. "Drink up."

His first sip startled him—she had hoped the hot water would grab his attention. "Hey, that scalded my tongue," he complained.

"Don't be such a baby." She eased back into the cushions.

He rested his head against her shoulder, and a pang of nostalgia hit her hard against the ribs. Her mother used to do the same thing, and they'd talk about their day while watching television. The feeling of familiar comfort, the warmth of breath brushing her skin. That connection never failed to show her how unbreakable their bond had been. Until that night when she lost it all to an arsonist.

It wasn't the right time to think about the fire, but how

the hell could she choose when to think about it? Those memories would never go away. "Does your mom want to see you?" she asked, to distract herself.

He raised his head. "She wants me to obliterate the bastard first. Her words, not mine."

"Totally get it." She placed her drink on the table. "I felt like that after losing my family. I wanted revenge, and I had the means to get it."

Adam sat up and looked at her. "What did you do? I remember you saying you found the criminal."

"Nothing illegal—don't worry." Finding the people responsible for her family's death had been a long, but satisfying journey. "The police told my aunt and me that it was arson. Someone broke the kitchen window and threw in a Molotov cocktail. My aunt demanded answers, but the cops couldn't find enough clues to nail down a suspect. They had told us that arson had been suspected with two other houses in the neighborhood but that's as far as they got."

He grabbed her hand and squeezed it. "You're trembling."

Reliving the memory had always left her emotionally wrung out—it wasn't surprising that it took a physical toll on her too. "I wasn't allowed to look at whatever evidence the police collected. They had the nerve to say I wouldn't understand, so I went one better. I studied my ass off, Adam. I took every forensic course I could get my hands on, and bumped it up with tactical force training. As soon as I graduated and got a job, I located my cold case and spent the next five weeks working on it until it was solved. I finally had a name, face and possible location."

Adam cocked a brow. "I hope you didn't conduct a personal manhunt."

"Of course not. I got the local Task Force team to do that. They brought the little monster in for prosecution."

He nodded slowly, then frowned. "Did he talk?"

"Yes, he did. Said it was some kind of initiation to join a gang that, at the time, was terrorizing my old neighborhood." She nodded to herself, remembering every detail. "He told the police everything, hoping to get a lesser sentence. I made sure that didn't happen."

"And the precinct you worked for caught the others?"

"Not only did we catch them, we found out who their boss was and nailed him too. It was the moment in my career that I'll never forget."

But it wouldn't bring back her family, no matter how many times she solved a case. They were gone, just like Adam's dad. The years of carrying that burden on her own, while proving her worth within the police force, dealing with sexist antagonism, bubbled up to the surface. A sob broke out of her, filled with pain, loss and fear—the terrifying fear—that she'd never find someone who would accept and understand her for who she was. Aunt Ki was one of the few who knew how hard this was for her. Mav had been the only friend who understood the pain of her loss.

"Shh," he whispered, his arms around her. "I've got you."

Cynthia leaned into Adam's embrace. In such a short period of time, a detective—a colleague—with eyes like glacier ice and the strength to match, wanted to be at her side, to support and care for her, when other men wouldn't give her a second look. His attentiveness had been the game changer, to allow her to work through her feelings and realize how much she cared for him in return. Knowing this helped her to finally calm down. She wiped her face with a hand. "Sorry about that."

"There's nothing to be sorry for." He rubbed her back. "You and I have been chewed up and spat out too many times."

"Tell me about it." She wanted to sit beside him and forget why they were here, to enjoy the peacefulness surrounding the cottage and his warmth, but he had other plans. "Come on," he announced, standing up and pulling her with him. "Let me show you the rest of the place."

Back in the kitchen, a door opposite the fridge led downstairs to a small basement. "Our camping stuff is down here," he explained, turning on the lights. "We also keep any booze down here too, since it's cool enough."

"What's that over there?" she asked, pointing to a smaller door to their right.

"That's the cold storage. Mom insisted on one to keep the veggies and other foodstuffs fresh." He opened it and turned on another light, revealing a small stone-lined rectangular space with wooden shelves. "Dad kept a few things on hand. He didn't like being without."

"And what's that? A hatch?" She pointed to a small square door in the ceiling near the opposite end. A ladder was propped against the wall beneath it.

"Dad was claustrophobic. Sometimes he'd get disoriented if he was in the cellar for too long. The hatch was his escape route into fresh air."

"And where does it open up to?"

"A small stand of pine trees at the back of the property."

"Very detailed, your dad."

"He certainly was."

The second floor contained four big bedrooms, while

the master suite occupied the full length of the house at the rear of the property. "Holy moly," she murmured, surprised by the simplistic beauty that continued from downstairs. "This is stunning."

"Thanks. Mom and Dad put a ton of work into it." Adam walked into the room, looking around. "With Dad gone, I don't know if we'll keep it."

"Are you kidding?" She grabbed his arm. "If anything, you'd remember your father every time you come here. Think of the good times you've had when you were a kid. I would."

"Ms. Logic and Reason." He smiled and caressed her cheek with a finger. "I appreciate what you just said."

Cynthia swallowed against the lump in her throat. The way he looked at her sometimes… "Yeah, no problem."

He bent down and placed a soft kiss on her lips. A simple gesture, but she tingled all over just the same. Would it always be like this? Lord, she hoped it would never end. "I hate being a party pooper, but I think you mentioned that your dad had a stash of weapons?"

He cocked an eyebrow at her as he led the way back downstairs. "Mom never knew about the guns. If she did, she would have thrown them all into the lake, if she had the nerve to even touch them."

Beside the fireplace, Adam stopped in front of a large oak chest. In it were several quilts, and he put these aside. "There's a false bottom," he told her. "We have a couple of Glocks and a SIG Sauer, and three hunting rifles. Dad liked to hunt deer in the winter." He retrieved the weapons and placed them on the floor. "Did you bring yours?"

"It's in my satchel." She shoved her hands in her jean

pockets to keep from fidgeting. "I'm finding it hard to believe that someone's coming after me."

"You're out in the field. And your work has brought in some serious criminals." He sat on the floor, checked over the weapons, then started loading the ammo. "You're not in the spotlight like the rest of us, but it looks like someone's been reading up on you."

"Great." She joined him on the floor and helped out. She picked up one of the hunting rifles, which had a telescopic lens mounted on top. "Which one is this?"

"Remington 7600. It's a pump-action rifle. I'll show you how to use it before loading it." He had finished with the smaller handguns and picked up the second rifle. "This one's a Browning BAR, semiauto rifle, a little easier to handle in my opinion. Just point and shoot. And number three is a Ruger 10-22. It holds ten rounds of .22 Magnum cartridges. These rifles do some serious damage so be careful if you choose one of them."

"All right." Damn, it was getting real.

He gave her a quick lesson on how to load and operate the rifles. Since they were heavier, she'd have to be careful when taking her shots. "I'm going to leave them in the chest with the rest of the ammo. The guns are safety locked and ready to use."

By the time he finished showing her around, including exits and the lay of the land at the rear of the property, the sun had angled itself toward the horizon. As a precaution, they checked the boathouse, and were surprised the boat was in the water. "Dad must have done that when he was here last," Adam surmised. "We have another escape route if it comes down to getting out onto the lake."

Adam kept dinner simple that evening—thick hamburgers charred just right with an amazing salad and blueberry pie from the gourmet store. "Delicious," she announced, kissing her fingers. "I'm really surprised you didn't become a chef. Why didn't you stick with it?"

"Wasn't interested. At the time, I couldn't stay in one place for long." He ticked off on his fingers. "Chef, fisherman, youth counselor, worked search and rescue for the Canadian Coast Guard."

"That's a hell of a lot of experience to gain." Jeez, what didn't Adam do?

"It was fantastic. Grew up really fast." He crossed his legs and sat back in the chair. "The Coast Guard job was my favorite. I loved being on the water and helping out. I'm still friends with my crew."

"I love hearing that." Her impressionable years weren't as exciting as his, but she had a different goal. Still, the girlfriends that Aunt Ki introduced her to so many years ago, along with the men from her former tactical team, were supportive and most of all, nonjudgmental. "I don't talk to my girlfriends as much as I should, and I need to rectify that. As for my RCMP buddies, we've been tight since training."

"You were in the RCMP?" Adam's eyes grew wide.

"The Emergency Response Team. I wanted a well-rounded education before applying for a forensics position. Even did a basic course with the Royal Canadian Navy."

"Huh. I'll bet they put you through your paces."

"I remember it like it was yesterday." Talking about the ERT reminded her of something. "Listen, I should have told you while driving up here, but I alerted one of my ERT guys about our situation."

Adam had an odd look on his face. "Alerted? What are you talking about?"

"Mav—Maverick Hitsugaya—was one of my team members. Really nice guy."

His body language changed from relaxed to pent-up tension in a beat. "Cyn, what did you tell him?"

She caught on to what he was worried about. Telling Adam about her conversations with Mav could piss him off, so she decided to remain silent. The Tannerite problem she would have eventually solved anyway. As for Mav's suggestion of a possible sniper's nest, it was just that—a suggestion. "I told him I might be in trouble. He's keeping track of me on his GPS."

Silence. The tension in the air had thickened and, judging by the look on his face, she figured he wasn't pleased. "What's wrong? Didn't we agree that we could use all the help we can get?"

"I would have liked our situation to remain within our team." He suddenly rose, taking his dishes to the sink.

Why was he upset? "Hey." She followed him, and scraped the remains of her meal into the trash can. "What is it?"

He grabbed her plate and rinsed it before placing it into the dishwasher. "Don't you trust me to keep you safe?"

"What?" Was Adam feeling insecure? She couldn't believe it. "Of course I do."

"Then why the outside help?"

Normally, at the sign of a macho ego, she would put a stake through it. But right now, she needed to back up and rethink what was going on. "I wanted us to have as many aces we could get our hands on. Adam, it's only the two of us. My former team is top-notch. If things get funky they'll back us up."

He gripped the rim of the sink. "I know you're right. It's just... I wasn't there for Dad." His face betrayed the grief he fought to control and failed. "But I'm here for you."

Chapter 15

"That's the last box," Cynthia announced as she stacked it with the others in the basement's storage room. "I'm surprised your dad left them by the front door."

"Probably wanted to go through them first." Out of curiosity, Adam flipped back the lid on one, and almost gasped at what he saw. His parents' wedding album. During the divorce, Mom and Dad had split the pictures, creating albums for each other as keepsakes. Opening the album would hit him with painful memories. He shut the lid.

"Anything else you'd like help with?" Cynthia asked.

"No, I'm good. Thanks for helping out." He watched as she washed her hands at the small sink in the utility room, headed back to the living room and sat on the couch. She reached for her ever-present satchel and retrieved her tablet and work phone. It was all about work with her, and it was bothering him.

Crimes would never slow down or take a break. She couldn't always be looking for the next case, the next clue. If Cynthia kept this up, she'd burn herself out.

He sat beside her and looked at the screen sitting on her lap. Images and written notes scrolled by too fast—she was looking for something. "What's up?"

"My irritation." She tossed the tablet aside and grabbed her laptop, then signed into the York Regional Police database. "I'm sitting here with viable clues to the bombing investigation, and they lead us straight to Captain Boucher. Yet listening to him and listening to my instincts…something's wrong. Something is missing, and I can't figure out what it is." She pulled up the folder in question, double-clicked it, then started scrolling through the information.

"Maybe you need to take a break from it." *Right, like telling a fish not to swim.*

She glared at him. "I'm on the run because my boss, who's the lead suspect, told me to leave the city. That I was getting too close to—I don't know, something he didn't want us to find out." Her finger tapped the Scroll key. "Whether it was his guilt or something else, I need to find the answer."

"My God, Cyn, I get it." Adam reined in his frustration. "But you're pushing yourself too hard. Even smart people need to rest their brains."

"It sounds like you're making fun of me." She snapped the laptop shut and stood. "I noticed your cottage has a study. I'll be hanging out there doing research. Maybe you should get some sleep."

"Cyn, come on." She was upset, he knew. Not with him, but with the mental wall she'd hit in this investigation. "I know you're doing your best, and I appreciate it—I really do." He followed, trying to think of what to say. "If anyone can crack this, it's you."

"But I haven't." She wheeled on him, tears shining her eyes. "Don't you understand? If I don't do my job, innocent people will have died in vain. I can't live—" She stopped, taking deep breaths.

"Hey." He stepped close and wrapped his arms around her. He kept the move gentle, not holding her tight, respecting her feelings. He kissed the top of her forehead. "Do you want me to bring you something to drink? Coffee? How about a snack?"

She looked up, tears streaking her face. He ached to wipe them off, but was worried she'd slap his hand away in annoyance. "That sounds great."

He had scored a point. "Give me a few."

Bruiser was at his favorite diner, shoveling down an early dinner and drinking a toast to Magnus and the others. His talk with one of the doctors gave him hope. Everyone had been moved out of intensive care and were recuperating, although he knew it would be weeks before they could all go home. But the families were relieved, and the tension and despair that had blanketed the waiting room for several days were lighter.

He hadn't stopped to be with his thoughts until now. A short text from Adam earlier today had raised the hair on the back of his neck—something about Boucher being a suspect, and Adam going into hiding with Cynthia until the investigation was solved. Bruiser's demand for answers had been met with radio silence.

His cell phone pinged. He leaned back in the chair and checked the message, but what he read sent chills down his back.

Hey, Bruiser. It's Boucher. Can you meet me at the Sunnybrook hospital, southwest corner about eight this evening? There's some stuff you need to know. Make sure you're alone.

Bruiser stuffed the phone back in his pocket. "What the damnation is this dude up to?" he mumbled. He had to decide quickly because of Adam's suspicions. He didn't have a weapon, and once he got into Boucher's truck it could be game over.

Finally making up his mind, he left the diner and jogged the short distance, reaching the location a minute before Boucher appeared in his navy pickup.

"Man, you still have that speed." Boucher leaned an arm on the open window. "I remember the track-and-field finals at York University like it was yesterday. You blew your competitors out of the water."

"Cut the crap, Greg." If Boucher was trying to distract him, it wasn't going to work.

Boucher looked around. "You getting in?"

That was the million-dollar question. "Don't know. Are you armed?"

Boucher shook his head.

"That means yes." Dude was still terrible at lying. Bruiser looked around him. He hadn't noticed anything suspicious, but that could change in a heartbeat. "What do you want?"

"Ten minutes." Boucher glanced into the rearview mirror. "Just to talk."

"We can do that right here." He spread his arms. "We're not in anyone's way."

Boucher gave him an odd look. "I'm worried I'm being followed."

Now *that* look, Bruiser recognized. Boucher didn't get into trouble. *It's too much trouble*, he used to say. When he did get himself into a situation, his terrified expression almost always propelled Bruiser into action to help his friend out.

And after so many years, it looked like Boucher needed his help again. It could also be a ruse.

"Look, man, I'll get in the truck." Bruiser waved his index finger at him. "But if I see or smell something fishy with you, I'm punching you into next week. You hear me?"

"Loud and clear."

"Where's your piece?"

"In the glove compartment."

Bruiser took a moment before nodding. He climbed into the passenger seat, opened the glove compartment and took out the police-issued Glock—it was loaded. "I'm going to hang on to this while you drive. I don't trust you right now, but maybe you can convince me otherwise."

"Good enough for me." Boucher merged the truck into traffic. "I assume you talked to Adam?"

He seemed calm now. Bruiser wasn't sure how to take that. "Where are we going?" he asked instead.

"I know you won't believe me, since you're holding the gun." He kept his gaze on the road. "So we're going to talk to someone you *do* trust."

Half an hour later, the truck parked in front of Cortellucci Vaughan Hospital. "What the hell are we doing at CV?" Bruiser demanded.

"I told you—we're going to see someone who can vouch for me." Boucher tilted his chin at the gun. "What are you going to do with that?"

Bruiser looked down at the weapon—there was no way he could bring the Glock with him. Hospital security was usually tight, and after hours even more restrictive. He stashed the gun back in the glove compartment.

"Come on." The captain led the way, his stride confident as he entered the building.

Bruiser kept an eye on his surroundings. It should be safe here, but it was always when you let your guard down that something bad happened.

They stopped at the security desk. "Captain Gregory Boucher with York Regional Police 4 District," he announced, showing his badge. "This is a friend of mine who knows the patient as well."

"Good evening, Captain. We'll need ID for your friend as well, sir." The security guard nodded at the sign-in list.

Bruiser reached for his wallet and pulled out his driver's license, then passed it to the guard.

"'Keith Roberts,'" he read out loud, and handed it back. "Sign in please."

Bruiser scrawled his name on the form. The guard said, "Captain Boucher, we need to cut your visiting time to fifteen minutes. Doctor's orders."

"Understood. We shouldn't be longer than that."

As the elevator traveled to the fourth floor, Bruiser was getting ticked off. "You mind telling me what the hell is going on?"

"When we're inside his room."

They walked to the end of the hallway, where a single police officer stood guard. Bruiser's nerves were on edge. Who was he going to meet who needed police protection?

"Captain." The officer saluted.

Boucher returned the gesture. "Is he awake?"

"Yes, sir, he knew you were coming." His gaze slid to Bruiser. "And that you were bringing a friend."

"Thanks. Go and take a break. Fifteen minutes."

"Thank you, sir."

Boucher had his hand on the door. "Promise me you won't lose it."

He definitely had a bad feeling about this, but nodded his agreement. When the door opened, Bruiser noticed the patient wrapped almost head to toe in bandages. One leg was elevated in a sling.

"Hey, I found Bruiser for ya." Boucher walked to the side of the bed. "Do you want me to raise the bed a little so you can talk?"

Bruiser craned his neck over the captain's shoulder as he pressed the remote. The bed hummed as its top half rose to a seated position.

Boucher moved to one side, giving him a full view of the patient.

A cold sweat traveled down Bruiser's back as he stared at the person in front of him. The patient's blue eyes were so deep in color they could freeze a body in its tracks. The only other body parts not bandaged were a mouth and the neck area. And it was the side of the neck, just below the ear, that Bruiser now stared at, spying a very distinctive tattoo. It was a Viking compass called the *Vegvisir*, and he only knew that because his best friend had one.

"Bruiser."

The man's voice was raspy, but he'd know it anywhere. "Magnus, you son of a bitch," he whispered, his throat swelling up with emotion. "How the hell...?" He stopped. He couldn't talk, he could only stare with wonder at the man who had saved his life. Tears burned his eyes, and Bruiser wiped them away with one fist.

"You crying over me, man?" Magnus joked.

"Shut up." Much as he wanted to, hugging his friend was out of the question. "What happened? How did you get out?"

"No time for that," Magnus whispered. "Is Adam okay?"

"Yeah." He glanced at Boucher, who had stood quietly in the background.

"You can trust Boucher. He got my ass out of the clubhouse and smuggled me to CV."

"Smuggled?"

"It's a hell of a story." Boucher's hand rested on Bruiser's shoulder. "This was a long time coming, but I didn't expect a bombing."

Bruiser rubbed the top of his head. "So no one knows you're here? Not even Leila? Or your brother? What about your son? Adam should at least be told you're alive."

"No, it's safer this way." Magnus shifted in the bed.

"Careful, Magnus, the doctor said no movement." Boucher approached the bed.

"What the hell am I supposed to do if my butt is itchy?" he demanded.

Bruiser couldn't help it—he laughed. He quieted down though, as the implications of the current situation played through his mind. "So, I'm the only one who knows you're here?"

"Yeah. Boucher trusts his team, but he needed to play this case really close to the chest. Although he told me his forensic investigator was starting to figure stuff out," Magnus said.

Bruiser turned to the captain. "By blaming you?"

"She didn't blame me. She presented the facts and fitted them into a plausible theory. I just didn't expect her to solve the main part so fast. I couldn't have her get caught in the crossfire when the time comes, so I told her to leave the city."

It was obvious there was much more to this than Bruiser was being told. "I guess that means you won't tell me what's going on, right?"

"I can't get you involved," Magnus said, his voice fading. "I can't lose anyone else."

"We have to go." Boucher lowered the bed to its original position. "The nurse needs to come in and make sure he's comfortable for the night."

The officer guarding the room had returned and was standing near a window when they came out. "Make sure no one goes in without the doctor's or my approval," Boucher told the young man.

"Yes, sir."

"Magnus agreed to help me out because all of our hard work in cleaning up this part of Toronto was about to go up in smoke," Boucher told him as they headed for the elevator. "It wasn't going to be easy, either. This new drug dealer is super smart and moves like a ghost through the area, so the bombing of the Chariots of Chrome was completely out of left field. It's not his MO, but he probably hoped to kill all of you to get everyone out of his way."

"So, you're working undercover." Bruiser had pieced together everything Boucher told him. "And Magnus was helping you. I can't believe I missed that," he muttered.

"You were supposed to."

Bruiser shook his head. How could he leave Boucher to face this unknown threat alone? "Listen, you know I can help—"

"You already have. You know your best friend is alive." Boucher gave him a rough hug. "Look after him, okay?"

* * *

Boucher stared at the rifle casing nestled inside the plastic evidence bag. "A .300 Winchester Magnum," he whispered.

After their meeting this morning, his phone had pinged with a text from Cynthia. Her unexpected message had shocked him, but after reading through the information, Boucher hadn't wasted any time, and got Hawthorne and several officers scouring the four locations she had listed. He didn't want to get his hopes up while taking Bruiser to see Magnus, but it was difficult.

Now he had a crucial piece of evidence.

It was close to ten o'clock at night when he checked his cell phone, but Boucher didn't care—this was too important. He hit a Speed Dial button.

"Oostermann," followed by a long yawn.

"Daniel, I need you at the precinct in twenty minutes."

"Seriously?" A pause. "It's almost ten."

"I know, but this is urgent. Wait for me at the front doors."

Daniel was leaning against a wall when he came down from his office. "Daniel," he called out, slapping the young man's shoulder. "You're looking awake."

"What's this all about?"

"We might have a solid lead in this bombing case." Boucher showed him the rifle casing. "I need you to work your magic and find me a print."

"Wow." Daniel took the plastic bag and eyed the casing. "What's this related to?"

Boucher headed for the elevator. "Cornwall told me that a bomb made with Tannerite can indeed explode if hit accurately with a rifle bullet," he said quietly as they headed down to the lab. "Even if this dealer was smart enough to make it explode with a watch as a timer, there was no guarantee it would've gone off."

"Wait a minute—hold on. The evidence we found pointed to you." Daniel hesitated. "Right?"

"I was a decoy." Boucher waited while Daniel unlocked the door to the lab and followed behind. "I was supposed to take the rap for the dealer in order to throw the police off his scent."

"But in the meantime, you were looking for evidence to bring the drug dealer in." Daniel switched on the lights and headed for the forensics room. "You were undercover."

"Deep undercover. I couldn't tell anyone, and it was damn hard not to."

Daniel pulled on a pair of gloves and retrieved a bottle of dusting powder before sitting down and carefully removing the casing from the bag. "I have to be honest, sir. How do I know you're not lying to cover your ass?"

Boucher understood Daniel's trepidation. Hell, he understood why everyone was tiptoeing around him. How could they know the truth if he didn't specifically direct them to his deputy commissioner running the undercover show? "You have to trust me, Daniel. Tomorrow morning, I'll bring the team in and contact the top officer in charge of the case. He'll explain everything."

Daniel nodded slowly, then opened the bottle and carefully sprinkled some of the powder onto the casing.

Boucher tried not to hover. "See anything?"

"There's one good print near the base." Daniel went through the motions until he had the fingerprint taped to a clean sheet of paper. "Ta-da."

"Excellent. See if you can find a match in the database." Finally, all the work he'd done to get to this point was coming to a conclusion. If the fingerprint didn't belong to the drug dealer, it would definitely belong to someone close to the criminal. Once Daniel got a hit, Boucher would immediately contact the local Emergency Task Force waiting on standby and get them to make the arrest...

"Sir, we've got a match." Daniel's voice was quiet.

"Let me see."

Daniel got up so that Boucher could analyze the results. He frowned, unsure of what he was reading, and leaned in closer for a better look, wondering if his eyes deceived him. "Daniel," he whispered.

"What's wrong, Captain?"

Boucher swallowed against the lump in his throat. In his years as a captain and former undercover agent, it was rare he got his intel wrong. If he did, he'd be dead.

"Is it someone you know?"

The question broke Boucher out of his daze. Damn right he knew the name on the computer screen in front of his eyes—knew it too well. Anger swelled within him until he shook from the force of it, his fists so tightly clenched he could break a finger if he wasn't careful. "This is *your* name."

"Yeah, it is. Surprised?" The distinct cocking of a gun.

Boucher slowly turned around. Daniel, a predatory grin on his face, gripped a .454 Ruger in one hand. In the other, a pair of zip ties dangled from his fingers. "We're going to take a ride."

Adam closed the study door, leaving it slightly open in case Cynthia called out. His lips still tingled from the kiss she'd planted there, her taste making him lick his lips with want. She had promised not to be long. He grabbed his own drink and sat his tired body on the comfortable couch. The table held various books and magazines. He grabbed one and flipped through it to pass the time, but a yawn caught him unawares. He put his mug and magazine on the table, then stretched out fully on the couch.

His restless mind decided that whirling with abstract thoughts was the best thing to do at the moment. He grunted in annoyance, but knew it wouldn't stop unless he gave in to some of the unexpected situations that took place over the past several days.

He hadn't spent time thinking about the implications. Everything and everyone were set on *go* and he had little downtime to truly process the tragedy. He was sure Timmins and Hawthorne knew some of the Chariots of Chrome members, or at least knew them as acquaintances. The police force was a tight-knit world. Dad's death still felt surreal—if he looked toward the front door, he'd bet the old man would walk through it.

The only thing that offered a semblance of comfort was cooking. And slowly getting to know Cynthia.

The story she had told him about her family made him realize all over again how dedicated she was to her work, even jeopardizing her health in order to get the answers she needed to close a case.

He yawned again, and settled deeper into the cushions. It had been a long day, and the drive had sapped the rest of his energy. If things went according to Cynthia's plan, she'd have an answer by the morning.

He stood at the entrance to the Chariots of Chrome clubhouse, cold sweat trailing a path down his back. The guys were laughing and drinking beer, like they usually did, oblivious to the danger at the rear door. He shouted a warning, but no one heard him. He knew exactly where the bomb was, but his movements were too slow, and when he looked down, he realized with horror that he was thigh deep in some kind of smelly muck. He gagged against the stench and yelled at Dad and Bruiser, who were looking at him with blank stares.

"There's a bomb behind you!" he managed to yell, but the volume of his voice was too low—no one could hear him. He fought against the sludge that tried to suck him backward, his arms pinwheeling as he fought to keep his balance.

He watched in slow-motion horror as a spark appeared out of nowhere and slowly landed on the bomb. He yelled even louder. "Run!"

No one heard him. The bomb expanded into a fireball and engulfed his dad, Bruiser and Jeffrey with greedy tongues of flame. He tried to turn around, but the muck held on to him in a death grip. He wasn't going to make it—he wasn't.

"Adam!"

He looked down, and screamed in horror as hands— Dad's, Bruiser's and Jeffrey's—oozed out of the muck below him. They latched on to his legs, trying to pull him back into the clubhouse. The flames crackled at his back, the heat surrounding him, singeing his hair. He used his arms to propel him forward, but it wasn't working, and he yelled, the fear overwhelming him as he was dragged further inside. He didn't save his father, and as guilt flooded him with remorse, he finally stopped fighting.

"Adam, wake up!"

Her voice again, this time filled with fight and an iron will. He reached out his arm toward the sound of sal-

vation. Would she save him? Was she an angel? It gave
him hope, and he fought against the muck and the hands
and stretched up.

Adam opened his eyes, gasping for breath. A heavy
weight sat on his chest, and he struggled for air. A dark
hand appeared and he grabbed it, hanging on for all it
was worth.

"Ow, ow! Adam, snap out of it!"

Something hit his cheek. It stung, and he concentrated
on the feeling until his blurred gaze transitioned into
Cynthia's worried expression. "Hey," she called out. "You
with me?"

He couldn't get his breath to slow down and his heart
thumped against his ribs like it was trying to break free—
damn, he must have freaked out. "What the hell happened?" he asked, wondering why she sat on top of him.
"What's going on?"

"You were having a nightmare." She crawled off, pulling her hand away, and sat close to him. "Are you okay?
What was it about?"

He wiped his face with a hand, and stared at the sweat
dripping from his fingers. He hadn't suffered from nightmares since he was a kid. "I was thinking about Dad
and the others," he whispered. "About the investigation.
About everything."

His heart finally worked its way down to a more normal beat, but his body was trembling. He gripped his
knees and started rocking, an old habit when he got really scared. He'd never been able to break it.

"Hey." A warm hand on his back. "It's all right. It was
a dream."

"I was at the clubhouse, Cyn. I knew about the bomb—

I knew where it was hidden, but I couldn't warn them." He gritted his teeth. "I couldn't speak—I couldn't move. Then it exploded and engulfed everyone." He turned to her. "Slow motion. You know when you're trying to run away and can't? That was me."

"Shh." Her other arm came around him, and he leaned into her, resting his head on her chest. "This wasn't your fault. You have to stop blaming yourself." She rubbed his back.

He wrapped his arms around her and laid his cheek against hers. She smelled wonderful. He turned slightly and brushed his lips against the soft skin. "Thanks for waking me up."

She looked at him, her brown eyes twinkling. "Hell, you were making so much noise, I had no choice." She brushed his hair back with her fingers.

His simple, thankful kiss worked its way through his body like fiery tendrils. The cold sweat that engulfed him moments ago turned quickly into a lust-filled haze. He braced her head with one hand and shifted their bodies so that she straddled his lap.

Cynthia made herself comfortable against him, then snickered. "For a guy who just had a bad dream, your body sure knows how to react when the situation calls for it."

"My body likes a certain someone. It can't help itself." It was true. He and Cynthia had gotten along so well the past few days—it felt like they'd known each other for years. He snaked his hands up underneath her shirt and caressed her warm, smooth skin. "What were you doing before you rescued me?"

"Looking over my notes and evidence." She rubbed her hands over his shoulders. The massage did its work, relaxing the tense knots along his upper body. She moved up, working her magic around his neck until he groaned, the warmth of her touch seeping into his muscles. He moved his head in a circular motion a couple of times. "That feels great."

"I would have suggested giving you a massage, but…" She glanced down at his busy hands as they unhooked her bra. Smooth globes of skin filled his palms, and he gently squeezed.

"Your mini massage was what I needed. It's loosened me up just enough to give you my undivided attention." He unbuttoned her shirt and removed everything to reveal what lay beneath. Cynthia had one hell of a hot body and he couldn't stop touching her. His determination to strip her naked had them half kneeling, half strewn across the couch. At long last, she was unclothed and lounging beneath him. Adam couldn't keep his eyes off her, finally wrangling his boxers off and then reaching for her.

"You're forgetting something."

He stopped, his haze of lust lifting a bit. "What?"

She used her hands to imitate rolling on a condom.

Everything stood in his way as he raced up the stairs, stumbling over a step in his haste to get to the bathroom. When he got downstairs, he dropped the box in his haste, and barely managed to get a condom on. He bent to pick her up, holding her against him, then turned around and sat down. Cynthia crawled onto him, alternating between kissing and biting his chest until he thought he'd erupt with desire. When she reached his face, he kissed her nose before caressing her lips with his own. He sucked on her lower lip until she moaned into his mouth, then swiped his tongue between parted lips. He couldn't get enough of her sweet taste.

She broke the kiss and rubbed herself against him.

Dark, glossy skin filled Adam's sight, and it got harder to breathe as his need to make love to her intensified. He grabbed her hips, holding her still as he looked up into her dark and heated gaze. "Damn, you feel so good," he rasped.

Cynthia didn't answer, but her body continued to gyrate against his heated flesh, her breasts rubbing his face and her fingers locked within his hair.

He couldn't take this any longer. Having a naked, squirming, willing woman all over him was something he only ever dreamed of. Even Else hadn't been this eager. Gripping Cynthia tightly, Adam then guided her down until the tip of his erection brushed against her. Her hands tightened in his hair, his scalp tingling with pain, and he didn't care. He thrust up until her gasp filled the air around them. He stayed motionless, watching her, his own body demanding more but not giving in.

"Adam," she purred. Her beautiful face glowed with desire, and the sexy sounds that whispered from between her full lips reflected the animalistic need in him to get his groove on. Her hips pushed down, needing no help from him. He threw his head back, in awe at the wondrous feeling.

"Cyn." It was hard to breathe, to think—all he could do was feel and move in time with the woman who captured his every waking moment. He wanted this to last, he wanted Cynthia to know he could make love to her every day and never be bored, but this wasn't the night to declare those feelings. She wanted him, and he was going to deliver.

He braced his feet on the floor, held on to her hips so tight she'd be bruised the next morning and drove into her, keeping his momentum steady. He wanted Cynthia to enjoy their lovemaking as much as he enjoyed watching her.

She wrapped her arms around his shoulders and locked her knees against his hips, uttering little grunts of pleasure with each stroke. Her mouth burned a trail of kisses across his neck, her hair a black wave that surrounded his face.

She shifted, and he went deeper. His orgasm simmered to the surface, and he gritted his teeth, fighting to hold back a little longer.

That wasn't going to happen. Cynthia picked up the pace, her slick body slapping against his as she rode him, digging her fingernails so hard into his shoulders Adam knew he'd have deep scratches. The sight of Cynthia abandoning the prim and proper forensic investigator, and transforming into the stunning, emotional goddess now astride him broke down the rest of his remaining defenses. Any chance of not falling hard for her was lost.

Adam mirrored her movements, so close to losing control he could taste it. Cynthia's body language had also changed—her breathing was rough, labored. Her legs tensed, telling him she was close. "Hey," he whispered.

She leaned down and he captured her mouth in a searing kiss that made him see stars. Her tongue demanded entrance and he opened his mouth, reveling in the taste that was all her.

Cynthia tightened her grip around him as her body shook, groaning into his mouth as her orgasm released its hold. Adam swore as his body shuddered beneath her, draining his energy from the sheer force.

They remained still for several minutes, with Adam fighting to catch his breath. Cynthia raised her head, her face and body completely relaxed and covered in a sheen of sweat. She rubbed his cheek with her hand. "Damn."

"Yeah." He eased their bodies down onto the couch, then grabbed the quilted throw that lay folded at one end, pulling it over their tired, sweaty bodies.

"I enjoyed that a lot more than I expected." She snuggled closer, then ran her fingers through his hair. "Are you feeling better?"

"Yes, thanks to you." He kissed her. "I think the nightmares will stay away tonight."

She stared at him, her gaze searching, questioning.

"I'll be all right." It was true. Something about this amazing woman made him forget all the bad things happening around him. Kept him sane and made him believe his future would be happier, brighter, with Cynthia in it. It was a lot of emotions hitting him at once, and Adam accepted them all without a second thought.

Chapter 16

Cynthia crawled out of Adam's embrace, trying her best not to wake him. She got partially dressed as she moved on silent feet back to the study, where her laptop and tablet lay.

Adam had been right—she'd been working too much, but that was how she was wired. That, and the constant need to prove her worth to Boucher and the police force.

She sat down and stared at the laptop's dark screen. Did she still need to convince others that she knew her job very well? Sometimes it was a resounding yes, but not as often as in the past, when she took on her first case. Or was she trying to prove something to herself?

No. She'd asked herself this question many, many times over the years, and the answer was always negative. Cynthia knew what she was capable of with a fingerprint and the right tools.

And that's why she sat here, ready to throw her equipment against a wall. She found herself facing a terrifying adversary, and more questions than answers to this bombing investigation. It filled her with anger—and a heavy dose of doubt in her abilities. It was all on her shoulders to find out the truth.

Maverick sounded so sure the captain wasn't her prime suspect, but why? What did her friend know that he insisted Boucher be provided with the clues to where the sniper might have been hiding when he set off the bomb?

"Argh!" She slammed her hand on the pine table. It didn't matter how many times she pored over her evidence, she came up with the same answer—Boucher.

Well, there was one thing she could do—text the captain to see if he'd taken the bait and found any rifle casings. If he answered her, it would be a pleasant surprise. If not—well, she'd need to come up with a different angle.

The thought of crawling back onto the couch and snuggling within Adam's warmth was tempting. She even got up and made it to the door before pausing to look back. The laptop taunted her. It almost felt like it dared Cynthia to ignore what needed to be done.

Cynthia glanced at the couch—Adam was still asleep, judging by his gentle snoring.

"Fine, you battery-powered piece of junk," she whispered. "Come to Momma."

She got it powered up, and while it quickly ran through diagnostics, she sent a short text to Boucher to find out if he'd discovered anything. She double-clicked a folder, then stopped altogether. The meditation practice she had done consistently for the last four years had been tossed to the side during this case. It was time to bring it back. In the past, it soothed the impractical thoughts in her head and allowed her body to relax. Then she could concentrate on her work with a fresh outlook.

It took longer than expected. Her brain wouldn't calm down, and it took several tries before she managed to mentally push the thoughts aside and breathe into the moment. She kept her mind still as she hummed quietly through her chant, finally feeling her muscles loosen and her consciousness slow down. By the time Cynthia finished and opened her eyes, she felt clear, her mind empty of the chaos that had dominated it.

This time, she had a goal to accomplish. She would look at everything again, but instead of growing frustrated, she'd write notes and look for any inconsistencies. She might have missed something.

Cynthia took her time until she had everything typed out, but in a shorter format that was easier to go over, and then she realized something.

No word from Mav. She had turned on her personal phone's GPS before leaving Adam's condo, so he knew where she was. He'd also said something about digging into more intel. She had no idea what he was looking for, so she sent him a text, letting him know she was safe, and inquired about his research. With any luck, he'd get back to her with answers she could use.

Cynthia's other mystery was the Viking pendant found by Daniel at the second explosion site. The piece of unusual jewelry had no fingerprints on it, and she hadn't had the opportunity to do a search for the artist. She would do that now.

The soft creak of furniture—damn, Adam must be awake. "Cyn?"

"I'm in here," she called out, typing the necklace's description into the internet's search box. It immediately pulled up hundreds of hits, but she should be able to narrow it down.

"What are you doing?" He walked in, wearing boxers and nothing else. The scent of his skin almost made her forget about what she was working on.

"I realized I hadn't finished work on something the guys found at the Kootenay Ridge crime site." She pointed at the screen. "They found a necklace buried under the meth."

"What?" He leaned closer to get a better look.

"It really stands out. I think the wolf heads are Geri and Freki, Odin's pets or protectors, or something." She clicked on a link that looked promising. "If I can find the artist, I can get a customer list to discover—"

"Don't bother."

"Excuse me?" What the hell was he talking about? "What do you mean, don't bother? This could be crucial."

"Because I recognize that necklace."

She turned in her chair, a question forming on her lips, but stopped. Adam's expression was wrong. A mix of sadness, resignation and what she thought looked like defeat. "Wait, do you know the owner?"

"Yeah." He moved to a chair opposite her and sat down.

Why did she have a bad feeling about this? "Hang on—don't tell me it's your dad's."

"No." His blue gaze fixed on her. "It's mine."

His? This wasn't happening—it couldn't be.

Cynthia stared at him, keeping her fear in check, but her mind raced down a dangerous, anxious path. If what Adam said was true, he was at least responsible for making and selling drugs with the perp from the Kootenay Ridge investigation. And bringing her to his cottage, out in the middle of nowhere, was perfect if he wanted to get rid of a body.

The calm she had managed to find only minutes ago went out the window. Thoughts warred with each other—logic versus emotion, doubt versus certainty. Her brain ran through the evidence again, searching, analyzing. It took less than twenty seconds, while Adam sat quietly, watching her.

Several things didn't add up, and Cynthia finally made a fateful decision—she would listen to his explanation. "Why do you say that?"

"Because it's true." He hadn't moved, kept his hands palms down on the study desk.

"I can easily say I don't believe you."

"You could, but I would come back at you with the knowledge of an inscription on the back of the hammer that says *Lancelot, strong and true—Dad.*" He paused. "Lancelot is my middle name."

"Lord." Cynthia hadn't expected that. This wasn't looking good at all. She didn't dare look around—he'd know she was looking for a weapon to defend herself. All she had was her laptop. She moved her hands so that they sat on either side of the machine. "What else do you want to tell me?" she asked.

"That I have nothing to do with the drug bust. I'm innocent."

"Don't all criminals say that?" Her snarky attitude immediately rose like a wall to protect her from the inevitable heartache and pain that were sure to come. Her decision to take a chance on Adam—on loving someone—waited to backfire in her face.

"I'm not a criminal, Cyn."

His icy gaze kept her riveted in her seat. She had to move, but wanted—needed—to hear what he had to say.

Adam frowned. "Instead of just condemning me, think about this, will you? My necklace was planted."

"Oh, I had thought about it. There were no prints, and honestly, the necklace was too clean—no meth residue on it at all, and none in the plastic bag it came in. Daniel said he found it buried beneath the drug packages, which already raised my suspicions it was deliberately put there." She closed her laptop. "And honestly, leaving something so distinctive at a crime scene is just plain reckless. What I want to know is, how did your necklace end up in Kootenay Ridge with the drugs?"

"Honestly, I don't know." He sat back but didn't get up. It looked like this would be a battle of logic. "Dad gave the necklace to me when I turned twenty-five and was about to move to Nova Scotia. He picked Thor because the Viking god represented strength and was a protector of mankind. It fit the job I was taking on with the coast guard." He shrugged. "Fits with what I'm doing now too."

Wow, he was calm. None of the classic signs of nervousness came from him—no fidgeting, no wandering of his gaze. He wasn't sweating or stumbling over his words. Of course, he could just also be good at this.

"It might have been stolen from Dad."

That surprised her. "Your dad? Why would he have it?"

"It came back with me when I moved into the condo. It was there with my other belongings. Dad might have taken it for a reason."

Adam had just blamed his father for stealing his necklace. She leaned forward. "And somehow planted it with this dude's meth stash in order to lay the blame on you?"

"No. If it was either of us, Dad would take the fall—he wouldn't set me up like that."

That statement she believed. "The captain was upset when he saw a picture of the necklace," she told him.

His eyes widened. "I'll bet he was. Dad told me Boucher was with him when he picked it up at the jewelers for my birthday. Did he say anything?"

"Nope, that's when the captain told me to hightail it. I'm sure he didn't think I'd be with you."

Adam stood. Cynthia rose as well and gripped her laptop. "I have an idea," he said. "Call Boucher and let him know you're staying with me."

"And what good would that do?" She was grasping at straws. Everything she'd found—all the evidence gathered and analyzed—led to Captain Boucher. And while the captain hadn't denied anything, his unexplained response to her accusation threw her for a loop.

"Because if the criminal *is* Boucher, he knows he'd have to go through me to get to you."

Cynthia sensed a question mark forming over her head like one of those comic talking bubbles. "Wait, what?"

"Come on, Cyn. Do you really think I'm part of some drug gang?" He took a step toward her. "Do you?"

This was why getting romantically involved with a colleague was a problem. How could she think logically with Adam standing there in his underwear? The thought almost made her laugh out loud.

"I had too many opportunities to count to get rid of you. If that was my intention."

"Yeah, I know that." While her logic was off course, her instinct was firing on all cylinders. She knew he didn't have anything to do with this. "It's just, you know, hard to ignore evidence."

"I get that. But you also know how I work. You know I'm thorough, organized. You don't think I'd leave something so obvious as this necklace to be found?"

She shook her head. It was true—she'd worked on his cases long enough to know his methods. And it did seem strange the necklace was in a clean, drug-free plastic baggie, buried under the meth stash. "It was a red herring."

He nodded, taking another step in her direction. "To throw you off the scent and fix that gorgeous, deep brown gaze on me."

"When the hell did Boucher find the time to plant that?"

"He might have gone to the crime scene with the others. Or maybe he was in league with the perp."

"Honestly, when this is over, I'm taking a damn vacation." She put the laptop down and crossed her arms.

"I hope you'll let me join you." He stood in front of her.

"I'll think about it." But she knew her smile said otherwise.

Adam had really believed in that moment, everything he wanted with Cynthia would go up in smoke.

Seeing the picture of his necklace on her laptop had sent ice-cold dread through every part of his being, especially after spying the inscription from Dad on the back. He had no clue how something so personal ended up at the Kootenay Ridge crime scene, but his highest priority was to convince the woman he cared about that he was not involved in any way.

And how the hell could he do that?

By being honest. She respected that—truth, no nonsense and a clear explanation of things. To be treated and seen as a colleague and investigator first. To most men, that would be a tough pill to swallow, but not for him.

His admiration for her skills had only climbed during these past few days, and watching how she struggled to figure out the identity of the arsonist who killed his dad only increased his desire and care for her.

He had thought about that while admitting the necklace belonged to him. He had remained calm despite the reckless beating of his heart, presenting the facts to her as Cynthia would have wanted. He had kept his cool while watching her figure out how to get out of the hot mess she suddenly found herself in, and almost swore in grief when she picked up her precious laptop to use as a weapon.

Ten anxious, nail-biting minutes later, logic, of all things, had won out. The urge to wrap his arms around her as she realized his innocence had to be restrained—it wasn't the time for it. And, judging by her smirk as she looked him over, he remembered he only had his boxers on. Yeah, sensitive, romantic hug could wait until later. "Guess we should go to bed," he murmured.

"I can't sleep. I'm all wired because I thought you—" She stopped.

"Well, I'm not." He traced fingers across her cheek. "So you can stop worrying."

The sudden ringing of a cell phone made him jerk in surprise.

"Holy crap, that's my work phone." She grabbed it from the table and looked at the number. "It's Captain Boucher."

Damn. Why would he be calling her at this time of night?

She put it on speakerphone. "Sir, what is it? Why are you calling so late?"

No answer, but heavy breathing reverberated through the phone.

"Captain? Sir?" Still nothing. Cynthia glanced up at him. "May I?"

She raised the phone to his face, keeping it on speaker mode. "Captain, this is Solberg. Are you there? Are you all right?"

"I knew it! I knew Cynthia was with someone. It figures it had to be you, Detective."

"Wait a minute. Daniel, is that you?" Cynthia demanded. "What are you doing with Captain Boucher's phone?"

"Hey, Cyn." His voice sounded almost cheerful. "How are you? I just wanted to check in to see that you were okay."

"Daniel, what are you doing with Boucher's phone? Where is he?"

"Oh, he's not feeling too good right now. Long day at the office."

The hairs rose on the back of Adam's neck. The way Daniel said that was…not right.

"Daniel, where *is* he?" Cynthia shouted into the phone.

"He's with me. We're coming up to the cottage."

What the hell did that mean? He signaled to Cynthia to keep talking as he walked out to the living room.

"What cottage?" she asked as she followed him.

"Don't screw with me, Cynthia." Daniel's voice through the phone's speaker had instantly changed to a cold tone. "You're hiding out with Solberg. I know where you're hiding, courtesy of the Toronto Police Stingray phone surveillance. And you can't tell me you haven't started putting two and two together when you heard my voice."

The pieces were starting to fall into place. Adam hurried to the chest where the loaded guns were hidden.

"Are you admitting your guilt to something?" She had put the phone down, and was hurriedly getting dressed.

Adam came back to her, rifle in one hand, while he gave her the Glock. He pulled his own clothes on as she kept talking to Daniel.

"You're so full of it, Cornwall. I'm not admitting to anything. You and Solberg, however, are going to have one hell of a good time when I arrive with the Desperados."

Chapter 17

Daniel Oostermann, the humorous little jerk, always cracking jokes and acting inexperienced around Cynthia. He was the bastard working with Captain Boucher and the one responsible for killing Dad and their friends?

Adam stuffed extra shells into his pants pocket while Cyn checked the Glock. "I don't want you down here when he arrives," he told her.

He knew he would get a look, and she didn't disappoint. "I can look after myself."

"I know that. But we—you—need a recorded confession from him. You can't do that while holding a gun."

She carefully tucked the weapon into the waistband of her jeans. "Then what do you propose?"

"You work with him, what do you think? Will he admit his guilt to me or you?"

She shook her head. "I honestly don't know. He might make fun of me for not figuring out his involvement, or he'd talk to you because, you know, man-to-man confession."

"Not helpful." The front and rear doors, along with the windows, had already been locked, and the security cameras turned on, so those bases were covered. "Daniel said he was bringing the Desperados," Adam murmured. He turned off the lights except for the high-wattage security lights positioned over the front and rear entrances and on the roof. "Any idea how many members in that gang?"

"Seven, that we know of. Eight if we count Larry."

Adam hoped the teenager wasn't involved. He took his personal phone out of his pocket and tapped on the app that displayed the home security on the cottage. The cameras were wide-angle lenses, and it looked like Dad installed a second pair. In all, they covered the road leading toward the door at the front, while the back view covered the dock and the woods to either side. Excellent. "Get your stuff and keep it with you. I don't want Daniel getting his hands on it and destroying what you've worked on. I also want you to download the security app for the cottage."

She returned in a few minutes and rammed her laptop and tablet into the satchel, then followed his instructions for the app. "Okay, I can see outside." She frowned. "The security lights don't penetrate the darkness very much."

"You're about to get a bird's-eye view from the attic." He noticed car lights coming down the dirt road. "Let's go."

"The attic? How the hell am I supposed to help you from up there?"

He led the way upstairs, taking them two at a time. "Mom has a studio room up here," he mentioned. They had reached the second floor, and he hurried to the end of the hall toward a tall painting. He pushed a latch, and it swung open to reveal a set of wooden stairs. "When they were married, she would hide up here if Dad brought friends over for sports night. Her only stipulation was that they didn't stay overnight. The one time she allowed it, she couldn't get any sleep with all the noise they made."

"And the mess too, no doubt," Cynthia chimed in.

When he flicked on the light switch by the top of the stairs, his throat tightened up with nostalgia. Nothing had been touched. Mom's wooden easel stood by the large windows. A table covered in painting utensils made him think she'd show up at any moment to work on a new masterpiece. A large leather chair and footstool resided at the opposite side of the windows, along with a small bookcase stuffed with her favorite novels. What surprised him was the lack of dust up here.

"This looks cozy." Cynthia walked toward the windows, looking around. "It's also clean." She glanced back at him.

He shrugged. "Guess Dad didn't want to get rid of anything." He shook himself out of his reverie and moved to one of the smaller windows. A bit of teasing with the latch, and it swung open. "This faces the front," he told her. "I'll turn off the lights when I head downstairs, so Daniel doesn't notice you up here."

"Right." She dug for her tablet and checked it over. "I'll record him. If you can get him to talk, we'll have him nailed."

"That's the plan." Now he had to work out in the next few seconds how to make Daniel confess.

"Hey."

Before he realized it, Cynthia had grabbed his shirt and planted a long, intense and thorough kiss on his mouth.

He wrapped his arms around her waist and crushed her to his chest, savoring her taste, her smell, her body. Anything could happen once he and Daniel were face-to-face downstairs.

"You'd better be careful," she whispered against his mouth. "Or I'll whup your sorry ass."

He laughed. "Pissing you off scares me more than taking Daniel down."

"Good." She smiled. "I'm glad you know your priorities."

Despite everything thrown at her—the evidence, the interrogations, the whole case—leading to Boucher, Cynthia had gotten it wrong.

And she still didn't know how Daniel was involved.

Music blared from outside. She looked out the window as three sets of headlights appeared, slowly meandering toward the cottage. Without streetlamps here, the area was pitch-black. Adam knew the woods, so he had that advantage.

She also had one of her own, pulling out her phone and dialing Mav's number. He picked up almost immediately. "What have you got for me, doll?"

"Trouble. I got a call from my captain's phone, except it wasn't him. It was my colleague, Daniel. He's almost at the cottage. I can see headlights about a half mile out and he's bringing a drug gang with him."

"The guys and I saw three cars turn onto the side road. We're tailing them. Hang on—did you say Daniel?"

Cyn closed her eyes. Oh man, what was he going to tell her? "Give it to me straight, Mav."

She heard paper rustling. "After you told me about finding Tannerite in the bomb, I played a hunch and started looking into Canadian Armed Forces' sharpshooters. I narrowed it down to the most confirmed kills and dishonorable dismissals over the past ten years. Three names came up—one of them was a guy named Daniel Oostermann."

This night couldn't get any worse. "So, not only was Daniel my lab partner, but he was also a sniper, and now a drug dealer and possible murderer? How do I find these guys?" she demanded.

"We know that's a rhetorical question, so we're not answering," someone shouted from the background.

Mav chuckled. "That was Hammer. Do you know how many in this gang?"

"Our precinct knows of eight, but we're sure there are more. Oh," she added. "Adam—Detective Solberg—will be at the front door confronting them, so don't accidentally shoot him. I'm upstairs in the attic recording everything."

"Solid plan. We're almost there, so don't get yourself hurt or worse." He hung up.

She placed the phone on the floor beside her and hit Record on the tablet. She grabbed the small chair by the easel and arranged it so she could see outside without being seen. She propped her arms on the wide window ledge for stability and aimed the tablet at the approaching vehicles. The security lights at the front of the property offered plenty of illumination to see everything below.

The cars finally stopped out front, arranged in a wide semicircle to surround the front door. She didn't see Adam, and the cottage interior remained dark.

The music was cut off. Car doors swung open to reveal several teenagers dressed in their distinctive Desperados style, and each wearing the headband that marked them as a member.

She almost cried out in distress when Captain Boucher was hauled out of the middle car by a huge male stranger. In the harshness of the security lights, this guy had tattoos that covered his arms, neck and face, something that was not part of the Desperados' MO. But it was Boucher that worried her. His bloodied, swollen face, hands tied behind his back and unbalanced stance told the story of a horrific beating. He was half dragged to the front of the vehicles and stood beneath the security lights like some macabre actor on a stage.

Daniel finally appeared, dressed in his usual khakis and dark shirt. He walked to the front door and hit the bell. The soft sound of chimes echoed through the quiet night.

"Hey, hey, anybody home?" he called out.

Silence, except for the sound of crickets and frogs.

"I know you're around here, Solberg." Daniel pointed two fingers to either side of him. The gang split into two groups, going around to surround the house, leaving Daniel, Boucher and the large man. "I just want to talk."

She heard a door open. "I don't know what's so important that you come to my personal residence at this time of night."

Cynthia watched through her tablet as Daniel backed away from the front door. Adam stood there, his body filling the door frame, his rifle gripped in both hands.

"Hey, now is that any way to greet a colleague?" Daniel glanced around. "Just wanted to make sure you and Cyn were all right."

"Her name is Cynthia, and yes, we're okay." Adam tilted his chin at Boucher. "The captain doesn't look too good. What happened to him?"

"Oh, I caught him snooping around the lab tonight. I think he was trying to destroy any evidence against him."

"He's lying, Solberg!" the captain yelled.

Daniel's tattooed employee stepped in and smacked Boucher across the forehead with a clenched fist. She zoomed the lens on Boucher, wincing as his injuries came into clearer view before refocusing on the full scene below.

"Who's the big guy?" Adam demanded. "And why are you hanging out with the Desperados? I've noticed they've surrounded my house."

"Damn, so you know who they are?" Daniel shrugged. "The guys have been helpful. And as for Peter here," he continued, pointing at the large man, "his assistance and personal experience with meth have been exceptional."

"So you've just admitted to selling drugs and being part of a criminal gang."

Daniel's eyes widened, then he laughed. "Well, well, I sort of said that, didn't I? You're just so easy to talk to. I'll bet Cyn likes talking to you too, if you know what I mean."

"Sleazeball," she muttered.

"Why is Captain Boucher beaten up like that?" Adam asked.

"Come on, Detective, use your brain. He found me out."

Cynthia worked that bit of information around in her head. That wouldn't make sense if the captain worked for Daniel. Oh, wait a minute it was slowly coming together, and she fought the urge to swear out loud in disbelief.

Captain Boucher had been working undercover and never said a word to anyone.

She kept the tablet trained on the scene below, and noticed Adam's realization cross his face. He stared at Boucher.

"There you go—I knew you'd figure it out." Daniel

strode toward Boucher and grabbed a fistful of the man's hair, yanking his head back into a painful angle. "Pretty damned impressive too. Had me completely fooled. All of the evidence pointed straight to him. Boucher said he would take the heat to prove his loyalty to me."

She heard two sharp sounds—Adam racking his rifle. *Damn, don't lose it,* she thought desperately.

"Are you telling me Boucher is responsible for the bombing?" Adam yelled.

"No! Adam, you have to believe me—I didn't have anything to do with that." Boucher crawled toward Adam on his knees. "Yes, I was deep undercover. The top brass in Toronto wanted this kept under the radar from everyone, and I volunteered."

Before he could get any closer, Peter, the big guy, stepped forward and grabbed Boucher's arm.

"I had to prove I was part of Daniel's team. I collected what he wanted, but I didn't know what the items were for. I didn't think he'd make a bomb."

"It was the easiest way to get rid of those old farts in the Chariots of Chrome gang. Boom! All in one swoop. They'd ruined significant deals I had arranged on my new turf," Daniel said.

Adam's rifle was pointed down, but she knew he'd be ready to use it when the timing was right. "There's no way you could have gotten inside. Dad had tight security around the clubhouse, and the guys would have been all over you in a flash."

"You're right." Daniel smirked. "Want to take a guess how I did it?"

He was playing games, and by the look on Adam's face, Cynthia guessed he was more than ready to start shooting.

Daniel pouted. "I can see you're not in the mood. Your daddy had regular deliveries twice a week. It wasn't hard to sneak in an extra box that morning. One of my Desperados was dressed as the regular courier and made sure to put the boxes by the back door.

"I also knew the back door would be open because I studied the old man's habits. The place isn't air conditioned, and opening the back door allowed a cross breeze. Along with a clear view of the box with the bomb."

Would she have even guessed it was Daniel? The revelation was already hard to swallow. But they were finally onto something—he'd just admitted to the bombing of Magnus Solberg's clubhouse and murdering several members.

"And the chain necklace Dad got for my birthday?" Adam asked. She heard his voice crack on the last word.

"Oh, that was my idea, too." Daniel snapped his fingers. "I told Boucher to get something that meant the world to you, and hide it with the drugs at Kootenay Ridge so that you'd get arrested and off my radar. I still don't know how he pulled that one off."

The captain smiled. "It wasn't Adam's. It was a duplicate."

That's right—Cynthia remembered Adam had mentioned Boucher was with his dad when he picked it up.

"The Rolex was one thing. Creatura had plenty—he wouldn't miss it, and could replace it whenever he wanted." Boucher coughed—it sounded so bad, she thought he might pass out. "But I'd never touch your necklace, Adam. I knew how much it meant to you. So I bought a duplicate and engraved it with the same message. Daniel had no way of knowing."

"Whoa! Now that is thinking on your feet." Daniel clapped. "Bravo, captain."

Cynthia grew concerned at Adam's expression—if looks could kill, Daniel would be nothing but a smudge in the dirt road. "I'm going to make sure your ass is in a solitary hole so deep, you'd better pray I can't find you." In the hush of the night's air, Adam's fury was so intense Cynthia felt the vibes from up here.

"Ooh, is that a threat? You're going to have a hard time going through with that."

"Arrogant bastard." Adam aimed the rifle at Daniel.

"Uh-uh, I wouldn't do that." Daniel nodded at his partner.

Peter, who still held Boucher, pulled out a monster .44 Magnum pistol and aimed the muzzle at the captain's temple.

Adam lowered his weapon, but kept it pointed in Daniel's direction.

"I'd say you and I are on even ground. Well, actually, no. I have seven gang members surrounding your secluded little cottage." Daniel looked up, and Cynthia ducked beneath the window. "You don't have a way out, Solberg."

Silence. She quickly put the tablet down and texted Mav.

Cottage surrounded. Eight guys minimum, assume armed. Our captain a prisoner. How much longer?

Several seconds passed, then, Five minutes. Thanks for the intel—we'll be ready.

It was going to feel like two hours. She carefully peeked

over the ledge, and saw Daniel walking to one of the cars. She got her tablet back in position.

"But you know what? I'm feeling sentimental. Boucher can join you."

What? What did he mean? She kept recording, watching as, at a nod from Daniel, Peter holstered his weapon and untied the captain. Boucher rubbed his wrists as he stood slowly, keeping his gaze locked on the big man.

"Why would you keep it a secret?" Adam asked the captain. Cynthia knew he meant the undercover work.

"The less all of you knew, the better." Boucher spat, and a smear of blood darkened the soil at his feet. "We've been working on this case for six months—the RCMP, the Ontario Provincial Police, Toronto Police and York Regional. Someone was moving large drug shipments into our area. Your dad…" He hesitated. "He asked me what was going on and I brought him in. He'd done a phenomenal job getting our city back."

"Yeah, and you got his ass killed," Daniel yelled. He held something in his hand—Cynthia couldn't see what it was, no matter how much she zoomed the tablet's camera to get a closer look.

"No," Adam finally spoke. "Dad knew what he was getting into. It was his choice." His smile was unfriendly. "I guess he gave your mules a good ass kicking if you were pissed off enough to kill him."

"And I'm more pissed off that I hired this little punk to work with us," Boucher retorted. "He actually knew how to do his job too."

"Duh. I went to school," Daniel said. "Besides, the irony." He made a dramatic show with his hands. "Fighting crime while committing crime. I loved it."

"I found out Daniel was a soldier in Afghanistan and

studied the drug trade there. He wanted in on a piece of the action," Boucher told Adam.

Adam fixed his gaze on Daniel. "Oh, I get it. You didn't like your army pension so you had to do something to make ends meet. Your new occupation is a big step down from your military days."

"Don't patronize me! I'm not going to explain myself to you." Daniel tilted his chin in a defiant stance.

"Why don't you humor me? You've already said I'm not getting out of this alive. And what about Cyn? You're going to kill her too?"

"You don't get to call her that!" Daniel ran up to Adam, and she held her breath as the two men squared off, faces inches from each other. Daniel hadn't even looked at the rifle in Adam's grip. "You're talking like she's your girlfriend, for God's sake."

Adam remained quiet. Her hands shook so bad, she had to lean the tablet against the window frame, but kept it aimed on the action. She still couldn't see what was in Daniel's fist.

"What if she was?"

Her ears perked up. What the hell was Adam doing? That little stunt wasn't going to earn him any points.

Daniel's expression did not bode well. "Fine, you can have her." He quickly walked back to the car. "Take Boucher too. I don't need him." He nodded.

Cynthia bit back a cry as Peter swung the Magnum up in one move and shot Boucher in the head. The captain's surprised expression froze on his face as he toppled over.

"Dammit!" Adam got the rifle up and shot at the big man. The guy stumbled back, clasping his leg, but managed to get his weapon raised, and returned fire as Adam dove back into the cottage. Cynthia heard the door slam shut.

"Hey, Cynthia, I know you're in there. I was going to ask if you'd join me, but it sounds like you prefer the tall, silent, Norwegian type." When he opened his fist, she gasped in shock—he held a grenade.

"Aw, hell no!" She dropped the tablet as she scrabbled for her phone to text Mav. She stuffed everything back into the satchel and ran for the door.

The explosion shook the cottage and knocked her down just as she got to the second-floor landing. Her satchel went flying through the railing, smashed into pottery on a table downstairs and skidded across the wooden floor.

"Cynthia!" Adam yelled.

"I'm here." She hurried down the rest of the stairs and snatched up her satchel as acrid white smoke billowed around the front door. "That was a grenade!"

"I know. We have to get out of here."

The faint tinkling of glass above reached her ears.

"Move!" she yelled, running through the living room. The second explosion blew more smoke down the stairs. She started coughing.

"Kitchen, now!" Adam led the way into the room, grabbed a couple of hand towels and soaked them under the faucet. "Hold that against your face."

She did what she was told. The cold compress made it easier to breathe.

"You running yet, Solberg?" Daniel's voice projected through a loudspeaker. "Let's get you and Cynthia hopping like rabbits!"

More breaking glass, and she watched in horror as two grenades broke through the kitchen windows.

"Downstairs!" Adam tore the door open and shoved her inside.

She managed to grab the railing before she lost her

balance, and slapped the light switch. Halfway down the stairs, two back-to-back explosions rang through her ears, and a heavy weight hit her from behind as Adam collided into her.

"Come on!" He engulfed her waist with an arm as he leaped down to the floor, and yelled in pain when he lost his balance.

"Adam, what's wrong?" Cynthia noticed he was favoring his left ankle. There was no way he could run on that. "Give me a second." She texted Mav about her situation and where they would appear once they climbed through the hatch located in the cold storage room. Smoke found its way around the closed basement door, along with the distinctive, crackling sound of flames as it tore toward them. This was not good.

"Is there an emergency kit with your camping stuff?" She raced across the small space and started rummaging.

"Check the shelf—should be a red metal box." He grunted in pain.

"Hang on." She grabbed the box and sat beside him. Within the kit, she found the bandages. "I have to get your shoe off," she said, grasping the short boot. "You ready?"

He nodded and glanced at the door leading to the kitchen. "Hurry."

She pulled quickly, wincing as Adam sucked in a tense breath. She started wrapping the ankle, making sure it was on tight. "Remember the extra help I told you about? My friends with the Emergency Response Team? They're on their way, might even be here now. I told Mav about the escape hatch."

"Think of everything, don't you?" He grabbed the discarded boot with one hand and carefully pulled it back on.

"Let's get out of here." She stood and offered her hand.

He grabbed it, and with one strong heave, got Adam onto his feet. She slung on her satchel, then wrapped his arm over her shoulders.

The cold storage room kept out most of the harsh, biting smoke. Above the stark glare of the light bulb, the hatch offered freedom—or death, depending on the situation above.

Cynthia checked her phone. No response from Mav, and looking closely, she still had cellular service. "Dammit, no idea if he and the others are here." She looked up, and rubbed her hands over her arms against the sudden chill that engulfed her. "I'll go first."

"Are you kidding me?" Adam limped over to stand much too close within her personal space. "What if one of those jerks is just outside? You might not get the chance to shoot before you're gunned down first."

"And what, you'll have better luck? Look at you." She stopped and took a breath—fighting wouldn't get them anywhere. "If Mav is here, he won't answer my messages. He'll be too busy. Meanwhile Daniel and his Desperados are bombing your cottage." She shook her head. "That sounds like the name of a rock band."

The ground shook as yet another explosion interrupted them. The light flickered erratically before shutting down. Cynthia used the phone's built-in flashlight to illuminate the space and to look into Adam's very anxious face. "I was about to say that I can look after myself, but that won't help, will it?"

"No." The back of his hand caressed her cheek. "Even though I know it's true."

"Adam…" She couldn't think of what to say.

"It's okay." He leaned down to kiss her softly on the lips. "I'm going to be right behind you," he warned. "Let me climb the ladder first and unlock the hatch, then you can go up and take a look around, see what's going on."

"Let me text Mav again. Even if he doesn't answer, at least he'll know where we are." She sighed loudly. "I hope he doesn't get in the way and I shoot his leg by mistake."

Adam's cottage, family memories—all gone up in a blazing inferno.

There weren't enough cruel ideas for punishment to take out on Daniel, but Adam knew he could think of a few extra ones to appease the fury that burned in him. However, his more immediate and important priority was the curvy, beautiful Ms. Cornwall, climbing the ladder to the escape hatch that opened within a thick stand of pine trees at the back of the property. The Glock lay nestled within one fist.

He came up behind her, his body tight against hers, and got ready to push the trapdoor up. Here, he caught the faint whiff of smoke and worried what they were going to discover. "The Desperados should be too busy admiring their handiwork."

"I hope so," she whispered. "It'll give Mav and the others the chance to put them down."

He couldn't see her face in the darkness, but the sound of her voice gave Adam a good indication of her mood—it reflected his. "Let's do it."

The escape hatch faced the lake, and was located about thirty feet from the cottage. When he opened it a crack, orange light flooded the cold storage room. "Oh my God," he said to himself.

The cottage was completely engulfed in flames. A moment later, another explosion rocked the night, almost knocking him off the ladder. He'd have time to mourn the loss later, after they escaped. "I see people standing close to the cottage," he said into her ear.

"I count five," she replied.

Suddenly, one of them, who stood farthest from the group, fell in a boneless heap.

"Make that four."

Adam looked around—with the trapdoor opened only by a couple of inches, it was difficult to see movement, even with the fire as a huge beacon. "Daniel knows what he's doing. He'll be on the move before the fire department gets here."

As if on cue, Daniel's voice rose above the conflagration. "Hey, Solberg, I hope you, your dad and Captain Boucher are swearing at each other in Hell for messing up!"

"We need to go," he said. "You have to text your friend to take Daniel alive."

"Right." She pushed the Glock through first, then carefully crawled out, staying on her stomach as she moved deeper into the thicker stand of pines. Adam looked around, caution a never-ending thought running through his mind, and saw another Desperado go down for the count.

When he turned back, Cynthia was waving at him to come to her, the Glock in her other hand. His foot hurt like hell, and putting weight on it was enough to make him bite his tongue in agony. Using his arms and one good leg, he got out with sheer will and strength, pushing the hatch up with his back, worrying that swinging it up fully would attract a gang member's attention. He used a few seconds to catch his breath before slowly crawling his way to Cynthia. "That was harder than I realized," he gasped.

"I had your back. No one saw us, and Mav just got back to me. He's coming to pick us up while the others get Daniel."

"You know, that Peter, the big guy? I'm sure he's not part of the Desperados gang."

"Exactly what I was thinking. I told Mav to grab him too." She patted her ever-present satchel. "The video will be enough to charge him and Daniel with murder."

Adam sat up and leaned against a tree. "Thank God you recorded everything. With the captain dead, there would have been no way to connect Daniel to any of this. He would have destroyed all evidence against him, and other people would have been killed."

Cynthia moved to sit beside him. "I still feel that it's my fault," she said.

"What?" He knew she felt responsible for not solving the case in the manner she was used to. "Cynthia, cut yourself some slack. You did your best with what you had."

"Did I? I didn't make the connection of Captain Boucher being an undercover agent. I was suspicious when he told me to run. I should have stayed and hung him over hot coals until he confessed."

Oh boy. "You know that's not legally allowed. Anywhere."

"I would have managed it somehow."

He wanted to kiss her—instead, he looked around, wary. "Any answer from your friend?"

She checked her phone. "Mav is taking a roundabout route to reach us. The others are moving on Daniel."

Suddenly, the crack of a gunshot rang above the flames and echoed over their heads.

"Dammit." Cynthia tapped on her phone, fingers skittering across its surface, then looked up, her expression filled with worry.

"Hey." When she looked at him, he touched her arm. "Take it easy. Think about your training with your former teammates. What do you think happened?"

She shook her head. "They should be hiding in the darkness, waiting."

"And the shot?"

She frowned. "Probably Daniel freaking out."

"Okay, let's stick with that." Adam wanted to keep her mind on the immediate situation, and not dwell on what she thought was her failure on the investigation.

Her phone pinged. She glanced at it and exhaled. "They neutralized all of them."

Adam had to wonder what that meant. Even though they were gang members, they were also teenagers. He wasn't sure how he felt about the ERT methods. "Your former team killed the Desperados?"

"Of course not. Shoot to kill is the last resort. The team tranquilized them."

"Why didn't I think of that?" He rolled his eyes, knowing Cynthia wouldn't see the action within the darkness.

"No need to take that tone, Detective Solberg." He caught the hint of humor in her voice.

"Cyn, you here?" a male voice called out.

"Oh my God, Mav." She scrambled to her feet as a shadow, darker than the surrounding trees, emerged. When Adam finally got a good look at the guy, etched within the glow of the flames destroying his cottage, he swallowed. This dude was *big*. He struggled to his feet to assess the ERT member eye to eye.

Cynthia ran into the guy's massive arms. "I'm so happy to see you!"

"I'm just glad you're all right, doll." She was totally engulfed in his embrace.

Doll? Adam felt his brow rise in disbelief.

"Mav, this is Detective Adam Solberg." She disengaged herself and stood beside him.

"Thanks for helping out." Adam held out his hand.

"Maverick Hitsugaya. Thanks for looking after our girl." Mav's hand almost surrounded his, and his grip was like steel, but Adam didn't budge. His dark gaze slid over Adam's shoulder. "It's too bad about your home, though."

He turned. The fire had burned through everything. There was nothing left but stone and frame, and as he watched, the torched wood screeched in protest as it started to buckle within itself. "Yeah, but it can be rebuilt." He looked down at Cynthia's concerned face. "We're alive. That's what counts."

Chapter 18

By the time the Port Carling fire, ambulance and OPP police arrived, there was nothing left of Adam's cottage or the RV—just a smoldering husk of his family's heirlooms. Under the harsh lights of the emergency vehicles, nine bound men were neatly lined up on the one-lane road, while Captain Boucher's body was covered where he lay with a large tarp.

"Jules insisted on bringing the big van," Mav told her when they approached the officers. "Good thing we half listen to him. We'll get the perps cozy. Where are we taking them?"

"To our precinct." Adam gave him a look. "Let me talk to the officers. You guys do your thing." He yelled out to the nearest policeman and soon, he was surrounded as Adam updated them on what happened.

"Seems like a decent enough dude," Mav said.

"Adam's okay." He was more than okay—he supported

and encouraged her to come out of her protective shell, to feel and care again. That's one hell of a guy.

Mav narrowed his eyes. "Uh-huh. If you say so. You'd better come over and talk to the boys or they'll be pissed."

"Ms. Cornwall, what kind of trouble did you get yourself into?" Staff Sergeant Victor "Hammersmith" Moore had trained in England's Special Air Service as a teenager before moving to Canada fifteen years ago. His confident attitude, years of combat experience and fierce loyalty made him a natural leader of the Emergency Response Team.

"It wasn't planned—I assure you."

Victor glanced at the burned-down cottage. "I'll take your word for it—maybe. Now come over here and give me a hug before I get really mad."

His grip was bone crushing as usual. "I've missed you, Cornwall."

"Me too." He let her go and she slapped the arm of the guy next to Victor. "You're quiet, as usual."

Lonan "Silent Runner" Ambrose nodded in greeting. "I'm glad you're okay."

"So am I." He wasn't one for hugs. She looked around. "Where are Jules and Ben?"

"Getting the patrol wagon." Victor hooked a thumb over his shoulder. "What the hell was this all about?"

"A bomb investigation that went sideways."

"Up in smoke, more like." He tilted his chin. "Is that Detective Solberg?"

"The one and only," she confirmed as Adam limped towards her.

"You must be Cynthia's former team." Adam held out a hand to Victor. "Detective Adam Solberg. Thanks for saving our asses."

"As I understand it, you kept Cornwall from getting killed." They shook. "Thanks, mate."

He nodded, then glanced down at her. "You okay?"

"Yeah." She noticed that his ankle had been properly bandaged and one crutch was perched under his arm. "What about you?"

"I'll live." He looked to where Captain Boucher's body was covered. "Can't say the same for the captain, though."

A horn blared behind them, and an enormous van drove around the police vehicles and stopped beside them. Two men hopped out.

"Cornwall, you wild woman!" Julius "Eagle" Doukas was outspoken, to say the least. "What the blazes did you get messed up in?"

"Long story." She wrapped her arms around his waist as he kissed both of her cheeks. "I'll tell you guys later."

"Back off, Jules, my turn." Benicio "Foxy" Iñíguez loved competition, and he and Jules always got in each other's way.

But one thing she could always count on with these guys—they had each other's backs and would never betray their teammates. They would die for each other if it was necessary.

Her ERT team left as soon as Daniel and the others were secured. "We came because you needed help," Victor told her. "This was strictly off the clock. If our boss finds out…" He didn't finish.

"You know I can put in a good word for you if you guys need it." She glanced at Adam. "Detective Solberg too."

"Thanks. We'll let you know if we need our asses pulled out of the fire." They each gave her a kiss on the cheek, and disappeared.

The rest of the night was an exhausting blur. Cynthia

barely remembered reaching the city, being driven by an OPP police officer. She did remember hearing Adam's loud, commanding voice at the precinct, giving orders for the criminals' lockup in the jail cells until transport to a maximum-security prison was arranged.

She thought about texting Timmins and Hawthorne, and actually pulled out her phone.

"Hey, what are you doing?" Adam put her phone away. "That can wait. Come on—you're staying at my place."

His place—that meant delicious food, but she wasn't hungry. It also meant sleeping in the arms of a man who she had grown to care for—the word *colleague* definitely didn't fit anymore. Unfortunately, the bed and pillow called her name before she could get her clothing off, and she fell onto the soft material, passing out almost immediately.

Royal Canadian Mounted Police–Toronto Airport Detachment—Etobicoke, Ontario

Cynthia sat in a chair hard enough to bruise her butt. Shifting only made it worse, and her movements also caught the attention of an officer who sat behind a large reception desk. She remained still, hoping Adam's interview would be over soon.

Today, she was at the RCMP office located in Etobicoke, giving her statement and providing evidence to a months' long undercover operation she knew nothing about.

Who would have thought that unassuming, follow-the-rules Captain Gregory Boucher was an undercover agent? But she guessed that's how it worked—agents needed to fool everyone, and he certainly did his job well.

She checked her phone. Adam had been in the deputy

commissioner's office for almost two hours. She wondered what they could be talking about that she hadn't already provided.

To hell with sitting—her butt cheeks were numb. She stood and stretched, then paced the length of the hallway, the watchful officer eyeing her from time to time.

Finally, she heard a door open. Unsteady footsteps echoed off the walls until Adam turned the corner. His limp was less pronounced as he reached her.

"Wow, you were in there for a while." Her smile died as she studied his face. "What is it?"

His unfocused gaze transformed into a look of incredulity when he stared down at her. "Dad's alive."

"What?!?" She kept her voice down so as not to alert the officer at the reception desk. She grabbed his arm. "Come on—let's get out of here."

The Artful Coffee Shop buzzed with customers as they walked in. Cynthia led him to the table they first sat at when they had met what felt like months ago. Adam dropped into a chair without thinking, crossed his arms on the table and laid his head down on them—tired, confused, relieved. It was too much.

"I'll get us something to eat and drink," she said into his ear. He felt her hand rub his back, comforting his frazzled nerves.

He sat up and blew out a shaky breath. The captain's murder at the hands of Daniel had infuriated him so much, that it took every ounce of willpower not to run outside and beat Daniel's face to a bloody pulp. Now, he felt sad, filled with remorse that he couldn't save Boucher's life. His boss had died while doing his duty to protect others—Adam would never forget that.

He remembered sending a one-sentence text to Bruiser about his and Cynthia's predicament. The big guy had asked questions, but Adam decided it was best not to answer—the less that was said, the better for his friend.

Now that they were back, he pulled out his phone and sent a short text. We caught the perp, but Captain Boucher was killed. Family cottage is gone, but Cynthia and I are okay. What about you?

He put his phone away when she returned with the drinks. "Cappuccino, extra strong. I figured you needed it." She smiled and went back for their lunches.

He wanted to think through his interview with the deputy commissioner, but decided to wait until he talked to Cynthia. They would also have one of the longest reports to write up, but it would be worth it.

He watched her in the line, pointing at items she wanted. The concept of time had been screwed. To realize that only eight days had passed seemed unreal. And during all of this, Dad was alive and recuperating at Cortellucci Vaughan Hospital because Boucher managed to get him there. How he did that was still a mystery.

"Here we go." She held two large plates and put one down in front of him. The delicious smell of fresh-baked bread, along with the aroma of the cappuccino, had his stomach growling with delight. "Thanks, Cyn." He waited until she sat down, ever conscious of her movements.

"No need to wait on me. Dig in—I'm sure you're starving."

He didn't need a second command. Three quarters of his sandwich was gone within five minutes before he finally slowed down and savored the meal.

"So, talk to me." Cynthia hadn't touched her meal yet. "What's this about your dad?"

He wiped his mouth with a napkin, giving him a few seconds to compose his thoughts. "The commissioner told me that Boucher asked for Dad's help to find out any info on the new drug dealer in the city."

"Your dad did that and didn't tell you? That seems..." She left the sentence unfinished.

"I guess Boucher told him to keep it secret. In a way, it was the best idea. The less I knew, the better."

"I'm trying to understand why none of us were brought on board." She turned her cup around in its saucer. "The DC said there might have been a mole in the precinct, but I could have investigated that."

"If you did and the mole got wind of it, he or she would have been gone without us knowing." He rubbed his forehead. "I hate it when they pull undercover stunts like this. They're not always reliable."

"They may not have had a choice." She started eating.

"Cyn, the captain is dead. That could have been prevented with better planning." He grew angry again. Listening to the DC talk about Boucher's stellar work upon discovering Daniel's drug dealing scheme had done little to appease him.

"Maybe." She finished her lunch, then pushed aside the plate to lean her arms on the table. "Or the captain knew exactly what he was getting into. We won't know."

"What did the DC talk to you about?" he asked, diverting from his interview.

"He asked a lot of questions on my investigative measures. I think he was wondering if I found out whether Boucher was an undercover agent." She shook her head. "It gave me the creeps...like, does this type of undercover work occur a lot? And if I found out about it, what then?"

"I don't know. I could say it's not your problem, but…" He didn't have an answer for that.

His phone pinged, and he checked to see a message from Bruiser. But what it said made him annoyed. "What the hell?" he seethed. "Come look at this."

"What's wrong?" She moved around the table and sat beside him, leaning over to look at his phone. "Who is it?"

"Bruiser. It looks like Boucher updated him on what happened." He kept reading. "He also knows Dad is alive, but was sworn to keep it secret until the perp was caught." Adam typed a quick reply.

"I think you should head to the hospital where your Dad's staying."

"I have to—don't I?" *What the hell was he going to say to the old man?*

"If you want company…" She shrugged. "I'll wait in the hallway, but offer moral support, you know?"

He leaned over and kissed her full on the lips. "You're amazing—you know that?"

She smiled. "I get that now and again."

The cab ride to the hospital started to fill him with anxiety. His dad, back from the dead so to speak, and waiting for him. There was no greeting in the world that Adam could think of to bridge the gap of the past several days. Before he knew it, they were walking down the hallway toward Dad's room.

He hesitated outside the door, fingers wrapped around the handle, and looked back at Cynthia.

"You got this." She kissed him on the cheek. "I'll be right outside."

The deep breath to calm his nerves didn't help, so he decided to go for it and opened the door before he changed his mind.

It was quiet, except for the steady ping of a monitor. Someone lay in the bed before him, their face and body fully bandaged.

He swallowed against the sudden dryness in his throat, then approached the bed, every nerve on edge. "Dad?"

The patient twitched, and a pair of ice-blue eyes opened. Their gaze slid in his direction. "Adam."

The patient was unrecognizable, but Adam knew that voice. He stood over his dad, fighting back the anguish and the tears as he let his own gaze travel over the man who meant more to him than his own life. *Far.* Pappa.

"Thank the gods you're okay. Do me a favor and raise the bed up so I can take a good look at you."

Adam pressed the button, watching until his dad nodded to stop. "How did you…?" He touched his fingers to his father's face, still doubtful.

"Son, I shouldn't even be here. Captain Boucher got me out. Still don't know how he managed that." He took a deep breath, a raspy sound that made Adam wince. "If you're here, that means Boucher was successful. He got the drug dealer?"

Adam nodded. "The perp worked as a lab technician at our precinct."

"Are you serious?" Dad was moving around too much.

"Hey, take it easy." He grabbed the glass of water from the table next to the bed and gently inserted the straw into Dad's mouth. "I know. None of us knew until Boucher found a crucial piece of evidence that tied it all together."

"The perp was a serious piece of work. Had the Desperados working for him. Little bastards were real pains." He sighed. "What happened?"

Adam gave him the rundown. When he got to Boucher's death and the destruction of the cottage, Dad's eyes reflected the grief he felt. "The poor guy. He should have seen this through to the end."

"Dad, how did you get out of the clubhouse when the bomb exploded? I saw what it looked like. Bruiser said you pushed him out and went back in to help the others." He touched his father's arm, desperate to reconnect with him. It was a miracle, but Adam had his dad back. He wouldn't take this second chance for granted.

"I'm sorry, son. No one had a clue what was going on, so don't blame anyone, all right? Boucher and I had a private talk outside the back of the club, making sure no one saw or heard us. When Jeffrey yelled that you were coming, I told Boucher to take off and come back the next morning—you weren't supposed to see him. Then Larry showed up and told me about that drug deal the rival gang was doing.

"Some of us were already at the club the next morning when Boucher came back. We chatted some more, and he left. Then Larry showed up, said he didn't know why the drug deal didn't happen, and I told him to beat it. Next thing, that damn bomb exploded.

"I got Bruiser and someone else out—can't remember who. I was trying to get out the back but the smoke was too much. Boucher rescued me and somehow got me transported to CV Hospital. When I finally came to, he made a point to visit to give me the lowdown on what happened. He didn't want to risk telling you, Adam. He was scared something would happen to you and the others."

"What about Bruiser? How did he find out?"

"The captain brought him here. I don't know why— Boucher didn't tell me. Maybe he knew his time was running short."

"Maybe." Adam turned to look out the window, unsure of his feelings. Dad hadn't trusted him to keep this undercover operation a secret, and yeah, it stung. But he also understood their motives—it seemed that Daniel had been a hell of a big deal to involve the RCMP, OPP and Toronto's top brass. It was a rare event, and thinking about it, he felt proud that Dad was involved in such an important investigation.

"Adam? You're not angry?"

Dad saved his friends' lives by being willing to risk his. Adam's beliefs in a higher power were skeptical, but Fate certainly looked out for his father. He turned with a big smile on his face. "Are you kidding? I'm proud to have you as my father."

He sighed. "That means a lot to me."

"So how long are you stuck wrapped up like a cannoli?" he teased.

Dad narrowed his eyes. "Don't give me any lip, young man."

He chuckled, glad his father hadn't lost his snark. "I have to go. They're transferring the perps to Toronto South Detention Centre. I want to be there to personally send them off."

Cynthia looked up from her phone when Adam appeared. "So, how's he doing?" she asked, rising from the hard plastic seat to meet him.

"A lot better than I expected."

"It's gotta be that Viking blood in him," she said, keeping a straight face.

His eyes widened a moment, then he laughed, sounding more relieved than humored. "Yeah, no doubt."

She was painfully reminded to call Aunt Kiara to let her know she was okay. Not talking to her since their last call threw off her schedule. Plus, she wanted to hear her voice, especially after what happened. "Do you know how long he'll need to stay in the hospital?" she asked, heading for the elevator.

"I think a month, tops. Mom's going to flip when she finds out he's alive."

The ride back was quieter than usual, and she wondered what Adam was thinking about. His dad, yes, and probably the family cottage. "What else did the deputy commissioner ask you during your interview?" she asked, hoping to gain his attention.

"Almost the same questions as you. Did we know about Boucher's involvement. What did we find out?" He looked at her. "The DC paid you a compliment."

"Oh?" Her interview had felt more like a torture confession. "I wouldn't have seen that coming."

"Why not? You did a fantastic job, as always. The DC was surprised you found as much evidence as you did. Boucher was supposed to cover his tracks."

"Hmm, he didn't do so great a job on that." She thought about the case, skimming over obvious findings, mulling the complex ones.

Adam placed his arm across the seat behind her. "My feeling is Daniel had a huge outreach. Who knows if that dealer on Kootenay Ridge worked for him?"

"True." Cynthia didn't know if they would get all the answers they needed to find closure. Daniel hadn't come across as the confessing type.

The precinct was abuzz with activity. Officers stood outside in several groups, their gestures indicating something was going on.

"Looks like we got here in time." Adam paid the cab driver and hopped out.

Cynthia followed more slowly, watching as some of the cops shouted at Adam and clapped him on the shoulder. She heard one of them congratulate the detective on solving the bombing case.

"Typical." The word came out of her mouth before she knew it. She was only the forensic investigator to them, after all. She would let Adam soak up the attention while she disappeared into the police station.

However, what wasn't normal were the five Emergency Response Team members standing by their van in front of the precinct. "Hey," she called out. "What are you all doing here?"

"We actually got called in for this job." Victor smiled. "Sort of poetic justice, don't you think?"

"I'll say." She gave him a peck on the cheek and glanced at the others. "Where are Daniel and his gang being escorted to?"

"Toronto South Detention. They'll be staying there until the trial. That's all we got."

"*Chérie.*" Ben kissed her cheeks. "How are you feeling today?"

"Other than ten rounds with the RCMP Deputy Commissioner, I'm well." She heard Adam's laughter, and against her better judgment, looked over her shoulder.

"It looks like your boyfriend's ankle is much better. He's not using crutches at all," Mav observed.

"He hated the crutches. And he's not my boyfriend." The five men stared at her.

"Perhaps it's not official," Jules said. "However, he has been checking you out while you've been standing here."

"That doesn't make a relationship." Yet somewhere

deep inside, a glimmer of hope left a warm feeling in the pit of her stomach.

"But the two of you have been in each other's company quite a bit, right? You stayed at his cottage," Ben stated.

"I had no choice!" She dialed down the volume. "After I told Captain Boucher about the evidence I found and how it implicated him, he told me to run. I had gotten too close. I called Adam to tell him what happened, not ask if he could protect me."

"But you let him." Victor said this matter-of-factly. "You could have gone with Mav or stayed with me, but you went with Detective Solberg. You know that's a huge step toward trust."

She shrugged. Honestly, Cynthia didn't want to discuss this—not out here.

"She knows." Mav tapped her chin with a finger.

"Heads up," Lonan warned.

She turned, and caught her breath as the YRP officers approached her. Timmins and Hawthorne flanked Adam, who stood within their midst. "What the hell is going on now?" she muttered under her breath.

"Forensic Investigator Cynthia Cornwall," Adam called out. "I've been talking to our law enforcement colleagues about the amazing work you've done in solving this case. Your dedication to York Regional Police 4 District has been exceptional. Don't let anyone tell you different."

She stared across the parking lot as dozens of uniformed men and women cheered, yelled and whistled at Adam's unexpected speech. He came up to her, a little too close for comfort, and placed a hand on her shoulder. "Damn, it's hard not to pick you up and kiss you right now," he said loud enough for her to hear.

Cynthia licked her lips—wrong move. Adam's narrowed gaze focused on the movement and his grip tightened. "You're not making this easy for me."

A discreet cough brought her rudely back to reality. "Time to bring the perps out," Victor said in a loud voice.

Lonan, Jules and Ben went into the precinct along with four tactical members of YRP. Cynthia moved off to one side, staying clear of the guys' path to the van.

"Hey, Cornwall."

The voice sounded familiar. When she turned around, Officer Spade stood a few feet away. Cynthia distinctly remembered his arrogant posturing when she'd finished her investigation of the clubhouse. "Yes, what is it?" she replied, not feeling friendly toward him.

He had the grace to blush. "You did good work. Guess you knew what you were doing after all."

"Thanks." It was a start.

"Oh look. Cyn and her detective have come to see me off."

His voice sent chills down her back. Daniel stood at the precinct's doorway, wearing handcuffs and shackles around his ankles. His usual neat appearance was disheveled, and his normally cheerful expression had been replaced with a look that boded ill will to anyone who got too close to him. Jules and Ben flanked either side as Lonan brought up the rear. Their grip was unyielding as they escorted him to the prisoner van. "That new orange suit you're wearing looks pretty good on you," she replied, keeping her voice neutral.

"Do you like it? It's a little big, but comfy." He hesitated before the opened van doors. "You know this isn't the end, right, Cyn?"

"Her name is Cynthia Cornwall." Adam's voice was behind her. "Remember that."

"Oh, so he is your boyfriend after all." Daniel stepped into the van and sat on the narrow metal bench.

"You can shut up now," Victor growled.

The Desperados gang followed, their heads bowed low in defeat. Cynthia noticed that Larry wasn't among them. "Do you think Larry's okay?" she whispered to Adam. "Was he involved?"

"I doubt it. Boucher would have said otherwise, and Larry idolizes Dad." He smiled. "I don't think he'd risk my father's anger."

The back door slamming shut heralded the end of this investigation. Cynthia had heard rumors that lockup at Toronto South Detention wasn't for the faint of heart. "We'll see you at the trial," she called out.

"Now now, Cornwall, that wasn't nice." Victor had a huge grin on his face.

"Arrest me."

"I'm so thankful Cornwall hasn't lost her sense of snark," Jules said, snapping his fingers. "I've missed you."

Oh God, these guys. "You'd better go before I get into trouble."

Victor was the last to climb into the van. "Excellent work, Cornwall, as always."

"Thanks, Victor. That means a lot."

"Detective Solberg." He stuck out his hand. "I'm glad you realize what a gold mine you have in Ms. Cornwall."

Adam smiled and looked down at her. "Don't I know it."

Epilogue

Port Carling—One month later

When Cynthia finally appeared, Adam's whole body stood at attention. She wore a red-and-black motorcycle jacket, the colors displayed in a bold diagonal pattern. The matching leather chaps couldn't hide the curvy silhouette that was all her. She carried a black racing helmet with streaks of red that were both subtle and bold—it certainly suited her.

"Sorry about that—I couldn't find my helmet." She cocked a brow. "What's wrong? Is there something on my face?"

He came around his motorcycle. "Just those luscious lips I want to kiss."

"Control yourself. We'll be late." She slipped the helmet over her braided hair. "And if you can't keep your mind on the road, I'll drive."

"Fat chance." Although he had plans on teaching her how to handle a chopper. Her experience with racing motorcycles would help.

He revved up and headed east to Highway 400. The charity ride would be a bittersweet one, as it was being held in Port Carling to support the main hospital. The charity rides held fond memories—riding with his dad and buddies, meeting other riders from across Ontario who shared the same passion for their motorcycles. Every year was a different location, but always for the same cause—to help others.

The sadness of not having his dad with him was replaced with gratitude that the old man would eventually ride again. Captain Boucher had made sure of that.

The captain's funeral had been attended by hundreds of officers from across Canada. He had been buried with full honors and a gun salute that still rang in Adam's ears when he thought about it. Boucher was divorced, but his ex-wife and two adult children were there. The RCMP Deputy Commissioner held Boucher's uniform, neatly folded with his cap on top. When the service was over, he had passed it to her, saying a few quiet words. That had been a touching moment.

As they got closer to the town, small motorcycle groups passed them, or were parked at the side of the road. Bruiser and officers from YRP would be waiting for them in front of Turtle Jack's, a popular restaurant.

"Is it usually this busy?" Cynthia asked.

"No. I think word of what happened at the Chariots of Chrome brought every rider across Ontario." This year was going to be special.

Adam saw Bruiser, head and shoulders above everyone around him. His monster bike, which garnered attention wherever he went, sat proudly on the street. Kids surrounded it, shouting questions and rubbing their hands across its gleaming chrome surface.

"Dude, I was starting to worry." Bruiser grabbed him in a bear hug.

"I had to wait on Ms. Cornwall." Adam kept his tone light and teasing.

"Fine, blame it on me." She pulled off her helmet.

"I see you're still hanging out with the detective." Bruiser winked.

"Yeah, well…" She shrugged. "He's not so bad once you get to know him."

"Now hold up," Adam argued, then quieted down when she started laughing.

"She knows how to get to you," Bruiser stated. "It looks like I won't need to teach her anything."

"You can be such a jerk sometimes." Adam missed the banter. He hadn't realized how important it was to him until the clubhouse went up in flames.

"The guys are hanging out on the patio over here." Bruiser led them down the sidewalk. Just as they turned the corner, Adam heard a distinctive laugh. It couldn't be.

Dad reclined in an electric wheelchair. His hair had been pared down to a buzz cut, which made him look ten years younger. Aunt Michelle and Uncle Henrik were here too, and it was the older woman who spotted him first. "Adam!" she yelled out, and tackled her way through guys twice her size to reach him. She grabbed his face and planted a loud, wet kiss on his cheek. "I'm so glad Henrik and I came out." She glanced over her shoulder. "A certain someone insisted on being here." She rubbed his arms. "I guess your mom isn't coming."

"This isn't her kind of party, Aunt Michelle—you know that."

Mom had been as shocked as everyone else when he told her Dad was alive. This time, her crying had held a happy, relieved tone that almost had Adam crying too. Whether or not that would follow up with a visit to her ex-husband, however, he had no idea.

"Hey, son!" Dad waved him over.

He turned to grab Cynthia's hand, but she had slipped away and was talking to Bruiser. Among the noise of the crowd and growling motorbikes, he couldn't hear what they were saying.

"Adam?"

"Yeah." He wanted to introduce Cynthia to his family, brag about how her work helped in nailing the monster who killed their friends. Instead, he walked up to his father and gave him quick hug. "How are you feeling?"

"Better than I expected. My leg's still torn up but the doctor said it's healing well. Said I could come out to watch the rally but I gotta be back by evening for my meds." He grabbed Uncle Henrik's arm. "This old troublemaker was nice enough to drive me up here."

"Only way to keep you quiet." Adam's uncle smiled.

"Adam, who's the lady with you?" his aunt asked.

He glanced over his shoulder. Cynthia and Bruiser were making their way toward them. "Forensic Investigator Cynthia Cornwall. Her extensive work helped to solve the investigation."

"Wait a minute—you're dating a colleague?" His father pointed an accusing finger.

Adam huffed—how was he going to explain this? "The captain kept me off the bombing case, said I was too close to it." He gestured at Cynthia. "Ms. Cornwall said she'd keep me in the loop as a courtesy."

"Isn't that against the rules?" Aunt Michelle asked.

"Yeah, but it didn't stop her." It felt like a lifetime ago, when he got that first text. A coworker sympathetic to the loss of his father had turned into so much more.

"You didn't stop her, either." Dad gave him a knowing look.

Adam rolled his eyes. "Pa," he pleaded.

His dad waved his hand. "Ms. Cornwall, may I talk to you?"

Adam mouthed the word *no* but it didn't work. Cynthia came to stand by his father's side.

"Magnus Solberg." He held out his hand. "Pleased to meet you."

"Likewise." Adam noticed the firm grip she used, and his dad's surprised look.

"So." Dad gave him a side glance. "You're joining the rally with my boy."

"It only seemed right. Some of your MC crew worked at my precinct. I thought it would be a nice way to give back."

The old man looked confused. "So, you're not here because you and Adam...?"

Cynthia smiled. It was a particular expression that Adam knew not to get too close to. "Adam and I what?"

Dad glanced at him, but Adam stayed quiet. No way was he going to get dragged into this.

"Well, you're dating my son, right?"

"I'm not sure how you came to that conclusion."

Oh crap. Adam turned at the odd noise behind him and caught Bruiser snickering behind his hand.

"Ms. Cornwall, you're here with Adam. What else would I deduce?"

She blew out a loud, dramatic sigh. "As usual, men thinking the same damn thing. Mr. Solberg, you can deduce more than that one idea, surely?"

Adam could almost see his dad's brain whirling with confusion. Uncle Henrik wasn't far behind.

"I like Ms. Cornwall." Aunt Michelle had an odd smile on her face, almost similar to Cynthia's. "I hope you enjoy the rally, dear."

"I'm sure I will. Coming?" she announced, walking past Adam to his bike.

He followed, his gaze checking out the swing of her hips. "I don't think I've ever seen Dad not have the last word."

"I'm sorry if I was rude, but hearing him make that blanket statement…" She didn't finish.

"Are you kidding?" He pointed at Bruiser. "You made Bruiser laugh. My aunt loves you. And now Dad knows better than to play games with you." He kissed her cheek. "He'll respect you more for speaking up. I'm sure that's why he still loves Mom, even though they're not together anymore."

"Yeah, well, as long as I haven't overstepped my boundaries with him."

"Don't you think it's me you have to worry about?" he teased.

She sidled up to him, and dammit, every intelligent thought in his head shut down. "Oh, I think I have you figured out." She wrapped her arms around his neck and molded her body and lips to his.

The cheers and wolf whistles faded away until it was only her. He swept Cynthia off her feet and swung around as she laughed and smacked his shoulders. "Stop it!" she yelled.

He sat her down on the chopper. "Now you know better than to give me the opportunity to show you off."

He was confused at her surprised expression. "You were showing me off?"

"Well, not like a prized possession or anything. I know better than that. Hmm, maybe I worded that wrong." He thought a moment, forgetting again that he needed to choose his words carefully around her. "I wanted everyone to know that…" He stopped, finally realizing that his feelings for the amazing woman sitting before him were more than just admiration.

"What?"

What would he tell her? The startling revelation made him feel unbalanced. "You're more than just a colleague to me. A lot more."

Ah, to have a camera. The look on her face

"Well, Detective Solberg," she replied as she was pulling on her helmet. "I know for a fact that you mean more to me than just a colleague as well."

Jeez Louise, as Aunt Kiara would say. She just admitted—again—that her feelings for Adam were more than more.

He'd caught her off guard this time. She remembered their conversation in the RV on the way to Port Carling— her confession to him, that she was ready to be with him on a constant basis—and his heartfelt agreement had surprised even her. They'd been through so much it hadn't been at the forefront of her mind.

But now, with everything behind them, she hadn't

hesitated in telling him how she felt, and it made her feel absolutely glorious.

He leaned over and flipped up her face shield. "Did you say what I think you said?" His stunning blue eyes held her and left her speechless for a moment, dammit.

"Yes. For the second time, actually." The sudden increased sound of engines marked the beginning of the rally.

He sat backward on the bike facing her, and cocked a brow.

She frowned at his unreadable expression. "What? Can't argue against facts, can I?"

Suddenly, Adam pulled off her helmet, hung it over the handlebar and wrapped her in his embrace. His kiss did it again—forced all logic out of her brain. *Lord have Mercy.*

* * * * *

#2263 COLTON THREAT UNLEASHED
The Coltons of Owl Creek • by Tara Taylor Quinn

Sebastian Cross's elite search and rescue dog-training business is being sabotaged. And his veterinarian, Ruby Colton, is being targeted for saving his dogs when they're hurt. But when the resurgence of Sebastian's PTSD collides with danger, romance and Ruby's ensuing pregnancy, their lives are changed forever.

#2264 CAVANAUGH JUSTICE: COLD CASE SQUAD
Cavanaugh Justice • by Marie Ferrarella

Detectives Cheyenne Cavanaugh and Jefferson McDougall are from two different worlds. When they team up to solve a cold case—and unearth a trail of serial killer murders—they're desperate to catch the culprit. But can they avoid their undeniable attraction?

#2265 TEXAS LAW: LETHAL ENCOUNTER
Texas Law • by Jennifer D. Bokal

Ex-con Ryan Steele and Undersheriff Kathryn Glass both want a new start. When the widowed single mom's neighbor is killed and the crime is posted on the internet, Ryan and Kathryn will have to join forces to stop the killer before his next gruesome crime: live streaming a murder.

#2266 THE BODYGUARD'S DEADLY MISSION
by Lisa Dodson

After a tragic loss, Alexa King creates a security firm to keep other women safe. Taking Andrew Riker's combat and tactical class will elevate her skills. But falling for the ex-marine makes her latest case not only personal...but deadly.

Get 3 FREE REWARDS!

We'll send you 2 FREE Books plus a FREE Mystery Gift.

FREE Value Over **$20**

Both the **Harlequin Intrigue®** and **Harlequin® Romantic Suspense** series feature compelling novels filled with heart-racing action-packed romance that will keep you on the edge of your seat.

HARLEQUIN
PLUS

Try the best multimedia subscription service for romance readers like you!

Read, Watch and Play.

Experience the easiest way to get the romance content you crave.

Start your **FREE TRIAL** at
www.harlequinplus.com/freetrial.

"Excuse me," she said softly, leaning back.

Adam didn't move.

"I need to get by," she added.

"I know." His voice held a low timbre, and the grin that slowly spread across his face was the teasing kind that made Cynthia shiver in her socks.

Lord. Undaunted, she put her hands against his chest and pushed. No luck. She tried using her hip to shove him out of the way. Nope. "Adam, come on," she said.

"There might be a toll you'll have to pay in order to pass."

"Oh, you mean like a gold coin?" Sarcasm usually worked to help get her out of sticky situations. If that didn't work, she'd have no choice but to put on her "office" attitude.

"Something a lot more fascinating than that." He lowered his head.

"Detective Adam Solberg."

He stopped—that got his attention.

"May I ask what you're doing?" Cynthia didn't know how she kept her voice from trembling.

He stared into her eyes. His blue gaze was so intense it could put the sky to shame. "Flirting with you."

Dear Reader,

What happens when the job you love takes an unexpected turn into territory you're unsure of?

For myself, I pivot and adapt. Cynthia Cornwall, forensic investigator, does as well, and that's one of the reasons she's considered the best in her profession. She's efficient, smart and gets the job done. It's taken a long time to prove her worth in the male-dominated field of law enforcement. However, her compassion kicks into high gear when she discovers one of her colleagues lost his father in the bombing investigation she's assigned to. Against her better judgment, she keeps the ambitious detective in the loop behind everyone's back. Normally she'd never even consider doing this, but it is with good intentions.

Detective Adam Solberg is skeptical, of course. Cynthia's keeping him up-to-date on his father's murder goes against all of her hard-as-stone rules. But as he learns more about her, he senses a kindred spirit, someone who's been through a similar emotional turmoil. And that's going to cause a big problem. Adam's plan of keeping their meetings neutral is slowly falling apart.

I love writing about two characters who have no intentions of falling in love, then having them realize they're meant for each other.

I hope you enjoy!

Charlene Parris